Fortune's Horizon

Andrea K. Stein

FORTUNE'S HORIZON

Published by **Muirgen** Publishing, LLC

ISBN 13 – 978-0-9909566-1-7

Copyright © 2014 by Andrea K. Stein

Cover Design and Interior format by The Killion Group
http://thekilliongroupinc.com

DEDICATION

For the two Kates, Marjorie, Reba, and Verleta, who always believed

Norm, who never gives up

And John and Kirsten who keep listening to my wild ravings

ACKNOWLEDGEMENTS

Super Editor Judy Brunswick

Latter Day Blockade Runner and Delivery Captain Tony Plummer

Dr. Philip E. Freedman, MD, who shared his knowledge of yellow fever. Any mistakes in medical references are entirely my own.

Rocky Mountain Fiction Writers critique partners – Aaron, Dianne, Harriett, Jan, and Jennifer

My wonderful beta readers, including the entire Breckenridge Book Club and the Dallas, GA, Moser clan

WORKING HERO COVER MODEL

A big thank-you to Chris, who's in emergency services in the Colorado high country. His special interest is avalanche dog deployment, and two percent of all sales of this book will go toward regional search and rescue resources.

CHAPTER ONE

Wednesday, April 15, 1863
Faubourg Saint-Germain, Paris
48°51'48"N, 02°19'20"E

Lillie Coulbourne chewed on her thumbnail and peered out the window of her hired hack. Where was Sarah Devereaux? The hardest parts of this blasted assignment were the waiting and the uncertainty.

Expatriate American Southerners spilled from luxurious carriages on the Rue de Varenne onto the huge turnaround of the Devereaux mansion while footmen raced to quiet horses and move conveyances. Her friend had to be caught somewhere in the crush of guests eager for an evening of music.

Fueled by her mission, Lillie gave up on Sarah's help and ran across the courtyard. She would have to find Captain Bulloch on her own.

Rough cobblestones cut into her flimsy evening slippers and made her long for riding boots and breeches. The real reason men made better spies had to be the clothing. She gathered in her heavy silk skirts, clutched her book to her side, and edged past the throng waiting to greet the Devereaux family. Scooting down the hallway, she stopped at a salon on the first floor and slipped through the door.

The thought of the secret notes in a small cavity midway through the copy of *Jane Eyre* she carried made her fingers burn through all the pages and binding. However, that was nothing compared to the feel of the folded paper crammed into her petticoat pocket. Every time the packet brushed against her knee, fear and curiosity warred within her. Curiosity was winning, hands down. She had to complete the handoff and then find a quiet corner to interpret the message for her eyes only.

She forced her mind to focus on the task at hand and swept the room with a glance. Sarah's mother had gone a little over the top with the mirrors. Every bit of wall not covered in dark, crushed velvet had a full-length, gilt-framed mirror embellished with curlicues, angels and flowers. If Lillie were to drop over dead in there, she'd be sure to go straight to heaven.

Drat. No sign of the captain. Although the Confederate master spy was based in England, he made frequent trips to Paris. One night at a ball given at the Devereaux home, he'd asked her to dance and by the time the music ended, had snared her into an elaborate game of passing decoded messages. Instructions for his blockade-runner enterprise were embedded in dispatches from the South she translated for the French Finance Ministry.

The door swung open behind her, and she froze as the voices of two men floated in from the hallway. As soon as she ducked behind a heavy, hand-painted screen in the corner, she berated herself for hiding. What on earth was there to be afraid of? Besides —

Good God, her side profile was reflected in one of the damned mirrors, and then over and over in all the others across four walls.

With a silent prayer, she inched as far as possible behind the screen. Gathering in her full skirts, she crouched low and crossed her fingers. Thankfully, she had chosen her dark burgundy silk for the musicale that night. Maybe she would blend in with the wall coverings.

One of the men closed the door, and they moved to a sofa across from her.

She silently repeated her favorite calming phrase — "I'm as good as any man, and I can do this to help the Confederacy."

The two men spoke in low, guarded tones, and she strained to hear. One of them sounded like Captain Bulloch, but she couldn't be sure. The second man had a distinct, English accent.

Suddenly, their tones became more intense, and she began to pick up snippets of conversation.

"I know you're firmly behind the cause, but I tell you, sir, the South is in severe straits. I don't know how much longer they can hold out. They just don't have the resources." The unknown voice paused then continued. "The people behind the lines seem to be losing the will to continue to fight."

She leaned forward to grasp more of the thread of their exchange, and without warning, a hand seized her arm and dragged her into the center of the room. Her cheeks burned in mortification, and, for once in her life, speech deserted her.

The stranger was so tall he nearly lifted her off her feet as he plucked her from behind the screen. Angry, blazing blue eyes rudely assessed her, and she prayed Captain Bulloch would save her.

"Miss Lillie, whatever possessed you to crouch behind that screen?" Her friend tilted his head, and a forelock of dark hair dipped across his face. He peered around the obnoxious man who had her imprisoned like a child. "Captain Roberts, please release her."

Bullock paused for a moment when his companion refused to comply and raked his fingers through his hair. "She probably didn't expect anyone to be in this room." He stared at her, the question hanging between them. "Did you?"

"Then why did she hide?" the rude man interrupted. Instead of releasing her, he tightened his grip.

"Why, I...actually, I was searching for you, Captain Bulloch." Despite the pain of a growing headache, she gathered her wits and jerked out of his hold. "I wanted to return this. So sorry to have intruded." She thrust the book into Bulloch's hands and wheeled toward the door only to be stopped short.

"How do we know she isn't spying on us for information to take back to Yankee operatives?" Bulloch's companion demanded while detaining her again with a painful grasp on her arm. Lillie turned and tried to wrench her arm free while giving the oaf her most scathing look.

That was a mistake.

His unblinking gaze radiated irritation from a deeply tanned face. Long, silver-blond hair tied neatly at the nape of his neck with a narrow black ribbon accentuated his rugged good looks and formal black evening attire. Her chest tightened, and she couldn't breathe.

"Whoa. Let's start over." Bulloch stepped between them. "Miss Coulbourne, this is Captain Jack Roberts, a colleague of mine. And, Jack, this is Miss Lillie Coulbourne, the daughter of a friend. We've been exchanging books from our libraries for some time now."

"I'm pleased to make your acquaintance, Miss Coulbourne," Captain Roberts said, then released her arm and gave a curt nod of acknowledgement.

"I'm sorry if I gave you a false impression earlier," Lillie said, "but I couldn't help overhearing your comments on the situation in the South." She softened her murderous glare under a warning glance from Bulloch. "Surely you must be mistaken," she continued.

"Oh? So you're one of those Confederate zealots waiting out the war in comfort here in Paris," Roberts said.

"I can't believe you said that." Bulloch ground out.

"Trust me. If I were a man, I would be back in Dixie, teaching those Union bullies a lesson," Lillie insisted.

"Pah!" Roberts shot back. "You would have to be a little more imposing than you are now to take on the Union Army."

"I assure you, I can shoot, fight, and ride as good as any man." Her chest pounded in irritation. She had to get away from this awful man. "Now, I'll leave you two gentlemen to your business."

"No need to hurry off." Bulloch motioned toward a large brocade settee. "Please join us."

"No, no — I've already intruded too long." She moved toward the door, fixing a wary eye on Roberts.

"Please stay, Miss Coulbourne. Don't let me frighten you off." Roberts ducked his head in contrition. "It's been a long time since I last wore formal clothes." He pulled at his tight collar and grunted in discomfort. "I apologize for my rudeness. I'm not accustomed to being confined. Makes me claustrophobic."

"And cantankerous," Bulloch added, with a wink at Lillie.

She flushed and fought a sudden urge to reach out and help the prickly captain undo his top button. "Um, I think I'm going to leave you two to your meeting. Miss Devereaux is waiting for me, and patience is not one of her virtues." She turned and fled the room as if the hounds of hell were on her tail.

Once she regained the coolness of the hallway, she leaned against the door and trembled. After a few moments, she straightened and moved toward the crowd in the front hall. She had to find Sarah.

CHAPTER TWO

"Sarah—." Lillie had to shout to be heard over the din of guests milling in the great receiving hall of the Devereaux mansion. Sarah acknowledged her with a welcoming smile and moved toward Lillie, stopping frequently to greet friends and acquaintances. Soon, a path parted as if she were Moses making the Red Sea negotiable.

When her friend came closer, Lillie glanced wistfully at Sarah's simple, sleek twist of honey blonde hair. Lillie's unruly dark tresses tended to spring into corkscrews as the night wore on.

Sarah moved toward her, arm-in-arm with Louis Mansard, Philippe Devereaux's secretary. The poor man tried to maintain a stoic front while attending his employer's daughter at events, but by the end of most evenings Sarah and Lillie found a way to evade him and sneak off on one of their adventures.

Lillie felt sorry for the quiet young man. He had the dreamy, light grey eyes of a poet. Black hair curled softly around his ears and ended at the nape of his neck. Although he was devoted to Sarah, she treated him like an older brother.

Sarah and Lillie barely had time to exchange a few words before Martha Coulbourne, Lillie's mother, glided up to them with a sly smile. There would be no peace or privacy now.

"Why, Sarah, you are absolutely glowing tonight. Is it true you have a new beau on your father's staff?" Louis lowered his head and pretended not to hear.

"Mrs. Coulbourne, you give me credit for more than I could possibly accomplish. If I had as many beaus as your gossip columns suggest, Papa would have to hire extra staff just to chaperone me," Sarah assured her.

"Louis..." Lillie rushed to fill the awkward silence. "Could you find us some punch? I'm parched."

When he beat a hasty retreat in the direction of refreshments, Lillie turned on her mother. "*Maman*, you go too far. You should be ashamed of yourself."

"And where have you been?" her mother demanded. "I assumed you were behind me when I left the carriage."

"Please don't change the subject. You cannot hurt innocent people's feelings just for the sake of another bit of gossip."

"Well, he is a gorgeous young man." Martha turned to Sarah for affirmation. Lillie's friend just rolled her eyes.

"You owe both Sarah and Louis an apology, *Maman*," Lillie insisted.

"Oh, for heaven's sakes, Sarah knows I mean well. I just want what's best for you girls."

"No, you don't," Lillie and Sarah replied in unison.

"You two will be sorry some day when you wake up and realize you're just two withered spinsters without any prospects in life." Martha smiled then and turned away, no doubt in search of more snippets for her column.

Lillie tried to ignore her mother's nagging but began second-guessing herself in spite of her best intentions. She supposed she should engage in more small flirtations, but how could she live frivolously while a war waged on without her a half a world away?

"A penny for your thoughts." Sarah said.

In answer, Lillie smiled broadly and tapped the end of her nose. The secret signal began during their childhood days on neighboring Sea Island plantations off the coast of Georgia. She spent much of her early years there with her paternal grandparents while her father served as an Army surgeon and her mother followed him.

"So, what mischief are we up to tonight?" Sarah moved closer while Lillie's mother disappeared into the crowd.

"Mischief?"

"You know you never use our secret sign unless something really good is afoot."

"Sarah, swear to me you'll never tell another soul."

"Why, Lillie, you know I would never—"

Lillie cut her off. "We both know you are a veritable town crier."

"Oh, all right, but it hurts to think you don't trust me." Sarah pouted for an instant.

"Today when I was interpreting dispatches, a strange message appeared for me alone." Lillie ignored her friend's theatrics and plunged into her tale. "I haven't had a chance to pull out the information with the cipher wheel. First, *Maman* wouldn't leave me alone before we left home, and then that awful man with Captain Bulloch delayed me until I thought I would have to shoot him."

"Wait a minute. What awful man?" Sarah's face took on the look of a terrier on the trail of a mole. "And you don't really have a gun with you tonight, do you?"

"No, I didn't bring a pistol." Lillie was about to burst if she couldn't sort out the message chafing against her knee. "He's some Englishman named Roberts," she said, making a half-hearted pass at smoothing back the frizzes forming around her face. "He's the tallest man I've ever met. I think he would tower over Papa."

"Oh no, that has to be the mysterious Captain Roberts. Please don't tell me you've developed feelings for him."

"Feelings?" Lillie sputtered. "Have you even been listening to me? He was rude, nasty, and he accused me of being a spy."

"Why, Lillie, I think you are smitten." Sarah laughed out loud. "Finally, the woman warrior falls into the same throes of unfulfilled passion the rest of us suffer."

"Don't keep me in suspense." Annoyance crept into Lillie's voice as she ignored her friend's accusations. "Who is this bothersome man?" she demanded.

"Well, I can tell you what I know. He suddenly appeared yesterday at dinner, and he and my father have been closeted in the study ever since. I'm surprised the two of them emerged to mingle with the rest of us this evening." Sarah paused and eyed her reflection in one of the endless mirrors lining the walls.

"For pity's sakes, stop preening and continue the story," Lillie urged.

"Let's see." Sarah held up the fingers of one hand and ticked off what she knew. "Captain Roberts is just the name he uses for blockade-running. He's actually a post captain on leave from the Royal Navy.

"Blockade-running?" Lillie's pulse raced. "He actually runs the blockade?"

"Yes — Wilmington, Charleston — he's one of the best. Papa said he's never been caught."

"Why is he here?" Lillie asked.

"He brings out cotton after he runs in supplies for the Confederate Army." Her friend gazed at her as if she were dense. "He's negotiating delivery terms with Papa, but that's all I know." Sarah flicked at a minor bit of dust on a mirror frame and then turned back to Lillie. "He's mysterious, he's bigger than life, and so handsome, I think Papa was a little peeved I spent so much time staring at the captain at dinner."

Lillie glanced over her shoulder to check for eavesdroppers. However, the crowd was so overwhelming, only the loudest conversations could be heard above the din.

"Where can we find some privacy?" Lillie pleaded.

"If we retreat to my room, Mother will be incensed, and my maid, Annette, will be there to devil us." Sarah paused and touched her chin. "My father's study is just the place. Follow me."

They threaded their way through the crowd, occasionally stopping to chat briefly, and then ducked through a side doorway and on down a long hallway. Oil lamps on either side of the study door shed a soft glow as Sarah turned the handle and Lillie followed close behind.

Captain Roberts nearly bowled them over as he strode out of the room. Sarah stopped short, but Lillie couldn't slow her momentum and trod hard on his polished boots. His only reaction was a frown. He held himself ramrod straight in spite of his considerable height.

There was a familiar bearing about him. Military, of course. He reminded her of her father, Charles Coulbourne, in the way he towered over everyone in the room and intimidated her in particular.

"You again?" He shook his head. "Weren't you able to steal enough information the first time?"

She recognized a force as immoveable as her own, but didn't care. Without hesitation Lillie rose on tiptoe to deliver a smashing slap to his face. She misjudged his height, however, and wound up landing a mere embarrassing smack to his neck.

Philippe Devereaux, Sarah's father, strode into the hallway, clicking the door shut behind him and moved toward them. Sarah backed away toward a window.

The Englishman abruptly stepped back from Lillie as if scorched.

"I apologize for my daughter and her friend, Miss Coulbourne," Devereaux said, as he moved between them. "I assume they were bored by the evening's festivities and sought to invade my office for their own nefarious purposes." He smiled indulgently. "I suspect they are guilty only of boredom and curiosity."

He turned and gave them both a warning glance. "Go on back to the musicale, before your mothers discover you're missing and assign you a week of confinement in your rooms." He ignored their sighs of frustration and returned to his guest.

"Captain Roberts, I appreciate your efforts on behalf of our association, and look forward to seeing you again after your next series of voyages." The two men shook hands and ignored her and Sarah.

"Now, if you will excuse my haste," Roberts said, "I have to make the coast tonight. We sail to Portsmouth at first light." As he turned to head for the front hall, a look of annoyance crossed his face at the sight of the two young women still lurking in the hallway.

Lillie returned the stare, as direct as his, and then turned back toward the musicale with Sarah, head down, close behind.

Captain Jack Roberts widened the slow smile spreading across his face. He turned sharply and, with a short nod to Philippe Devereaux, headed out into the night. He loped toward a waiting hired carriage in the circular entryway. After directing the driver to the Gare St.-Lazare, he climbed inside and turned to his weather-roughened companion who had been patiently awaiting his return.

"Tell me, Edward, do you ever get lonely and tired of endless adventures? Do you ever just wish to settle into anonymous domesticity, perhaps with a small fishing smack in Cornwall?"

Of course, the question was moot. Both battered veterans of countless engagements, neither spoke, but just settled in for the long ride ahead.

"Do we have an agreement on the return cargo?" His friend broached the topic that brought them all the way to Paris from Portsmouth.

"Yes." He broke the companionable silence.

"Did they meet our price?"

"Absolutely. We leave within the month."

Jack leaned back and stretched his long legs in front of him as far as the cramped carriage would permit. He immediately nodded off for a short nap. Years of sea battles and hair-raising storms had left him with the ability to carouse with fellow officers into the wee hours, fall quickly to sleep, and awake refreshed, ready for whatever the day would bring. His body had become accustomed to taking advantage of any short interludes to rest before the next challenge.

This time, his usually uncomplicated slumber was interrupted by the vision of a girl with the face of a Botticelli cherub surrounded by a cloud of dark, unruly curls. Her eyes were the peculiar violet shade of the sea at dusk.

He enjoyed the appearance of nubile young women in his dreams as well as the next man, but this one woke him with a start. She was walking the deck of his ship. He sat wide-awake in the dark puzzling over the memory. If twenty-three years at sea had taught him anything, it was the presence of a woman aboard rarely boded well.

The two men soon disembarked and made for the express train to Le Havre. The hands of the huge clock on the station tower warned they would have to sprint to make the eight o'clock train. Disappearing into the steam of arriving engines, they pulled themselves onto one of the second-class carriages. The compartment contained only a dozing elderly cleric, not likely to disturb their relative peace on the northbound trip. What a relief.

Lillie's cheeks still burned from her second collision with Captain Roberts. Her reaction to him niggled at her, but his clean, male scent seemed to circle her like a stalking wolf. Good English soap mixed with something else she couldn't quite put her finger on. Fingers ... wolves ... the hand pressing on her arm snapped her back to attention. Sarah leaned closer, a silly grin on her face.

"I asked if you were still thinking of him ... and you are, aren't you?"

"No," Lillie said, her voice crackling with denial. "Let's sneak back to your father's office during the intermission. Our mothers will be occupied with the music, not to mention the gossip. They'll never think to look for us there after your father made us leave."

Some time later, they bent over Sarah's father's mahogany desk while Lillie painstakingly deciphered the code. When the words of the message were finally complete, both sucked in gasps and straightened quickly.

"Will you help me?" Lillie asked.

Sarah's face clouded with fear, but she replied without hesitation, "Of course."

"Then tomorrow, at eleven," Lillie said, "collect me in your carriage outside the ministry offices at the Tuileries."

CHAPTER THREE

Thursday, April 16, 1863
Palais des Tuileries, Paris
48°51'50"N; 2°19'34"E

Lillie sat tucked into an alcove at the end of a long gallery where the glass doors cracked open a bit onto the narrow balconies overlooking the Tuileries gardens. An early spring heat lay heavily over the city, and the lush greenery beyond was beginning to bud with color.

Her heart still pounded at the memory of the terse message she and Sarah had uncovered the night before. Someone wanted to meet her at the Cimetiere du Pere-Lachaise that afternoon. She was so nervous she could barely sit still long enough to translate the day's dispatches.

She shoved back a long, corkscrew tendril of hair liberated by the humid breeze trickling through the alcove. Not more than a few hours ago her hair had been confined to two secure plaits at the base of her neck.

Once again, she cursed the accident of her gender for stranding her in the jaded Parisian court of Napoleon III. Instead of waiting out the war of Northern aggression like one of the elaborately dressed dolls in Madame Solein's shop window, she longed to wear the grey uniform of her beloved Dixie and fight like a man.

Out of the corner of her eye, Lillie watched the elderly Monsieur Berliot from the Finance Ministry. Sprawled artfully across a nearby brocade and gilt sofa, he sagged over his embroidered waistcoat while soft, snuffling sounds emanated from his open mouth.

She smiled at the sleeping bureaucrat and leafed through Confederate dispatches on the small writing desk, translating them into French. On the last page she found the phrase, "complete victory," inserted in the final paragraph. She sneaked a look at the napping Frenchman and slid the cipher wheel out of the hidden pocket sewn into her petticoat.

After positioning the wheel on the right edge of the desk, she lined the left side with four dip pens. One rolled sideways, and she straightened it, keeping the shining points aligned.

The translations were tedious but could be just as crucial to the war effort as physical combat, which brought her back to the task at hand. She set the A of the cipher wheel on the outer ring to the letter of the keyword being used, in this case, "victory." The outer letters represented the cipher text, and the inner letters represented the plain text.

Not knowing the precise meaning of the secret messages for Captain Bulloch embedded in the dispatches, Lillie assumed they concerned the procurement of ships and supplies he managed for the Confederacy.

She folded the odd slips of paper gleaned from the day's dispatches and stuffed them, along with the wheel, back into the pocket in her petticoat.

"Monsieur Berliot, do you know the time?" she inquired loudly while eleven chimes rang out from the polished, gold mantel clock.

The Frenchman started and sat upright before pulling a bell cord for a servant. Moving stiffly and stretching his back, he walked over to her and peered at the stack of papers on the desk.

Although his step was spry, his eyes were still heavily lidded with sleep. It was hard to guess his exact age. In his prime, he must have been a powerfully built man, but now his shoulders stooped, possibly from many long hours of bending over accounting ledgers for the French government.

"So, mademoiselle, I see you work very quickly today. We can scarce read the dispatches as fast as you translate them. So talented for one so young. Did you grow up speaking French?"

"Yes, sort of. Maman taught me at home. She made a game of challenging me to converse in as many different languages as possible. And, of course, I much admire the novelists of your country."

Although she would certainly never let the elderly bureaucrat or her mother know, she was currently devouring Flaubert's <u>Madame Bovary</u> in the privacy of her room each night.

"You are an unusual young woman. You sit inside all day translating boring matters of state, when others your age are out enjoying the Paris spring."

"Since I am not a man, this simple labor for my homeland is the least I can do. Otherwise, I assure you, I would be on the battlefield."

Lillie rose, smoothed her skirts, and reached for her bonnet lying on the window seat. She ran her fingers over the new green and pink ribbon trim she'd found in one of the stalls at Les Halles and turned toward Monsieur Berliot.

"You need not concern yourself with accompanying me home today," Lillie assured him. "The Devereauxes are sending a carriage."

"At least let me escort you down to the portico and wait until they arrive," he insisted. He paused while she pulled on gloves, then led the way down the steps with a light pressure on her arm. She quelled the urge to race pell-mell out into the fresh air because he always had difficulty with the long, winding staircase.

Counting slowly to ten under her breath, she smiled until her face ached.

Lillie still was not sure what to make of the strange note burning a hole in her pocket. The message specified she was to meet a contact at the cemetery that afternoon at one. Alone. She cringed at the thought of a solitary walk through the final resting place of famous and infamous Parisians.

Once more, she went over the plan she and Sarah had sketched the night before. On the pretext of an afternoon luncheon, Sarah would accompany her as far as the cemetery entrance and then wait while she completed her secret errand.

Finally exploding into the fresh air, she breathed a sigh of relief at the sight of the Devereaux carriage waiting beneath the side portico.

She viewed the Tuileries gardens under an early spring sky heavy with the promise of rain. Touches of mist hovered near a pond. Young girls fed the ducks while their nurses sat nearby on iron benches. Streaks of a stubborn afternoon sun pushed through threatening clouds and warmed the park while the intense blues and pinks of the flowering bushes along the walkways were muted to pastels in the softening mist.

After polite goodbyes to Monsieur Berliot, she bounded down the steps to the carriage only to be stopped short by Sarah's brother, Wade, holding the door for her with a mocking smile.

"Where is Sarah?" she asked.

Her friend leaned out of the carriage window and shot her a warning look.

"My brother has been good enough to come along today as chaperone. Mother worries so. I don't know how she has survived motherhood this far."

"The truth is," Wade said, "Mother knows you two cannot be trusted to lark about the city on your own with nothing more than an easily bribed servant in tow." His cutting look silenced his sister.

Wade helped Lillie up into the carriage where she took her place next to Sarah while they both cast sullen looks at the tall, golden jailer opposite them. He chuckled softly as if at a private joke and acknowledged their angry stares.

He knocked on the roof and leaned forward to give directions to the driver.

Lillie's mind raced. How could she keep her appointment if they could not somehow contrive to get rid of him?

"How do you two feel about skipping a boring lunch? Let's move directly to the sweets at Stohrer." He leaned forward, looking more like a co-conspirator than a chaperone.

She and Sarah exchanged wary looks. Could he possibly suspect their plan?

"Do not beat about the bush. What do you want from us? Why are you being so accommodating?" his sister demanded.

He opened his mouth as if to reply, and then sat back with an enigmatic smile and rested his hands on his thighs.

To Lillie's annoyance, her attention strayed inadvertently to the buff colored trousers that hugged his athletic figure to advantage. She turned her head to conceal the flush creeping up her cheeks and tried to concentrate on the problem at hand.

Memories sprang into her head of a time not so far distant when they had been inseparable childhood friends. However, his childish teasing and baiting seemed frivolous in comparison to Captain Roberts' exploits in support of the Confederacy.

She began to panic and feverishly racked her brain for a way to keep her appointment without alerting him to the scheme she was about to embark upon. Lillie sneaked a look at her father's pocket watch hanging on a long, black silk cord around her neck. It was already close to 11:30. She had just an hour and a half to get to her meeting.

Her father gave her the watch two years before during the tearful parting when she and her mother left for France. He had sent them to Paris to avoid embarrassment over their Confederate sympathies. He was a field surgeon who had remained with the Union Army in spite of the defection of his fellow West Point officers and friends to the Confederacy. Her mother had remained a rabid supporter of the Southern cause and wrote a gossip column for newspapers in California.

In desperation, Lillie doubled over as if in pain, causing Sarah to bend forward and feel her forehead.

"It must be the fish your mother always insists on having for breakfast." Her friend threw her a conspiratorial look. "We must turn around and deposit you back home."

"No," she insisted. "Please, stop the carriage. Let Wade find a hack to take me home. I don't want to spoil your outing."

"Nonsense," Wade insisted. "We'll take you home. Mother would never forgive me if I allowed you to ride in a public conveyance unescorted."

Lillie gave him an anxious look while she racking her brain for alternatives.

"Oh, I see. You two have plans." As the silence lengthened, he scanned their faces as if seeking a clue. "So, where are we really going?"

"You mustn't tell a soul," Sarah said. "Lillie is meeting a beau at Cimetiere du Pere Lachaise."

"That's right," Lillie chimed in. "I met the most wonderful gentleman the other day. Maman would never approve, but I just want to see him again, to talk to him." God bless Sarah's fast thinking.

"Who is this 'wonderful' man? Do I know the blackguard? I swear I'll call him out for pressing himself upon a well bred young woman without her parents' approval."

"Heloise and Abelard." In sudden inspiration, Lillie spat out the name of the famous lovers.

"What?" He shot her a look of disbelief.

"Heloise and Abelard's grave. We're to rendezvous there. If you want to meet him first, Sarah and I will wait at the entrance."

"We'll be safe with our driver," Sarah added, taking a breath as if to go on before her brother stopped her with a look.

He leaned out the carriage window and gave instructions to make haste for Boulevard de Menilmontant, near the entrance of the final resting place of many of France's great and infamous citizens.

"I suppose you don't even know where the graves lie, do you?" He snorted and studied the pathways after she produced a touring map.

During the quiet ride to the eastern edge of the city, Lillie worried so, she thought she might really become ill. As soon as they reached the entry gate, Wade stalked off into the cemetery and began trotting to the east toward the lovers' site.

As soon as he disappeared from view, Sarah leaned forward and engaged the driver in conversation. Lillie slipped out the other side of the carriage and raced through the gate to take another route leading northwest through the cemetery toward the prescribed meeting place.

Light mists from earlier in the day were now more substantial and shrouded the paths in fog-like wraiths moving slowly with the breeze.

A man suddenly appeared out of the thickening fog. Heart pounding, Lillie held her breath, convinced he was the one. Instead, he merely tipped his hat and murmured, "Mademoiselle."

She pushed on until she was in front of a tall monument topped by an imposing bust. "Honore de

Balzac" was chiseled into the grey stone monument behind the black iron fence. When she lifted her face to study the stern lines of the sculpture, her arms were pinned firmly to her sides from behind.

"What do you want from me?" she asked, refusing to jerk or scream.

"You must not see my face. It could be fatal for both of us." His warning came in a hoarse whisper. "When you travel to London with your mother, you will meet with Algernon Summer, a marine solicitor at Lincoln's Inn."

She forced herself to relax and absorb what he was telling her but couldn't help sneaking a look down at his hands. They were rough and dirty with broken nails – certainly a far cry from Captain Bulloch.

"He will arrange passage for you on a blockade runner into Charleston to deliver documents and gold bond certificates to an agent near there."

"But where?"

"Details will be revealed as you need to know."

"I can't—"

"Ah, so you really aren't 'as good as any man.'" The tone of his voice turned spiteful. "You'd rather enjoy life in Paris while Confederate soldiers die for lack of ammunition and blankets."

"I don't know who you are, but you're wrong. You don't know me at all." In spite of her anger, tears squeezed out the sides of her eyes and rolled down her cheeks. How did this person know so much about her?

"All you have to do is seek Solicitor Summer, and the rest will fall into place."

He disappeared just as quietly as he had appeared. She rubbed her arms where he'd gripped them, then concentrated on getting her body to stop shaking. Smoothing her skirts in preparation for facing Sarah and Wade again, she sucked in a breath and then raced behind a secluded bush to retch. After she wiped her mouth with a handkerchief, she turned to dash back through the cemetery to the waiting carriage.

Fear clawed at her, and a childhood memory surfaced: Lillie was seven again, staying with her grandparents at their plantation bordering the Devereaux holdings on Sea Island. Her father was off on a military campaign, and her mother had gone with him.

At thirteen, Sarah's brother, Wade, had been kind and doting toward them, but his dark side could appear unexpectedly. He enjoyed torturing helpless creatures, from his father's hunting dogs to the field laborers.

He cornered her once during a game of hide-and-seek at dusk in an old abandoned outbuilding. Appearing out of nowhere, he dangled a dead snake in her face. When she froze in terror, he knocked her down on the dirt floor and forced her to submit to rough fondling and pinching until Sarah stopped him. She could still feel the nausea of helplessness and her frantic struggle to edge away, escape. That incident had strengthened her determination never to let herself be ensnared again in a situation like that.

A kind of calm came to her during the long walk back. With each step, her resolve strengthened to take up the gauntlet the mysterious man had laid down.

She was puzzled as to why he had not shown his face. But then, if she were ever captured, she could truthfully deny knowledge of her contact.

Just then, she rounded a corner and spied the carriage near the entrance. Her friend's warm smile took the edge off her fear, but just as she reached for the door, Wade swung down to help her up. Her stomach churned. This ordeal was not over yet. It had just begun.

He boosted her up the steps, his hands squeezing tightly at the sides of her breasts. She was rewarded with a smirk when she shot him an angry frown over her shoulder.

Sarah gave her nervous looks the minute she was safely inside. Wade settled into a shadowy corner and projected a sulk of boredom.

"Did you ever find the grave where you were to rendezvous with your beau?" he asked, clots of sarcasm in his voice.

"I'm sure she didn't mean any harm, and—." Sarah interrupted him.

Her brother cut her off abruptly. "Stop your blithering," he said, squelching her attempts to smooth things over. "I'm on to your clever little deceptions. Your pathetic attempts at deviousness failed, I might add."

"Will you tell on us?" Sarah ventured, in spite of his censure.

"I don't know. I'm thinking about it."

The wind whipped through the thick canopy of trees overhead and flipped their leaves over to a pale shade of green. Lillie's grandmother always said that was a sign the trees were showing their petticoats before the rain.

She leaned out the window to let the wind gusts cool her face and was startled by the sight of the same man she'd encountered earlier on her way to Balzac's grave. He nodded to her, smiled, and then walked on toward the entrance gate, swinging an ivory-topped black cane and whistling a familiar tune.

"Couldn't we offer that poor gentleman a ride? He will soon be soaked." She turned and appealed to her companions.

"What gentleman?" Sarah asked.

Lillie swung around to point him out, but he had vanished. The cemetery was empty and eerily quiet, the winds temporarily stilled before the onslaught of the storm.

"I swear, he was just outside, walking toward the gate. Didn't you see him? And what was the tune he was whistling?" She paused, guessing from their horrified looks they were convinced she had gone mad. "All right. I guess I've had a hard day. I may have been imagining things, but I won't be able to get that song out of my head until I can remember what in blazes the name of the tune is."

"You look as if you've been dragged behind the carriage instead of riding in it," Wade said. "You're shivering, and your shoes are a mess from running through the grass and mud. Your face is as white as if you had actually seen a ghost."

She opened her mouth to protest, but he was already leaping to the ground to speak to the driver.

"Where are we going?" Lillie asked when he climbed back inside the passenger compartment.

"You two have wreaked enough havoc for one day. It's time to sit, remain quiet, and obey."

The carriage turned out of the gate and headed back west into the city.

Lillie was so absorbed in her thoughts, she forgot to worry about where they were going. Finally glancing outside again, she relaxed at the familiar sights of Boulevard de Sebastopol. After two short turns, the carriage pulled up in front of Stohrer on Rue Montorgueil.

"Come on. You need some sweets to restore the pink in your cheeks. And besides, I can't take you home with empty stomachs."

Lillie followed him inside with Sarah in tow and let the warmth and smells revive her. The air filled with the scents of fresh-baked buns and chocolate wafting from the patisserie ovens. Sarah leaned against a case of tiny fruit tarts and eyed the perfect jewel-like glazed apricot, apple and wild strawberry flavors. Lillie debated a while, then chose a flaky cream-filled pastry decorated like a crown.

"Could you package one of the baba au rhum cakes for me?" she asked the clerk. Glancing at her friends, she added, "Sweets always distract Maman."

They settled with their prizes around a table and ordered tea. Wade devoured a tart in each flavor, while Sarah savored an apricot sweet.

"So, what is your intention?" Lillie asked with a pointed stare at Wade. She took a bite of her crown and then licked the pastry flakes from her lips. "Will you tell my mother about our adventures today?"

"It all depends on your behavior from now on. No more trysts in cemeteries, no more sneaking off to meet beaus."

"And your report to our mother about me?" Sarah demanded.

Lillie nearly laughed in spite of herself. Of course Wade would not reveal their adventures. To do so would also incriminate him. She smiled fleetingly, and he stiffened.

"Are you enjoying a private joke at my expense?" he asked.

"No. However, it has occurred to me you can't tell our mothers, because you were there too."

"I will say we had a pleasant lunch today and a ride through the park." Cruel lines formed at the edges of his almost smile, and he turned to his sister. "The real question is how you will keep from blabbing. You know you're incapable of keeping a secret."

"He's right," Lillie added. "You need to invent a story you can tell with a grain of truth."

Her friend frowned at both Lillie and Wade but didn't deny her shortcomings. "I will just have to plead fatigue and retire immediately to my room so I can compose a plausible tale before Mother wrings the truth out of me."

"Since Maman and I leave in a few days for London, I think I will get up early tomorrow and go to the book stalls." Lillie paused and casually tapped the end of her nose. "I can't imagine being stuck in stuffy old London with nothing to read."

Sarah leaned back into the cushions with a knowing grin.

"I guess I know where you two will be tomorrow morning," Wade said with a sigh. "Just don't let mother know. I refuse to follow you around Paris at an ungodly hour of the day."

CHAPTER FOUR

Thursday, April 16, 1863
Faubourg Saint-Germain
Devereaux Mansion

Julia Devereaux sat in soft splendor in a fragile dusty rose satin evening dress. Her flawless skin belied her years, and her gentle, muted drawl never failed to entrance Wade.

He moved stealthily toward the low banquette where she sat with a book and gently covered her eyes with his hands.

"Stop it, Wade. You'll destroy my coiffure." She tried to turn away from him, but he moved his hands lower to the tops of her shoulders and held her still.

"You are a wicked, wicked boy," she said.

"But not nearly as wicked as you, Mother."

She ignored his caustic remark and continued as if nothing had transpired between them.

"We're having a late supper this evening with some friends. Won't you please stay?" She raised her hand glittering with rings, placed it over his, and patted him in a mollifying gesture. Her gaze never left the pages of her book.

"No, Mother, I'm meeting some friends at Tortoni's for the absinthe hour."

"How did the little outing go this afternoon? Did the girls cause any trouble?" she asked.

"No, Mother. You know my special talent is crushing rebellion." He moved to her and sat on the edge of the delicate bench.

Julia overlooked his dark mood. "I just wish we could find a suitable match for Sarah. It's time she quit adventuring off on her own with that Coulbourne girl. We need to get her settled into a suitable life before there's a scandal even your father can't handle."

At the concerned look in her eyes, Wade hastened to assure her. "Sarah's only nineteen. The war at home cannot last much longer. I promise you I will watch over my baby sister, and as for Lillie, I think we can find a way to minimize her involvement in Sarah's life."

"I knew I could count on you." She rubbed his hand again, lifted her eyes to his face for the first time, and asked, "When will you be home tonight?"

"Late. Don't wait up for me, and don't worry."

Wade walked out into the circular courtyard in front of his family's mansion, preparing himself mentally for the other half of his life as a double agent. After giving brief instructions to his driver, he climbed into the carriage and began to formulate his next move in the elaborate chess game set in motion that afternoon.

When they rolled down a dark side street, he knocked on the roof of the carriage at the next corner. The driver reined in the horses to a stop, Wade opened the door, and a small, dark-haired man slipped inside.

"How did the meeting go?" Wade did not waste time on pleasantries.

"That bit of fluff was very pliable once I threatened her." His companion leaned forward and winked at him. "I must say she was very tempting under all those stays."

Wade drew back with his fists and sent him sprawling to the floor of the carriage. He shoved a wad of francs into his pocket, grasped the man by his collar, and shoved him out the door while the carriage was still moving. He looked back to see the runner lying in the gutter, groaning, with blood seeping from the side of his head.

Once Wade's heart stopped pounding, he forced himself to re-gather his thoughts. He would see his plan through to the bitter end, and by the time he was through with Lillie, that leech of a man would be the least of the dangers to Miss High and Mighty.

In truth, though, he really didn't care what happened to her, or for that matter, the Southern cause. He just wanted to be the one to profit from picking up the pieces at the end of the war.

Some time later his carriage rolled through muddy streets in a district a half-hour from his family's Paris mansion. Directing the driver to wait next to an apparently abandoned warehouse, he then approached a battered old door. A rat scrambled over the soft leather of his boot, and he kicked it back into the refuse-lined gutter. He pounded on the door loudly once, then four times in close succession after a short pause.

A tall man dressed in drab brown unlatched the heavy door to reveal rich mahogany paneling down a narrow, gas-lit hallway.

"State your business," the man demanded brusquely. He resembled no servant Wade had ever encountered, and made no effort to hide the pistols barely concealed inside his coat.

"I'm here to see the committee."

"Follow me."

"I like a man of few words," Wade said. His broad-shouldered guide just turned and scowled at him.

They proceeded down the hallway to a book-lined study where four men shared a round of brandy and cigars. His host looked up and nodded toward an overstuffed chair near the fireplace.

"We've been waiting for you, Devereaux. Sit and tell us what you've uncovered."

Wade sank into the chair, stretched his arms toward the fire, and then gratefully accepted a glass of dark amber liquid from a tray. He took a strong swallow and then gazed directly at the man across from him.

"I think the Coulbourne chit has access to bonds and gold from the French. She means to smuggle them back into Charleston on a blockade runner." The die was cast. He could breathe again.

"In the name of all that's holy." The other man cursed. "With enough cash infusion, and French support, they could prolong this war for years."

"Exactly." Wade could barely contain his excitement. "We can seize her and finally expose her family."

"Surely we needn't put her in prison, though. She is so young. I will arrange an exchange." Wade's contact sank back into his chair and blew rings of smoke toward the ceiling.

"Anyone in particular in mind?" another member of the circle asked.

"Let me think about it for a while." The elderly Englishman cast a critical look at Wade. "So, Devereaux, what is your price if you manage to pull this off?"

"I would like to take over the Coulbourne Sea Island plantation when hostilities cease."

"We'll put your request before the commission and let you know. But you have to implicate old Bonie and the rest of his gang at the conclusion of this affair. That has to happen, or our deal is off."

"You have my word."

April 17, 1863
Le Marais

Lillie's mind raced. Even the soft spring morning couldn't calm her. She and her maid, Giselle, dawdled their way toward the booksellers' market. It would not do to adopt her customary fast gait. She might betray her mission.

Instead of her usual late rising, her mother had been up with the dawn, whipping the household into the massive packing project for their London trip. Applying all of her persuasive skills, Lillie had convinced her mother she needed to venture forth to replenish her reading supplies.

Turning the corner, Lillie picked up the pace and hoped she was not being followed. If Sarah had correctly interpreted her hints the day before to meet her at the bookstalls, they might still figure out a way to get her mother's blessing on the blockade run. If only her friend could come along to London.

"Mademoiselle, what a long silence, and what a serious face. If you keep frowning, we will have to apply more creams to keep the wrinkles from your forehead."

Lillie looked over and immediately regretted the speed of her walk. Giselle struggled to keep up, but she hadn't uttered a single complaint.

Suddenly she caught sight of her friend, Sarah, with her maid in their carriage. Lillie dashed across the street toward them, dodging traffic. Sarah leaned out of the window, waving frantically and hanging onto her bonnet.

"What brings you out so early?" Lillie asked.

"It was such a beautiful morning, and since it was impossible to sleep with the all the clatter of spring cleaning, Annette and I decided to take a drive. I saw you and realized we haven't had a farewell tea." Sarah fussed with the ribbons on her bonnet, nervously curling them around one of her fingers.

Lillie turned and beckoned to her maid peering anxiously from across the street. After Giselle joined them, they found a sidewalk café and ordered cakes for the two servants. After choosing pastries for themselves, they sat at a separate corner table. Accustomed to being used as foils for the girls' questionable activities, Annette and Giselle settled into a session of gossip, rich confections and tea.

"This had better be good, and it had better be fast. Everyone is on to us, and Mother has been a terror about our adventures." Sarah frowned while she swirled lemon and honey into a fragile teacup scattered with delicately painted violets. "Wade smoothed over yesterday's adventure with Mother and waved as I left this morning. I'm afraid he'll exact a terrible price if I have to support you in these escapades much longer." Unblinking, Sarah stared across the table, waiting for an explanation.

"You have to come to London with us," Lillie pleaded, and crossed her fingers under the table, praying she could convince her friend. Everything depended on Sarah's support.

"I think all the suspense and tension of the last few days have unhinged you." Sarah's mouth opened wide and she sighed with exasperation. "I'm beginning to believe there may be something to Mother's contention. Too much thinking and reading muddles a woman's mind." She ignored Lillie's scathing look and continued. "I can tell you she will never let me accompany you and your mother. She's already plotting ways to confine me to my rooms – lessons on the harp, elocution, even Italian, for heaven's sakes."

Jumping ahead of her friend, Lillie blurted, "What is your mother's greatest fear?" She went on as if her friend had not even spoken. "What is the worst thing that could happen to you? It's an unsuitable man, I tell you. That's the key."

"No, no, no. I can't worry Mother so." Sarah's eyes widened in recognition of what Lillie was suggesting. "And besides, I don't have a beau. There aren't even any admirers on the horizon."

"You have the perfect man at your fingertips. You've had him all along," Lillie insisted.

A blush began on Sarah's cheeks and spread downward.

"See, I knew it. Even *Maman* suspects. Your father's secretary, Louis, worships you. You know it." She regretted her words instantly when tears began to roll down her friend's cheeks.

"You are so cruel. How did you guess?"

"Let me see. You are cooped up in a musty old mansion. Before *Maman* and I moved here, you were limited to contact with your family and their friends. The only eligible male within miles of your parents' fortress is poor Louis."

"Shush. What if someone overheard us?" Sarah glanced around frantically, searching the café for acquaintances. After a quick look at the two maids to ensure they were not eavesdropping, she turned back to Lillie. "No one must ever know. My father would fire him and make sure no one else ever hires him."

"Nonsense. We're both nineteen. If we can't enjoy a little romance now, when will we? And as for Louis, he is a wicked-smart accountant and attorney in his own right. Your father might censure him, but he knows he's an asset to your family's rice and cotton business. Your mother would calm down eventually."

"You don't understand. You've lived an entirely different life from mine." Sarah scooted her chair sideways, away from their maids. "Your father's fellow officers taught you to ride and shoot. Your mother drags you on sea voyages from California, to Panama, to New York. And now, the two of you are in Paris, managing your own lives. I've never experienced anything even close to what you have."

"Does Louis know how you feel about him?" Lillie asked.

"You are incorrigible," Sarah said, defeat in her voice.

"You haven't answered my question."

"No, maybe. Well, yes."

Lillie thought she could detect a note of yearning in her friend's answer.

"All right, then. We're making progress." Lillie leaned closer.

"Can you tell me now why it's so important I come with you to London?" Sarah pleaded.

"I need your help with *Maman*. I am about to embark on an adventure I'm not sure she will condone."

"You mean you have something planned which might be worse than what we've already done?"

"I'm afraid so."

"Don't tell me. You really did meet with a spy in the cemetery." Sarah stared at her, eyebrows raised.

Beads of sweat popped up on the bridge of Lillie's nose. Losing her nerve for a few seconds, she wavered, then plunged ahead, holding her finger to her lips for complete quiet as she bent forward across the table and whispered her plan into her friend's ear.

"No." Sarah raised her hand in a gesture of finality. "You've gone too far this time. What you're proposing is madness. You could be killed, or brutalized. Your mother would never consent to such an adventure."

"Which is why I need your help to distract her. Once the details are finalized, she'll come around. She wants to help the war effort as much I do. And besides, women play important roles all the time," Lillie said. She blew away a frizzy curl edging toward her mouth and added, "Look at Mrs. Greenhow, the famous spy. She carried messages that turned the tide at the battle of Manassas. This adventure of mine pales in comparison to some of her exploits."

"How are you going to arrange this affair?" Sarah asked, a faint hint of resignation creeping into her voice.

"I'm to meet a solicitor in London who has all the details. Then I can tell *Maman*, once my plans are complete. She'll be happy to help the South but worried, and will insist on coming along. You have to help me talk her out of interfering."

"Me? Your mother would never listen to me." Sarah clasped her hand over her chest, her mouth gaping.

"Why not? She's going to be writing about the London season, so she will have entrée to all the best parties. What better way to enjoy the excitement and gossip than through your eyes?" Lillie asked. "She doesn't need to know the real reason you're there. She'll use her connections to line up the best of the eligible men to meet you, which will give me time to execute my plans."

"Wait a minute. I'm not looking for a husband," Sarah insisted.

"I know you love Louis, but you can pretend to need a husband. Who knows? This might be just the thing to push him to offer for you," Lillie said.

Sarah hesitated, a frown creasing her forehead.

"For heaven's sakes, if you do as I say, and help me, you'll get Louis in the end anyway. Trust me."

"Aren't you afraid she'll expect you to find a husband, too? After all, you're not getting any younger, either."

"She's given up trying to marry me off." Lillie glared at her friend, irritated at her assumption. "And, besides, none of the men I find attractive ever measure up to her high standards. Once she knows I'm on a mission to help the South, the rest will fall into place. Trust me."

"So, what exactly am I supposed to do?" Sarah asked, defeated.

"Distract her."

"And how do you propose I do that?"

"Make her think you're desperate to find a husband. *Maman* will jump at the chance to interfere in your life, and she'll leave me alone for a while," Lillie said.

"All right," Sarah crossed her eyes and stuck her tongue out at Lillie. "You've worn me down. What do we do next?"

"We're going to play a little game of cards tonight."

"What?" Sarah asked, and let out a whoosh of air in exasperation.

"We have to upset Louis enough to get him to show his true feelings."

"No, Lillie," her friend wailed. "Not again. I hate it when you tease him."

"He'll get over it. Just trust me."

Lillie laid out her campaign, and then they made plans to meet that evening at Sarah's home to put the first step into play.

Lillie watched Louis from beneath lowered lashes, checking her hand of cards once again to pull off a final bluff to infuriate him enough to leave the table. He had been conscripted to join his employer, Philippe Devereaux, in a game of Whist with her and Sarah. As Sarah fidgeted, she nudged her friend's tapping foot under the table to signal her to be still.

Depending on the young secretary's short temper at cards to bring him to his feet to end the game, she kept fueling the fire. She also counted on Julia Devereaux's constant need to monitor her daughter's movements. At the moment, Sarah's mother sat in a far corner of the room and appeared to be absorbed in a book.

"Lillie, please make your bet," Philippe insisted, "while we're all still young enough to finish the game."

"All right." She looked directly at Louis. "I will call your ten and raise you fifty." She reached toward her piles of multi-colored buttons that served as stakes.

The other two players threw down their hands, defeated, but Louis rose to the bait.

"I'm calling you. Show us what you've got." The ante pile in the center of the table was mounded high with buttons.

With an innocent smile, she laid out a pair of twos.

"That does it." Louis tossed his two kings across the table. "I'm not playing cards with you ever again. I should know better than to be fooled by two conniving females." Sputtering, he pushed away his chair and backed out of the room, making his apologies to the Devereauxes.

She glanced toward Sarah, who cowered in her chair as Louis headed for the door. A well-placed kick under the table sent her friend scrambling after him.

Sarah's father looked up, alarmed, when she raced out into the hallway in pursuit of Louis. Julia Devereaux lifted her head, put down her book, and placed her pince-nez back onto a hook on a silver brooch on her bodice. After pushing out of her chair, she fairly steamed toward the fleeing card players, with Lillie in close pursuit.

Even though she had instigated the drama, she was still shocked at the scene outside the card room. Sarah was on tiptoe in a clumsy embrace, clinging to Louis's tall frame, while he smiled and placed a kiss on top of her head. This was going much better than Lillie could have hoped.

Sarah's mother stood in the middle of the hallway, alternately shrieking at Sarah and Louis, and shouting for her husband.

"Yes, Julia?" Philippe calmly joined them and looked from one to the other. "Is someone injured? Have thieves broken into the house and taken hostages?"

"Well, no, but—"

"Then please desist your caterwauling. You're frightening the servants."

"What are you going to do about your daughter and that, that vile excuse for a secretary," Julia asked, exhaling a huff.

"I'll tell you exactly what we're going to do. Sarah will go to her room to ponder how she might have handled this incident differently. Louis will escort Lillie and her maid to their home. And you and I will retire to my study for some cognac and conversation." Philippe punctuated his orders with a look at each of them in turn, which Lillie interpreted to mean he would tolerate no argument.

Julia's frown softened. Lillie expelled the breath she'd been holding, and some of the color returned to Sarah's pale cheeks. Louis stood to the side with bowed head, studied a boot, and scuffed it from side to side, as if trying to straighten the carpet.

The following morning Lillie and Sarah sat in Lillie's bedroom and shared a hidden stash of chocolates. Their mothers were downstairs in the parlor. Muted sounds of debate wafted up through the levels of the townhouse.

Opening her window and leaning out, Lillie tried to pick up threads of the conversation below, but gave up after a fruitless few minutes.

"They're shouting, but I can't understand the gist of what is being said." She turned to Sarah and made a face. "See, your father didn't fire Louis after all, did he?"

"Oh, right, right. As usual, your analysis of the situation was precise. You're the one who should have a command in the army. Are you never wrong?"

"It's simply a matter of lining up all the facts in my head and then juggling them until I see a pattern."

"Well, poor Louis nearly fainted of fright after he returned last night and Father called him into his study."

"Did you sneak back to investigate?" Lillie's eyes sparkled with excitement at the thought of Sarah getting into the spirit of things.

"No. I do not enjoy provoking everyone around me into a frenzy as is your usual state of affairs." Sarah tried to look stern, but faltered and admitted, "I did send Annette to eavesdrop outside the door."

"What happened? He didn't punish Louis, did he?"

"No." She paused a moment before ending the suspense. "No. You were right, of course. Annette said he was warned in the most serious tones that any contact with me must end, or he would face the consequences."

"And then?"

"Father and Mother retired to discuss how to handle my punishment."

"So, what will it be?"

"Please, do quit badgering me. You don't think I would listen in on my parents' most private conversations, do you?"

"Why not?"

"My maid was too terrified to stand outside the door of their private quarters."

Sharp taps on the bedroom door cut short their conversation. When Lillie peered out, Giselle looked from one to the other and motioned for them to follow her to the first-floor parlor.

Abandoning any pretenses to gentility, they clattered down the stairs hard behind the maid and spilled into the parlor to face their mothers.

"You seem to have outdone yourself this time, Lillie." Martha took charge of the situation. "You've finally managed not only to corrupt poor Sarah, but also nearly ruined a young man's prospects with Mr. Devereaux."

Lillie stilled but never broke eye contact with her mother.

"Do you have anything to say in your defense?"

"*Maman*, I'm sorry about my behavior at cards last night, but bluffing is part of the game. Louis just took it too seriously. Then Sarah tried to soothe his ruffled feathers, and—."

"Manipulation is your forte, Lillie, but someday you will meet someone who pushes back, and then—" Her mother stopped short of finishing her warning.

"Sarah is not blameless in this farce, either," Julia said. "Her father and I have decided her restlessness must end. "Since we have no idea how long this wretched war will stretch on, the only option left for us is to provide her with something constructive to occupy her time."

Lillie turned to her own mother, only to be met with a stern stare.

"Philippe believes Sarah should accompany you to London for the season. She cannot be expected to put her life on hold indefinitely. Perhaps London is a better place for her to meet young people in our own social strata."

Lillie and Sarah exchanged guarded looks. Lillie wanted to whoop and holler but instead maintained a meek façade by lowering her gaze and examining her shoes in detail. Somehow, against all odds, she had gotten her way: Sarah would accompany them to London. She was so excited she had a hard time sitting still while the two mothers outlined their plans. Her friend sat with eyes glazed.

"You haven't much time to get ready," Martha warned Sarah. "We leave on Wednesday morning."

"Annette is already supervising Sarah's packing, and I've sent word to my sister, Louisa, in London, to hire a pair of seamstresses to begin designing gowns," Julia said.

Giselle knocked on the parlor door and pushed her head around the corner. "Monsieur Varenne's carriage awaits, Mademoiselle. Shall I tell him you are ready to go, or should he return later?"

"Oh, no. Just get my cape and gloves. I believe I left my bonnet on the bench near the doorway. I will meet you there," Lillie said.

"Tell him this is the last day you will be able to work," Martha said, as she interrupted Lillie's usual mad dash for the door. "We'll need every minute over the next few days to get ready."

Lillie grabbed her things from Giselle and raced down the steps, her mind moving as fast as her feet. She hoped that day's translations would not contain any more jarring revelations.

CHAPTER FIVE

Wednesday Morning, April 22, 1863
Gare St. Lazare, Paris
48°52'37"N; 2°19'28"E

Lillie stood next to Sarah in an early morning haze made up of two parts engine smoke to one part fog. She wrinkled her nose at the acrid smell while gazing wide-eyed at the mound of trunks surrounding them.

Two porters patiently passed them hand-to-hand up the steps to a third man to stow aboard the train. She gave up calculating how they could all fit on the single car they were boarding.

Martha directed the porters, complaining all the while. Julia stood teary-eyed to the side, patting Sarah on the shoulder as if she were leaving forever. Lillie was so tense at the thought of finally setting her scheme in motion she was having a hard time keeping her breakfast down.

"Sarah, how do you do it?" She sneaked a sideways glance at her friend, envying her serene appearance.

Trains pulled into the station with hissing brakes, while those leaving engaged in ear-splitting whistles.

"How do I do what?" Sarah turned to the side of the pile of trunks, away from some of the din, and leaned her head toward Lillie.

"How do you stay so calm while I am like to burst with excitement? We're on our way. We did it."

"Oh, Lillie, you poor thing. This is just the beginning. You still have to convince your mother to let you do this on your own. I'm afraid you've set yourself up for disappointment."

Fortunately, their mothers were squabbling with the conductor over the position of the private compartment they had reserved for the trip north to Le Havre.

"And just look at you," her friend lowered her voice. "How will you content yourself to live in rough men's clothing for weeks on end when you take such pleasure in all those new, beautiful frocks? Forget about this wild adventure of yours. Stay with me, and we'll take the silly London season by storm."

Lillie glanced down at her traveling suit. There was a lot of truth in Sarah's words. She fingered the delicately embroidered fawn percale of the skirt, savoring the fine touch. In a few weeks, the only clothing she could wear would be the crude woolen pants, jackets and underwear of a sailor and soldier. Not a pleasant thought, but it couldn't be avoided.

Sarah swept up her voluminous skirts to ready herself for the precarious ascent to their car. They gave up trying to talk in the midst of loud whistle blasts from the conductor, signaling ten more minutes before departure.

Lillie squeezed Sarah's hand hard before they climbed aboard. Julia joined them briefly for a tearful good-bye and then left with her groom.

Once settled into their private compartment, Martha sat down and eyed them suspiciously.

"I know you two are up to something. It's only a matter of time until I find out what it is."

"*Maman*, I have no idea what you are talking about." Lillie widened her eyes into what she hoped approximated an innocent stare.

"We shall see," her mother said.

Thursday, April 23, 1863
Crossing English Channel

Lillie leaned against the rail of the ship and swept her gaze across the horizon as they approached Portsmouth. Both her mother and Sarah were laid low in their cabin with *le mal de mer* from the rough channel crossing. She never suffered from the affliction, having spent much of her childhood on ships, crossing from her father's world in the West to her mother's in the Southeast.

But now she stood and viewed the mist at the far shore signaling the entrance to the harbor. Staring without seeing, she let her restless mind to range over the many possible outcomes of her danger-fraught scheme. What if she lost her nerve at the last minute, or worse, in the middle of the mission? She tried not to think of the hardships she might have to endure, but focused instead on the brave soldiers who needed ammunition and food. The gold she would carry could go a long way toward easing their suffering. And who knew? The diplomatic transmissions might be the beginning of open assistance for the Confederacy from the French government.

50°53′47″N 1°23′48″W
Portsmouth Harbour

Moored to the left and closer to shore, a long, sleek ship with three smokestacks and two schooner rig masts gently rode the swells at anchor. *The Kate* was undergoing vigorous testing, closely monitored by her captain. He supervised preparations for his next run into Charleston harbor as if his life depended on it.

In fact, it did.

Jack stood on the deck deep in thought, and then leaned over the side rail. He shouted to his chief engineer, Derby, over the clanging of reinforcements to the steel hull. "Mind the fittings. Go over them twice. If they don't hold, we're finished."

"Aye, sir."

His pre-voyage paranoia drove many of the crew to distraction, but all obeyed without question. His incessant reminders and commands were merely the way he ticked off in his mind the remaining tasks before they set out to sea.

In his considered opinion, the secret to returning with ship and crew intact was constant review of the endless minutiae involved in ensuring seaworthiness. In the case of blockade running, this also included imagining the many disasters that might occur and trying to provide backup contingencies for a safe return.

Another possible disaster suddenly occurred to him. He leaned over the rail again and shouted for Derby to join him in his quarters.

Charles Derby had been with Jack through many skirmishes at sea. He had become a solid fixture on his subsequent blockade runs, having been put on temporary leave from the Royal Navy between wars. Short and barrel-chested, the savvy engineer had a volatile temperament to match his wildly thatched red hair. However, Jack could not imagine facing a disaster at sea without him.

"Aye, sir. As soon as I can find someone with a strong enough back to hoist me up to the deck." The burly Scot's attempt at humor brought a smile to Jack's face.

"And where would I find someone with sufficient might to haul your girth over the gunnels?" He good-naturedly wrapped the line of Derby's sling around a pulley for leverage and then began hauling the solid engineer back aboard.

In his thirties, Jack was in good health and strong from a life of hard labor at sea since entering the naval service at thirteen. His only outward concession to age seemed to be the silver streaks in his light blond hair.

As soon as Derby cleared the rail and landed safely on deck, Jack turned and moved aft toward his quarters. Jack's long stride forced his friend to rush to keep up.

He pushed back crimson damask curtains from the portholes in his cabin. The weak spring sun washed the interior of the saloon and illuminated the large table used for the officers' mess.

At the moment, however, the surface was covered with ship's plans and charts. Carved rosewood panels along the walls glowed with a high sheen of polish. Plush red cushions lined comfortable benches along the walls on which hung softly shaded landscape paintings.

"Have you thought any more about our discussion of how to maximize engine power and minimize boiler damage?" Jack leaned over the table and shoved aside a pile of rolled papers before taking a seat.

"I may have a solution." Derby paused and waited for his words to sink in.

"But?"

"It's no been tried much, but I think it worth at least a trial at cruising speed before we encounter any trouble." After years in the Royal Navy, Derby still reverted to his Scottish brogue when under pressure.

"Go ahead." Jack leaned his lanky frame back, putting his hands behind his head and stretching his legs out beneath the table, waiting for his engineer to continue.

"What we need to do is to refit the boiler with a superheater."

"What?"

"A superheater. It's a fairly new concept, but I know it should work. It's so simple."

"This had better be good. *The Kate* is a brand new ship just commissioned from the yard." He eyed Derby warily as the engineer searched through the pile of plans on the table. He pulled out the sketch of the boiler and pushed it in front of him.

"You know our ships can't come to us fitted for resistance to attack." Derby gave him a shrewd look and continued. "Once the steam builds up," he said, pointing to a mass of pipes within the boiler, "you get condensation the further it travels from the heat source, and with condensation, the temperature falls."

"Dammit, Derby. Get to the point. I'm not an engineer."

"In short, when we're trying to outrun blockaders, we'll be able to get more power out of her for a much longer period of time." By then Derby had turned to face him, abandoning the plans.

"How much will this cost?"

"A lot."

"And how long will it take?"

"A month, maybe three weeks if we push it."

"Done. Start today."

"But it's just one part of the solution."

"For the love of God, spit it out. What else do we need to do?" Jack groaned inwardly, calculating how much this would eat into his share of the profits. However, he could not complain at his success over the last dozen trips into Charleston and Wilmington. His personal worth was at well over a million pounds sterling. Doing battle with the Russians had never paid this well.

"The second problem, as you well know, is the scaling caused by the remains of the seawater we use for cooling. With a circulating loop system for the steam, we could minimize the salinity of the water in the boiler."

"Which would mean . . .?"

"Less scale buildup."

This last bit of information he understood only too well. It was a constant annoyance at sea and had brought him to a standstill a number of times. The engines were useless until the water in the boiler could be blown out and fresh seawater pumped in to replace it. If the wind died and rendered the schooner's backup sails useless, they could drift for days.

"Is there anything else on which you would like me to splurge my money?"

"No, sir."

"And how much longer should the modifications take?"

"With any luck in getting the parts we need, it could take three weeks to a month for both projects. But I can't promise."

"We set sail in three weeks, first to Bermuda, and then Charleston."

"But you didn't hear me..."

"Three weeks, Derby. And you'll have to manage in my absence. Blasted inconvenient, but my mother and sister have been badgering me for months to attend some events at Clarendon. The Season, God help us, is nearly upon us."

"Aye, sir." Derby turned and blustered toward the cabin door, muttering oaths beneath his breath.

"Three weeks, Derby. No more. You were the best-damned engineer in the service. No one but you could even come up with such a plan, let alone pull it off."

Derby turned away, muttering, but Jack didn't doubt for a moment the work would be finished on time.

Even though the day was hardly bright outside, it took Jack some time to adjust to the murky light of the harbor tavern. He hated wasting time in such establishments, but information gleaned from double agents could be invaluable, could make the difference between success and failure.

He spotted Wade Devereaux at a table in the far corner, nursing a drink and periodically scanning the room. As soon as the younger man glanced up and noticed him, he rose, and moved through the gloom to meet him.

"Captain — how long have you been in port, and when do you leave?"

"Those are interesting questions. Why do you ask?" He narrowed his eyes and stared hard at Wade. "For all you know, I may have retired to the country to count my coin."

"Come now. It's not about the money, is it?" Wade sat down and leaned back, tilting a time-scarred chair. "You could return home and live quite comfortably on your naval half pay, not to mention the allowance you must get from your family."

Jack was tempted to lean across the table and swat the disrespectful pup to the floor, were it not for drawing unwanted attention.

"My family and my finances are none of your concern. Get to the point." The throbbing vein at his temple was a sign none of his friends would have ignored, a sure precursor to a fit of temper.

"I hear you're doing extensive improvements to your ship before you make another run." Wade continued his arrogant snooping without apparent regard for the consequences.

"All right. What do you want? And what is it worth to you for me to do it? Quit wasting my time and get to the point."

"I prefer to think of us as old friends joined together for mutual benefit."

"Listen. You are nothing more than a little weasel. The only reason I tolerate your very existence is for the information we occasionally share. If not for your occasional usefulness, I would have called you out long ago."

"I had no idea sailors were so talented with pistols."

"Pistols are not what I had in mind. It would give me great pleasure to bloody your precious face with my bare fists." He paused for emphasis before standing to stare down at his adversary. "I will ask one more time. What do you want?"

"A certain person has papers which must get into Confederate hands." Wade talked quickly, and then paused. "And this person has good French gold to pay the captain who could get this done by the most expedient means available. If you are boarded at sea, he must not be taken; the dispatches must not be found."

"No. Not on my ship."

"You haven't even heard the best part."

"I don't need to. The last 'passenger' you represented to me caused my ship, my crew and myself endless peril." He rose to leave.

"In addition to your usual passage fee, we are willing to pay a bonus of five-thousand pounds in gold."

"My God, what is this person carrying?" He turned back and gave Wade an incredulous look.

"You don't need to know. Just trust me when I say this is so pivotal to the war effort, influential persons in high places are willing to go the limit to make it so."

Monday, April 26, 1863
51°30'26"N, 0°7'39"W
Mayfair, London

Lillie stared into the full-length mirror propped in the corner of the room she shared with Sarah. She was wearing her third outfit of the day, having discarded the previous two in heaps on the floor. Giselle nervously followed her around the room, providing new options as soon as she tossed down the old.

Three hats lay askew on the bed's counterpane, while delicate lace and knit gloves were strewn on the floor. She still stood in her stocking feet, an assortment of shoes lined up along the wall.

Sarah sat on the massive four-poster bed, her eyes wide, watching her friend's continued frenzy.

"Don't just sit there with your mouth open. Get over here and help me."

"If you could tell me what you're trying to do, I might be abler to come up with some suggestions. You won't even say where you're going."

"Out, and I need to look serious, worldly, rich, in charge of my life."

"Then I know exactly what you need." Her friend jumped from the bed and dragged Giselle back to a huge wardrobe, which nearly covered one wall of the room. "You need to wear the one thing in which you feel most comfortable. The rest will follow."

"All right, but hurry." She rolled her eyes in disbelief and began tearing at the buttons on the dress she still stood in. "I have only one more hour to get to my appointment."

Ten minutes later she stood in the hallway of Sarah's aunt's Mayfair townhouse, waiting for the carriage to circle around to the front from the stables facing the alley.

Louisa Williams, Julia Devereaux's sister, was the wife of a wealthy English lord with plantations in South Carolina. She had insisted Martha and the girls stay with her for the season.

Peering one last time at her reflection in the hallway mirror, she felt as though she would suffocate in the midst of a dizzying array of furniture, plants and bibelots crammed everywhere. Her sensibly heeled boots sank into layers of Turkish carpets.

However, she was pleased with the image staring back at her. She was ready.

CHAPTER SIX

Sunday, April 26, 1863
London, England
51°30'62"N, 0°10'0"W

Lillie settled back into the cushions of the Williams
carriage and plucked at a piece of lint on her navy blue
Ottoman silk. Thank God Sarah helped her choose
what to wear. But would the right dress disguise the
hammering of her heart and the shaking of her knees?

She was headed for Lincoln's Inn, center of the
English legal profession, to meet Solicitor Algernon
Summer whose firm represented shipping companies.

She pressed her face against the carriage window
and glanced back along the street. She was certain she
was being followed. The Pinkerton detectives were
bulldogs once they were convinced she and her mother
might be up to something. Agents followed them
everywhere, and censors at the American Embassy
read all their correspondence.

As if avoiding Union agents were not difficult
enough, she had to plan this outing without *Maman's*
or Aunt Louise's knowledge. She'd chosen this
particular morning because her mother would be at
the dressmaker's shop for hours. Venturing forth on
such a mission without Giselle as chaperone had also
been a risk. She timed her departure just after Aunt
Louisa left on morning rounds of calls.

Thomas, the family's elderly driver, climbed down to inquire as to where she would like to go.

"There is a street lined with drapers' shops near Lincoln's Inn. I know I've seen it. Do you recall where that might be? I need to do some shopping for *Maman*."

"To be sure, Miss Coulbourne." He pulled a handkerchief from his pocket and dabbed at his already sweating brow. "That would be Walnut Street."

"Now I remember. That's where it was. If you could drop me off at one of them, I will look through several for what she wants." Now she would have an alibi for how she spent her morning.

"And since the morning is so beautiful, I think I might enjoy a brisk walk to Lincoln's Inn Fields. Could you meet me there?"

He looked askance at her but helped her inside the passenger compartment and then climbed back up to the driver's seat. The young groom who had been holding the horses leapt onto the jump seat, and they trotted through the park toward the city.

Once inside the shop, she surveyed the bolts of fabric covering every available surface. The tinkle of a bell mounted on the shop door summoned a tiny woman with heavily rouged cheeks who bustled from the back room and looked at her expectantly.

"Yes, Miss?"

"I need something to complement the blue stripe of *Maman's* favorite chair, yet not clash with the reds, blues and greens in the carpet."

"Aye, that's a tough one. But, let me see." The woman dug into her stock of fabric bolts beneath the counter. "I think one of these might do."

The three options fished from the jumble below included a dark blue background with a field of red flowerets accented with white, a cream-on-cream stripe which she condemned out of hand, and a dark red paisley with touches of blue and green. She had no idea what would suit her mother, but chose the paisley.

She fussed about the price until the woman good-naturedly agreed to a bit of a percent off. The clerk cut the required yardage and wrapped it in tissue paper.

After arranging to have her purchase delivered, she slipped out the back door to foil the Pinkertons loitering outside the front of the shop and turned north toward Serle Street and Lincoln's Inn Fields.

The morning sun had not yet burned off all the fog, and random wisps mixed with smoke from coal fires spread a light ochre patina over the neighborhood. In spite of heavy smoke and dust, the London air always verged on outright dampness.

Ever-present smells and soot of thousands of coal fires filtered gently down. The grime covered sidewalks, stoops, sills, and anything white a hapless walker was foolhardy enough to wear outside.

A servant bustling along the street toward her coughed into a kerchief while she moved quickly among street vendor stalls, searching for fresh flowers. Lillie studied her from a distance and savored the smell of hot chestnuts roasting on a brazier.

The woman's shock of fair hair was combed back from a widow's peak. Without a cap, the flyaway tendrils might puff toward curliness. Her complexion had the dewiness of constant exposure to mists and rain. The white apron at her waist already had begun to collect bits of settling coal dust.

Lillie wondered how this same woman would fare back home. Would she be a servant, or would she be the mistress of her own life?

At Serle Street she approached the main gate near Lincoln's Inn and turned to the path leading to the offices around New Square. She noted the four-story building housing both offices and residences of barristers and some offices for solicitors.

Stopping at the entrance to the stairs at Number Twelve, she studied a list of ten names. Her gloved finger moved down to one listed simply, Algernon Summer. A bead of sweat lined her brow as she slowly climbed to the third floor.

The door swung open on her first knock, and a clerk ushered her into a waiting room.

"And you would be here to see...?"

"Solicitor Summer, Algernon Summer. I'm Miss Lillie Coulbourne. I have an appointment."

He offered her a seat on a leather couch in a reception area. She lowered herself stiffly, keeping to the edge so as not to sink into the cushions and need a hand to get up again.

Books lined the oak-paneled room except for one wall where two tall mullioned windows overlooked the street and square below. A Turkish carpet covered polished wood floors while silver-capped decanters of port on a tantalus reflected the morning sun streaming through the windows.

"Would you like some tea while you wait?" The clerk hovered like some large, fluttering brown moth.

"No," she answered quickly. The heat in the waiting room was stifling. "But could I impose upon you for a glass of water?"

"Certainly." He disappeared into a rabbit warren of corridors off the waiting room.

She rose from the couch and wandered among the bookshelves, browsing titles. The unease in her stomach subsided a little. She ran her fingers lightly over the bindings and read the titles, stopping occasionally to pull one from the shelf.

After returning the volume to the shelf, she tipped the glass of water the clerk had delivered and poured the cool liquid down her parched throat.

"He will see you now," he said, interrupting her pause for breath after a long sip. "This way, please."

She followed him through a passage lined with paintings of clipper ships whose owners the firm represented. Having spent much of her childhood sailing with her mother between her father's posts in California and their plantation properties in the Carolinas, she had traveled aboard several of them. She peered at the brass title plates on the frames and smiled at memories of the various voyages.

Her last long sea trip had been three years earlier when her father had sent them packing to flee the volatile pre-war climate in California. They sailed down the coast, crossed the Isthmus of Panama, and then embarked on another ship to cross the Atlantic to France.

Her boots sank into thick carpeting and she half-skipped to keep pace behind the long-legged clerk, following him to the very rear of the maze of law offices.

He opened the heavy oak door for her and then softly closed it behind her with a muffled click.

A man rose from behind a large teak desk rubbed dark with oil. She clamped her mouth shut to hide her surprise at his youth. Solicitor Summer could not be much older than thirty, with close-cropped coppery brown hair. His mutton-chop sideburns, instead of lending seriousness to a young, handsome face, served only to heighten the effect of the soft curve of his cheekbones and jaw.

"Algernon Summer, at your service." He extended his hand and took hers warmly in his. "I'm so glad to meet you, Miss Coulbourne. I feel as though I know you after reading your newspaper columns."

She could not speak for a moment. Why on earth would he have read her columns back in the *San Francisco Evening Bulletin*? She wrote infrequently, her columns being more travelogues than her mother's gossip.

"Please call me Lillie," she insisted.

He motioned her toward a chair pulled close to his desk. After sitting, he leaned back in his own chair, remaining silent for thirty or forty seconds.

"You know, we will have to manufacture a reason for your trip here. I believe you were followed," he finally said.

"They're always following me," she protested. "They have no idea why I'm here."

He stood and moved from his desk to the ceiling-to-floor window behind her chair. Why was he gazing out at the park for such a long time? Had he changed his mind about helping her?

"Never underestimate your adversaries," he said. "If the ship is stopped by Union blockaders, the captain will eventually be released, as he is still a British naval officer. But you — you could be hanged." He turned from the window to stare at her. "You don't have to do this."

"There is no way I would give up now." Lillie gestured wildly with her hands. "I've wanted to do my part to help the cause ever since Fort Sumter." Her face flushed in agitation.

"Very well," he said. "A benefactor, who wishes to remain anonymous, is underwriting your mission," he added, and moved quickly to complete their business.

"Now, what questions do you have?" he asked. "We haven't much time. Arrangements to transfer the bonds and funds should not take long, and there is the matter of some documents you will be carrying from the French government."

"What do the documents contain?" she asked, trying to stem the excitement in her voice.

"I don't want to know and neither should you, but they might very well change the course of the war." He turned and bent to a small safe behind his desk. When he stood again, he held a packet bound shut with the seal of France.

"With such valuable items entrusted to me, how do I know I can trust your organization?" Her mouth suddenly felt dry.

"Miss Coulbourne, dangerous waters are our specialty. All of the captains I represent are experts at getting out of tight situations. I assure you their records for successful, safe delivery are the best in the business."

He narrowed his eyes and studied her. "Are you sure you are committed to this mission?"

"Yes, I will do it," she said in a rush. This was it. After all her glib talk of "do or die for Dixie," it was time to stand up and be counted.

"Since you've accepted," he continued, "you must make arrangements to disguise yourself as a man. Would you be willing to pose as a crew member, perhaps a cabin boy, the son of an old friend of the captain?"

"What?" She didn't like the sudden change in direction of the conversation. "Why do you think it would be safer for me to go aboard in disguise than to sail as a passenger?" His sudden nervousness was puzzling.

"Of course, I planned to wear sailing clothes to simplify my time on the ship, but to represent myself as a man? I don't know." Her voice trailed off.

"The truth is, this captain refuses to allow women on his ship. He had an unpleasant experience last year with a female spy and has vetoed any women passengers ever since." His forehead wrinkled in a frown.

"In fact, he is wary of carrying spies at all. The only reason he has agreed to the presence of an agent on this trip is the very generous bonus on top of passage fees your benefactor has offered."

"And you expect me to risk this captain's ire along with all the other challenges I will have to face?" she asked.

"Please trust me, Miss Coulbourne," he said. "This man is the finest blockade runner in our fleet. Considering the danger of your documents being found should the ship be boarded, he is the only captain you would want at the helm."

"We must make arrangements immediately," Summer added. "There is not a minute to waste. Our ship, *The Kate*, sails in three weeks from Portsmouth. Can you be ready to leave by then?"

"Yes, but there is a minor problem," Lillie said.

"Problem?"

"It's my mother. She doesn't know I'm here. I couldn't tell her my plans before our meeting. She will want to meet the captain before giving her blessing," she said, and then hastily added when he frowned at her request, "but of course, he can't know why."

Summer reverted to his previous habit of waiting for her to fill the vacuum of silence with chatter. She would not give him the satisfaction. She bowed her head and studied one polished boot toe poking out from beneath her skirt.

She finally raised her head defiantly and was surprised to see him smiling as if enjoying a private joke.

When he rose to lead her to the door, curiosity overcame her, and she asked, "What sort of man is he?"

"The best." He gave her a steady look and added, "I would trust him with my life. In fact, I have."

"Then your word is enough for me." She turned toward the door again.

"You should go home and prepare for the voyage. I will have a messenger sent to Lord Williams's residence with an invitation for a weekend house party at the captain's family home in Wiltonshire. My wife, Miranda, is a distant cousin of his stepmother, Caroline. She will make the arrangements, and he will never know you are his new cabin boy

Once you're on board the ship, it's up to you to maintain your disguise," he added, "May luck be with you, Miss Coulbourne. And of course it's still not too late to change your mind."

Lillie did not even acknowledge his last offer. She would make the run.

Standing on the walk in front of the Lincoln's Inn complex, Lillie craned her neck to pick out her carriage among all the conveyances in hectic midmorning traffic. For the hundredth time, she cursed the accident of her sex and how it made her an object of curiosity.

She hated the stares of passersby when she lingered alone on a public street. Crossing the thoroughfare into the park area, she sought a secluded bench where she could watch for Thomas guiding the familiar, reliable team.

She leaned forward for a better look, and the bench suddenly shook as another person planted himself on the far end. She focused on the jam of carriages to avoid eye contact, but sat up with a start when her fellow bench-sitter began to whistle. She risked a sideways glance.

It was the man she'd encountered swinging his cane in the cemetery in Paris. The name of the tune he whistled suddenly popped into her head. It was her father's favorite, a rowdy ditty of the California mining camps. He had sometimes taken her along as a child when he volunteered his medical services in the camps.

"Miss Coulbourne, please do not stare at me," the stranger said. "Just listen carefully." He let his warning sink in. "We haven't much time."

She leaned over to pick a flower at the corner of the bench and then turned her body to the side to inspect her prize. Anyone watching would not suspect they were carrying on a conversation, albeit one-sided.

"I know you'll sail for Charleston soon. I'm an old comrade-in-arms of your father — James Weatherby. He asked me to teach you what you need to know before you embark on this adventure."

She said nothing, but kept her head bent over.

"He said you would know he sent me if I told you his favorite name for you."

She lifted her head expectantly, still gazing in the opposite direction.

"Poppet."

A shockwave went through her at his knowledge of her family.

"One week from today, you will leave the house after everyone has retired for the evening. Wear all black and exit from the rear mews. My carriage will be waiting."

She chafed with annoyance at his commanding manner and turned to flash him a cutting look, but he was gone. Only a neatly folded broadsheet remained on the bench along with the many questions crowding her mind.

While Lillie returned to the Williams townhouse, she rehearsed over and over in her head how to explain her lengthy absence. She needn't have worried. The entire household was in an uproar. Her absence was the least of their worries.

Martha alternated between gushing at Sarah's Aunt Louisa and firing off commands to poor bewildered Giselle.

"Where have you been?" Her mother cut short her attempt to answer. "Never mind — we haven't a moment to spare. This invitation is more important."

"An invitation? Who sent it?" Lillie asked. Surely Solicitor Summer couldn't have contrived to have one delivered so soon. She didn't even remember telling him the address. The whole meeting had gone by in such a blur.

Her mother ignored Lillie's question and motioned the four of them to join her in the downstairs parlor. Once they were settled in, she passed around the cream-colored vellum card, and they took turns reading the contents. On the outside was an elegantly engraved coat of arms featuring rampant griffins and a knight's helmet.

The message inside said simply: "The pleasure of your company is requested Friday next for a weekend retreat at Clarendon, country home of the Dowager Countess Wiltonshire." All four women, as well as Lord Williams, were included on the invitation.

"Haven't I been telling you cultivation of social contacts is everything?" Martha fairly vibrated with excitement and looked around in triumph after reading the contents aloud. "I knew the aristocracy would come around to seeing the importance of my columns."

Lillie stifled a smile and glanced around the room. Amazement registered on Sarah's face, while her Aunt Louisa's expression spoke of something altogether different.

"Who led you to believe such an invitation would be forthcoming?" Louisa's look was noncommittal, and she directed her question to Martha. Her soft, soothing voice contrasted with the forward thrust of her chin. Although she had no children of her own, she always knew exactly when Lillie and Sarah were plotting and refused to accept their improbable explanations of questionable comings and goings. Her tiny, delicate figure belied a stern, commanding presence.

"My columns are read widely in the expatriate community and now, apparently, in upper circles of English society as well," Martha continued.

Lillie studied her mother, and her earlier optimism plummeted. How could she broach the subject of the blockade run now? The invitation had nothing to do with the column, but was all about the latest predicament in which she found herself. She had to get her mother alone as soon as possible and begin the tangled web of explanations.

"*Maman*, could we discuss this later this afternoon? I am faint with all the excitement and could use some fresh air in the garden to sort out my thoughts. Would you come with me?"

"Of course, but I..."

Lillie and Martha found their way to the rear garden nestled between the townhouse and mews. They sank onto a wooden bench at the edge of a small reflecting pool. Fat carp circled endlessly in a soothing dance in search of food. With no inspiration forthcoming from the depths of the water, she turned to face her mother

"*Maman*, I want to run the blockade into Charleston Harbor in order to check on my property, and to smuggle money to the Confederacy."

Her mother remained strangely quiet, not even interrupting to challenge the plan. Martha's clear blue gaze revealed nothing. The silence stretched out.

"For heaven's sakes, please," she said, losing her nerve. "Say something."

"What do you want me to say? 'God speed, go with my blessing'?" Her mother regained her voice and gathered momentum. "I suppose you expect me to stand by helplessly while you destroy your reputation, your fortune, your life?"

Of all the possible reactions she had feared, this one was the least likely. Her mother should have been excited about the adventure and insisting upon going along.

Lillie sucked in a breath, taking in the pungent odors of the kitchen garden herbs.

"I've made up my mind. I will prove myself 'as good as any man,' and for once in my life, be the captain of my own destiny." She squinted into the afternoon sun and waited for the explosion that would surely follow.

"You cannot —"

"I'm nineteen. Would you rule me for the rest of my life? I have decided. The ship leaves from Portsmouth in three weeks. Please say I have your blessing. Don't make me beg."

"Then I will come along." Martha clamped her mouth shut in a thin line.

"No, you mustn't." Lillie faltered, but a moment later she added, her voice croaking, "I need you to stay here with Sarah and provide my alibi."

"Your alibi?"

"Yes. I want you to hire a female companion who resembles me. You can say I'm ill and go out in public with her heavily veiled. That way, no one will suspect I'm gone."

"Then I insist on meeting the captain." Her mother gripped the side of the bench, her face pale and pinched.

"I knew a face-to-face meeting would be the price you would exact."

"—Which explains the invitation."

"But you must promise me you won't tell him I'll be on his ship." Lillie leaned forward and covered both of her mother's hands with her own.

Martha pulled a lace handkerchief from her pocket and dabbed at a tear at the corner of her eye. "What you are proposing is madness. Although your father and I have not always been in accord, I feel certain he would agree with me this time."

"You're wrong about Papa."

"I suppose the two of you have been plotting behind my back again." Her mother's look changed from tortured to bitter.

"No, of course not." Would they ever cease this tug-of-war over her father's affections? "But somehow, I believe he knows of my plans and is working behind the scenes to ensure my safety."

"How do you know? His letters to me have said nothing of this."

"I cannot say. You must simply trust me on this," Lillie said, and closed her eyes against the colossal headache building at the top of her head. She pressed her fingers against her temples and added, "Let's just go spend the weekend at Clarendon. I'm convinced once you meet him, all your fears will be allayed."

"I'm still not sure," Martha insisted.

"Can you at least agree to delay judgment until after you've met the poor man?" Her mother was probably right to doubt, but whatever lay ahead, Lillie knew her fate was sealed. He would have to be an ogre spewing fire for her to change her mind now.

"Yes." Martha reluctantly nodded her consent and then grasped both of Lillie's hands in her own.

Looking down at the fingers clasped in hers, Lillie was startled at the similarity of their hands. She hoped that was all she'd inherited from her mother.

CHAPTER SEVEN

Friday, May 1, 1863
Wiltonshire, England
51°43'0"N, 0°45'0"W

Mud squished up over the ankles of Lillie's smart leather boots while she strained to push with all her weight against the wheel. Deep ruts from early spring rains along the road to Clarendon had undone their driver's best efforts to keep them on the road.

She grinned at the thought of the look on *Maman's* face when she finally arrived at the estate looking like her grandpa's old hunting dog, covered in mud. The second driver on the hired carriage pushed alongside her while his partner coaxed the horses to pull them out of the rut.

"Keep them pulling. I can feel the carriage starting to move," she said with a grunt.

The two men had annoyed her, dithering and wringing their hands after landing in the first rut. They'd refused any help from their passengers, had balked at even letting her and Sarah get out of the carriage to lighten the load.

When they all leaned hard into the wheel one last time, it budged, only to issue a loud crack and roll out of one rut into another. Unfortunately, the second rut contained even more muddy slop than the first one, most of which ended up on her dress.

A quick pass across her face with her hand loosened most of the globs of mud settled there. When Sarah gawked at her from the side of the road, the look of horror on her face confirmed Lillie's worst suspicions — she was a wreck.

"Come on - just one more push." Lillie used her best wheedling tone.

"We'll walk for help," one of the drivers said. The man next to her shook his head in apology. "Nothing more we can do here, Miss."

The sound of a solitary horseman coming up behind them brought a halt to her pleading. She spun around in hope.

He cantered along the wide avenue lined with massive oaks. Sunlight filtered through the thick canopy of leaves behind him, masking his face.

The moment he dismounted, she recognized the man. Lillie and Sarah exchanged silent looks of dread. This was the same tall Englishman who had held her in such disdain in Paris at the Devereaux mansion.

Maybe he wouldn't recognize her, maybe—.

He walked directly to her side, leaned over, and wiped a finger across her mud-spattered chin.

"Ah, so we meet again, Miss Coulbourne."

Her stomach dropped. Could this be some horrible coincidence? He was a blockade runner captain, he would be sailing back into a Southern port soon. Please, God. Don't let him be the same captain she would have to serve under.

Even as she sent that little prayer winging, she knew. In a few weeks she would have to work in disguise with this infuriating man. Every time she encountered him, he got another look at her.

As if he could read her thoughts, he took a firm grip on her chin, pulled a handkerchief from his pocket and dabbed at the worst of the mud coating her face. After wiping as much as he could with the cloth, he moistened his thumb and rubbed away the remaining evidence.

"Not perfect, but it will have to do."

"My lord —" She started to object to his ministrations and tried to jerk out of his hold.

"Just Jack, please." He stared at Sarah and directed his questions to her. "Miss Devereaux, perhaps you can explain to me how your hoyden friend managed to get herself into such a state."

"We were on our way to spend the weekend at Clarendon when we were delayed by this unfortunate accident." Sarah shifted her gaze between Lillie and Jack. Then she added somewhat lamely, "The rest of our party in the other two carriages did not see the accident, and so, she was just trying to help."

"Right." Abruptly releasing her, he turned toward the two drivers. He hitched his horse to the team and then stripped off his riding coat. His vest followed, and then he rolled up his shirtsleeves.

Relieved at no longer being held and cleaned like a small cat, she stepped back to take her place behind the wheel to help push and stared expectantly at him, waiting for his command to lean in.

"What do you think you are doing?" He strode over and pulled her to the side of the road where Sarah stood.

"I'm going to help," Lillie said. Do you want to get us out of here or do you want to wait all day for another man to come along?"

"How old are you?" He ignored her question entirely.

"Why should it matter?" Why did he have to tower over her so? With the late afternoon sun slanting behind his head, she couldn't gauge the expression on his face.

"Can you not answer a simple, civil question?"

"I will be twenty in June, sir. Why would a gentleman ask such a question?"

"I'm trying to determine what sort of imbecile child I'm dealing with. So, do get out of the way and allow us to remedy this unfortunate situation before the day grows much older. My stepmother will have my head if I don't get you two safely to Clarendon with enough time to change for dinner."

She formed a retort but stopped at a look from Sarah. Instead, she leaned against a tree, folded her arms and glared in the direction of the odious man who had thrust her aside as if she were of no account.

Imbecile, was she? Why were women always assumed helpless? With her assistance alone, the hired drivers eventually would have been able to extricate the carriage from the ruts.

Moments later, with the addition of his horse to the team, Jack managed to roll their conveyance onto a more level patch of road.

While her friend hastened to climb back aboard with his assistance, she could not bring herself to let him hoist her up the steps.

"Miss Coulbourne," Jack said, "you really are too old to use mutinous ways to vent your disapproval. I would think someone who will be 'twenty in June' would have been long enough out of the nursery to understand and accept the ways of polite society."

She stifled a gasp of indignation and moved quickly to his side. She thanked her lucky stars that when next they were in close proximity, she would be disguised as a man, and on better footing with this pompous Englishman. She would survive the weekend by avoiding him as much as possible.

"There, now. That wasn't so difficult, was it?" He offered her his arm, and then gave her a boost up into the carriage. "See, you can behave as a proper young lady when you set your mind to it. Can't you?"

She turned and gave him a forced smile over her shoulder. Anyone who knew her would not be fooled.

"Lillie, please. Please get in, so your mother and Aunt Louisa don't go into spasms wondering what happened to us. This gentleman has been most kind to help." Sarah flashed him a dazzling smile and then sent a dark look Lillie's way.

She would climb docilely back into the carriage with his assistance. However, she would not, could not, let him see how he was affecting her. She would show him she was no frail miss. She would — she missed the last step and ended up tumbling back into his arms.

Unaccountably shaken by his encounter with the young American woman, Jack climbed back onto Nelson and urged the gelding into a trot alongside the carriage to make sure no further catastrophes befell them. He hadn't yet darkened the door of his family home, and already the weekend loomed ominously ahead of him. Fortunately, his friend, Edward, would be joining him. Maybe they could find a quiet corner to play cards, smoke the cigars he'd brought back from his last voyage, and avoid most of the unpleasantness.

If his first encounter in Paris with the violet-eyed spitfire were not bad enough, finding her in mud-spattered disarray at the side of the road had nearly undone him. What was he thinking? He was thirty, for God's sakes.

He momentarily shifted his focus from Nelson, which was unfortunate. The wily beast used the short lapse to edge his way precariously close to a steep drainage ditch at the side of the road. To avoid a plunge into the watery channel, he had to jerk the reins, and Nelson recovered clumsily. They made a wide circle and fell back in behind the carriage. Dealing with this blasted animal was another reason to remain at sea.

After regaining his dignity, he looked toward the carriage only to see the impudent, dark-haired minx staring out of one of the windows. She smiled a wicked smile at him but quickly withdrew when he returned her look with an imperious stare.

Jack wanted to ignore the ill-mannered little chit, but he could not forget the warm softness of her body in his arms when she had catapulted from the steps of the carriage. Perhaps it was time to visit his old friend, Elizabeth, the innkeeper at his favorite harbor haunt in Portsmouth.

"Don't think for one minute I believe you're actually reading the French novel on your lap." Lillie leaned back into the squabs and eyed Sarah, whose cowardly head was buried in a book.

"Fine. What is the problem now?" Her friend looked up and set her reading aside.

"Can't you see how he treats us like infants? It is not to be endured. You must promise me you will help me avoid him this weekend at all costs."

"What makes you think he will seek you out? You do not seem to be one of his favorite persons, either."

"Can't you see how little he thinks of women?"

"Why do you care? And, besides, he probably has some frumpy English wife tucked away in the countryside."

"Well then, why isn't she traveling to Clarendon with him?"

"I think you are sweet on him," Sarah said.

"Are you daft? He's done nothing but give me stern looks and call me an imbecile, an imbecile, for heaven's sakes. No matter what I do, I offend him. And, not to change the subject, but did you see how his comical horse nearly unseated him? He really ought to spend more time with the poor creature. The two of them are going to fly over the side of a cliff some day at the rate they get on together." She stopped her tirade with a sheepish look at her friend.

"I was wrong. You are way beyond sweet on him." Sarah raised a lace-gloved hand and added, "No more denials.

"You are in a dangerous state of mind. Don't forget you will be spending long weeks at sea with this man. He must not find out you are a woman. Even if he had feelings for you, he would not tolerate your presence on his ship. You know what the solicitor told you. Developing an attraction for him could destroy all your plans."

"Do you honestly believe I'm attracted to him?" Lillie chewed on her lower lip. She hated it when her friend was right.

"Yes, and furthermore—." Sarah stopped mid-sentence and gaped out the window. "Oh, do stop babbling. You must see this."

Lillie poked her head out the window. As the road curved out of the towering oak tunnel, the late afternoon sun reflected off a palatial manor, making the windows glitter and the outside walls glow as if painted in soft pink and golden hues.

When the carriage passed through the gates into a park filled with fountains and neatly trimmed hedges, she leaned back and squeezed shut her eyes. What had she done? She had a whole weekend to get through, and she was nauseous with dread. She might as well be a fish out of water. Rubbing elbows with English aristocracy was beginning to wear thin.

She scuffed furiously at the remaining mud caked on her skirts and boots, but managed only to spread the mess around. She gave up trying to look presentable.

When the carriage finally came to a halt at the front entrance, they waited for their drivers to come around and help them down. Instead, when the door opened, it was Jack who reached for Sarah's hand and helped her down. The foyer was full of servants, as well as

Maman and Aunt Louisa. Everyone talked at once, and Lillie's mother rushed forward.

Jack stared into her face splotched with dried mud when he leaned into the carriage. Without a word, he swept her up in his arms and strode through the mass of chattering women relatives at the door.

"She's fine. A bit of a difficult afternoon. Everything's ship-shape. No injuries. She just needs to get sorted. Let me take her to her room so she can rest and restore herself before dinner."

He nodded to a servant who moved to lead him to one of the rooms prepared for the guests.

Lillie's mother ran after him, rushing to keep up with his long strides. "What happened?" she asked, her voice full of alarm.

"Just a bit of bother on the way here. Carriage struck a rut or two, and she managed to step in a puddle of mud."

Lillie looked up at him from her perspective in the cradle of his arms and mouthed a silent "Thank you."

Jack could not imagine what possessed him to pick up the prickly Miss Coulbourne and carry her into the house. Maybe it was the look of embarrassment in the depths of those lavender eyes. The only thing that could compare with that color might be the shade of the sea off Portugal one night many years before, just after the sun slipped below the horizon.

Or maybe it was the look of cool amusement on his stepmother's face. He hadn't hesitated. Somehow, he had to protect her from the questioning stares and condescension that surely would have accompanied her walking into the hall in her mud-soaked state.

Hell, the sight of Clarendon after months, or years, at sea still had the power to bring him up short: Magnificent chandeliers, dark mahogany paneling, and thick beams gave a majestic look to the grand hallway entry and never failed to intimidate him.

He had been sent off in shame at thirteen to serve as a midshipman in the Royal Navy after having proven an embarrassingly inadequate student at the private school chosen by his father.

When they neared her room, he refused to wait for the servant to fumble about. Jack pushed the door open with his boot and gently deposited her on the massive four-poster bed. She let out a sign and sank into the soft feather ticking, then suddenly swung her still-booted feet over the edge to limit the damage. She looked up with those damned eyes, and he had to look away.

"Right." He turned to leave her to the ministrations of her mother and maid, only to hear her impudent voice call him back.

"Sir? My lord. No, Jack." She seemed in a great deal of difficulty choosing the right title.

He spun around and waited expectantly.

"I want to let you know how much I appreciate what you did for me. I promise to make it up to you. I think I'll start by working with your horse."

His jaw sagged. "Nelson?"

"Yes. He is a fine creature, but he could use some lessons in obedience."

Jack could not believe the subdued young woman he had deposited in bed not five minutes past was now insulting his horsemanship. And on top of everything else, contemplating her in that very bed made unbidden feelings flood his body.

"My dear Miss Coulbourne, Nelson and I have managed to get on together reasonably well for a number of years now. However, I am a sea captain, not a country squire accustomed to surveying his domain from the back of a horse. He can be stubborn at times, but we seem to suit quite well, all things considered.

"I cannot imagine taking riding lessons from a child at my advanced state in life. But of course, I appreciate the thought."

Lillie, her mother, and Giselle stared at him oddly, so he shut up, and they all stood in awkward silence.

"I just meant it would give me great pleasure to work with your horse for a few hours while we are here," Lillie said. "I would never presume to give you riding lessons, my lord. Perhaps I could just give you a suggestion or two."

"You do not owe me anything. I was happy to ease your discomfort by helping you to your room. And, please, I'm not anyone's 'lord,'" Jack insisted.

"Really, Lord Jack, she is quite good with horses. It is her passion. You should let her work her magic on this Nelson," Martha said.

"Right," Jack said, resigned, "but please - I do not have a title. I am simply Mr. Finch-Barton. If you are determined to deal with Nelson, let one of the grooms know when you require the bully's presence. They will find a suitable saddle for you." He gave up trying to dissuade her from the madness of teaching the damned horse anything useful.

Annoyance flooded him in spite of his vow to remain gracious throughout the weekend. And now the small one's pushy mother was calling him "Lord Jack." If only he could find his friend, Edward, and hide out in the billiard room with a good snifter of brandy. He made his apologies and fled.

Sarah was right. Lillie had to end this dangerous attraction. She sank back into the luxurious feather bed, her lower legs hanging over the edge, and had fallen into a half-nap when *Maman's* anxious face loomed over her.

"Lillie, get up. We have to get you ready for dinner. Even though the countess was most gracious at your slovenly arrival, she is not the sort of woman to overlook another social lapse if you are late for dinner."

"*Maman*, you've been here just a few hours. How do you already know so much about our hostess?"

"Why, Lillie, my darling, you underestimate your mother. In order for me to maintain clarity in my writing, I must get to the essence of the people I meet." Her mother was smiling the artificially sweet smile Lillie had come to dread. "And don't even think about forming an affection for Lord Jack. Not only is he the third son, but he is also engaged in mercenary activities."

"What makes you think I've formed an affection for him?" Lillie sat up so abruptly the room commenced to spin.

Her mother did not answer, but just smiled.

"You must promise me not to mention anything about Jack's profession while we are here." Lillie grasped her mother's arm. "I do not want him to know I will be his passenger. I can assure you I will stay as far away from him as I can manage this weekend.

"And, besides, the only reason we are putting ourselves through this ordeal is for you to meet the captain. Let's just get through the weekend with as little fuss as possible.

"And for goodness sakes, quit calling him 'Lord Jack.' He hates it, *Maman*."

"You have exactly twenty-five minutes to dress," her mother continued, as if she had not heard her daughter's complaints and warnings.

Lillie held her head, pressing her fingers into her temple for some relief. This was just the beginning. How could she possibly get through the rest of this nightmare weekend?

After Martha swept out of the room, she jumped off the bed to find Giselle laying out her clothes. A steaming tub of water tempted her in the far corner.

She shed her mud-soaked traveling dress and sank into the water with a sigh of relief. Her maid held her hair up and began skillful spot repair of the mud damage in her heavy, dark curls.

Nothing like a short nap and hot water to lift a girl's spirits. She had begun to rally her strength when there was a knock at the door. Her maid adjusted the screen around the tub and went to investigate.

"Lillie, you'll never guess who we've drawn for partners." Sarah's bright, annoyingly chipper voice floated across the top of the screen.

"Please," she groaned. "Tell me it's not the 'odious one.'"

"Yes, and I'm to go in with his friend, Edward."

"Is there a gun anywhere out there?"

"Of course not. Why would you ask such a horrible question?"

"I was hoping you could just shoot me and get it over with. At the rate this whole affair is going, I'm probably going to be shot as a spy eventually, anyway. If we do it now, then I won't have to endure all the torture in between."

"It's only dinner," Sarah said. "We can maneuver them between us at the table so they'll talk to each other and ignore us."

Lillie stood, reached for the drying sheet her maid handed her, and moved resolutely toward her clothing.

Jack stretched his long arms across the ornately carved billiard table, lining up a ball and aiming for a side pocket. He not only missed his target, but also scratched the felt.

"Get hold of yourself, man. I've never seen you in such a state. What the devil happened today? Is your family dogging you about your commercial ventures again?" His old friend, Edward Harken, prowled around the table, looking for an advantageous shot.

Jack straightened and observed his fellow officer. They'd been close since they served together on a naval ship chasing slavers off the coast of South America.

"It's nothing," Jack finally said. "It's only that I'm having a hard time adjusting to coming home again. I've never really lived here that much, only seven or eight years as a child. I've never been comfortable in the midst of all this, this —" Words failed him. Instead, he turned with his arms out, pointing to the sumptuous room around them.

"Since when have you become egalitarian? I remember many a night in this very room, carousing with friends until the dawn. This beautiful old place never seemed to bother you then."

"You're right. I suppose those blasted Americans have me on edge. Why my stepmother invited them for the weekend is beyond me. Do they always assume money is an excuse for bad behavior?"

"What sort of bad behavior?"

"The Coulbourne women. The mother is merely pushy, but the daughter is beyond the pale. I happened upon her and her friend's carriage on the estate drive. It was stuck in some nasty ruts. Instead of staying put as any other proper young Englishwoman would, she got out into the mud with the drivers and made a total mess of herself trying to push it back onto the roadway."

"Sounds like the sort of woman I could use on a long trip." Edward put his hands in front of his face in feigned defense while laughing at the look of fury on Jack's face. "Not to change the subject, but we'd better get dressed for dinner before you shatter your brandy snifter with that tense grip. Chin up, old man. It's only three days, then back to your ship. Speaking of your ship, how are the changes going?"

"Derby, as usual, has things well in hand. He has some interesting ideas on boiler improvements we're in the process of testing. In fact, we should be leaving within the next two weeks, depending on the results of the sea trials. What about your ship? Will you be making another run?"

"It depends," Edward said thoughtfully.

"On what?"

"On a certain young woman in Portsmouth."

"Have you gone mad? A young woman, at your age?" Jack asked, sputtering.

"Why not? This will be my last series of runs through the blockade. I've had enough. I'm ready to settle into life on land, learn how it feels to put my boots up in front of my own hearth," Edward said. "With any luck, England will choose not to fight any more wars until the worms are picking over my bones. Blockade running has left me reasonably well off."

"But, a young woman?" Jack asked again.

"Yes." Edward's look turned belligerent. "Am I so old you think I can't handle a younger wife?"

"Of course not. Who is the lucky girl?" Jack's voice softened.

"Remember the boarding house in Portsmouth?" Edward asked.

"Yes."

"Remember Mary Ann, the innkeeper's daughter?"

"Mary Ann? Why, she's just a child still playing with dolls," Jack said, the sound of a censor creeping back into his voice.

"That was ten years ago, Jack. I stayed there last spring for a few days for old time's sake. I assumed she would still be a little girl, but she's turned into a conniving, green-eyed vixen with freckles across her nose. She's taken control of my life, and I wouldn't have it any other way."

"Right. So, when will you be needing my services as witness?" There was an odd tightening in his chest. After all their adventures together, he couldn't believe his old partner in battle was leaving the fray.

"You want to stand for me?" Edward asked.

"Of course. I wouldn't miss it for the world. Once you realize you've made a complete fool of yourself, you'll need lots of good Irish whisky. When will the nuptials take place?"

"Well, there's the uncertain part. I explained to her I should make another run with this new ship being commissioned. A final go would set us up with a farm in Cornwall, but she doesn't want to wait."

"Why should a month or two make a difference one way or the other?"

"She should know soon." Edward blushed bright red and studied the pattern in the rich carpeting covering the billiard room floor. After an embarrassing moment, he looked into Jack's face. "I may be a father by early next year."

"For the love of God. How old will you be when this child is grown? Fifty or so? After all we've been through, you'll be lucky to be alive still." Jack broke out laughing and clapped his friend on the back.

"Let's go back to our rooms and get ready for dinner. I can hardly wait to see what horrors my sister and stepmother have cooked up for me. With my luck, they'll insist I escort the highly annoying Mrs. Coulbourne."

CHAPTER EIGHT

Friday Night, May 1, 1863
Clarendon
Wiltonshire, England
51°43'0"N, 0°45'0"W

Jack strode down the sweeping staircase toward the drawing room as if to a court martial. Why had he agreed to engage in this tomfoolery again?

He was in full formal naval dress uniform and already tugging at the blasted tight collar to salvage what comfort he could for the ordeal ahead.

He glanced at Edward. The annoying cuss was almost prancing toward an evening of excruciating boredom. The vapid grin on his face had to be the sign of a man lost in the throes of infatuation. And he wasn't even going to see his love. He was just thinking about her. It was going to take a lot of brandy after dinner to wipe the nonsensical look off his face.

"For heaven's sakes, could you please have the good grace to at least pretend to be in as much agony as I am?" He paused in their progress toward the drawing room and plucked at his friend's sleeve.

Edward turned to him with a faraway look and a quizzical expression.

"You aren't listening to me," Jack said. "For all I know, you don't even remember where we are. Now I can see why you're reluctant to get back into the game. In your present state of mind, you could lose your ship as well as your worthless hide before we make it into Charleston."

"Why badger me?" Edward asked. "Would you feel better if I adopted your dour outlook on life? I'm tired of roving the seas with a ship full of souls depending on my every decision. Is it such a crime to want to sit in front of my own hearth of an evening and dandle a rosy-cheeked babe on my knee?"

"Right. But do you suppose you could bestir yourself tonight to help an old comrade-in-arms make it through the next four hours?"

"Oh, I see the problem," Edward said with a laugh and gave him a good-natured punch to the arm. "Let's get on with this. I can't wait to meet this outrageous young woman who has managed to get under your skin. For an old salt who thinks nothing of seizing a ship from Russians armed to the teeth, you're not very brave at the prospect of one small chit."

Jack glared at his friend as they entered the drawing room and were surrounded by a circle of chattering women.

Proceeding directly to his stepmother, the dowager countess, he favored her with a slight bow and a warm smile. She gave him a soft peck on his cheek.

"Jack, it's been too long since you've been home. We miss your rousing tales of the sea."

His father had remarried late in life, and his stepmother was only a few years older than Jack. Her smooth creamy skin and sparkling dark eyes belied the widowed status imposed upon her by the death of Jack's father the previous year.

"I hope you have been well, Caroline. Where is that young scamp of a brother of mine?" Jack asked, and peered around the room.

"You've been away too long. Teddy has outgrown his tutors and is boarding at Cheam in Surrey," she said with a sigh.

"I certainly hope he comports himself better than I did. I'm afraid I embarrassed the family with my poor attempts at scholarship when I attended there."

"You, sir, are a bold buccaneer, born too late for the era of dashing privateers." She put her hand on his arm with a mischievous smile. "I'm only teasing. And you don't have to pretend to hang on my every word. Go over and check on the poor young woman you saved from shame this afternoon. They are acquaintances of my niece. The girl and her mother write gossip columns for American newspapers. I thought they might enliven a stuffy weekend."

He moved to comply as if condemned.

"And, Jack, would you and Edward please escort Miss Coulbourne and Miss Devereaux in to dinner?"

He started to protest, but she put her finger to her mouth to shush him and pushed him toward Mrs. Coulbourne who was regaling Lord Carlton St. James with stories of her adventures in Paris.

When Jack worked his way across the room, he came up short. Blast Edward. He was standing close to Lillie and Sarah, their heads bent together in laughter, as if sharing a private joke.

Was it not enough that just a few minutes before he was mooning over his own lady love? Now he was pressing himself onto the youngest women in the room. Was there no end to the man's audacity?

"Ah, here is the captain now." Edward looked up when Jack moved to join the trio. With a mischievous gleam in his eye, Edward turned to him. "I've just been relating some of your exploits to Miss Coulbourne."

Lillie turned to acknowledge the new arrival, and was momentarily bereft of speech. The trim, dark blue uniform with fitted double-breasted jacket and trousers molded to his towering figure. Masses of gold buttons and medals dazzled.

"Whatever am I to call you now?" Her blunt question brought conversation to an embarrassing halt.

He looked down at her, a frown of irritation forming at the corners of his mouth.

"Why, we all call him the right honorable Captain Jack." Edward broke the uneasy silence with a quip.

"Miss Coulbourne," Jack said, with a glare for Edward, "for the course of this evening, and this evening only, you may call me anything you like. However, I do prefer to be called merely Jack when I am not on the deck of my ship. I do not claim any special title, other than the courtesy term, 'the honorable.' Fortunately for me, my eldest brother has taken on the onerous responsibility of being Lord Wiltonshire until his son, Charley, assumes the burden some years hence."

She groaned silently. She had offended him again. How could she ever break this cycle? Worse yet, why did she care?

When she looked up, his piercing, icy blue eyes glared through her like ice shards. Lillie fought a crazy urge to sit down with him in a quiet corner and confess all.

Instead, she said the first thing to pop into her head. "We'd probably call you just Mr. Finch-Barton back home."

"It's settled, then," Edward interrupted without giving Jack a chance to protest. "Your suggestion is probably better than he deserves. Now, let's move on to dinner. Your stepmother is giving us nasty looks." He held out his arm to Sarah, and Jack moved to Lillie's side.

The moment she slipped her arm into his, she trembled with the same heat that had seized her when she tumbled from the carriage step into his embrace.

"Try not to let the surroundings overwhelm you, my dear," Jack said, and patted her gloved hand. "We really are quite simple folk once you get to know us."

She expelled an involuntary sigh. He had mistaken her tremor for an attack of nerves. Little did he know she had survived presentation at Napoleon and Eugenie's court in Paris with nary a jitter.

Jack made a valiant effort not to allow his eyes to stray to Lillie's décolletage, barely covered beneath a filmy silk wrap. The exposed skin of her shoulders glowed above a shell pink confection of a dress. Layers of soft pearls covered her neck and wrists.

But it was the sight of her eyes that required all his strength to ignore. Fortunately, they were not trained on him at the moment, snapping out a challenge and turning a dark purple. It would take a lifetime to tire of watching them change.He banished his wayward thoughts when they arrived at the long dining table. Hand-lettered cards marked their places, propped against tiny crystal holders graced by single, miniature pink-budded roses from the manor gardens.

He turned to pull out a chair for her and placed his hand at the small of her back to guide her into her seat. At the sound of her sharp intake of breath, he wavered. Had he offended her with an unwelcome touch?

"Forgive me for startling you," he said, bending close to her ear to mouth his apology.

She did not reply but simply flashed him a brilliant smile before turning to talk to the gentleman on her right, the Reverend Walker.

His action dismissed, he sat down and bent himself to the task of making desultory conversation with his sister, Letitia, on his left.

"Why, Jack," she said in a low, conspiratorial tone, "I think you've lost your composure."

"What do you mean?" he asked.

"You know exactly what I mean — the delectable young woman on your right," she said. "I think you are about to become a casualty on the ocean of love. There is no defense against what I saw pass between the two of you when you came across the dining room. And, after all, she is a very wealthy young heiress. You could stow away your sea boots for good."

"What an outrageous assumption. I—"

"Mr. Finch-Barton, when will you be returning to your ship?" Lillie asked.

"I beg your pardon, Miss Coulbourne." Jack turned with a guilty start. "What was your question?"

"When do you plan to put to sea again?" She slipped off her gloves.

He could barely breathe. The complete bareness of her shoulders, arms, and now her hands unnerved him. Blast it. He could not keep his mind on the thread of their conversation.

"I believe my brother sails at the end of the month." His sister intervened on his behalf, saving him further embarrassment.

"Just so," Jack said. "We're waiting for a few changes." He paused, grateful for Letitia's interference for once. His palms began to sweat, like a shy schoolboy. Would this ordeal never end?

Lillie barely heard Lady Letitia's reply. She looked down at Jack's hands. They were large but finely formed, with long, tapering fingers. The backs of his hands were weathered and tan. The calluses on his palms revealed a life of hard labor spent out in the elements.

She lifted her gaze to his face only to catch him looking back at her. She was mortified. She'd been caught staring.

"So, Miss Coulbourne, how much longer will you be staying in London?"

"We'll leave soon, when the war ends."

"The conflict may take much longer to resolve than you think," Jack warned.

"What have you heard?" she asked, alarm in her voice.

"When did you and your mother last visit the South?"

"The year before we left for Paris."

"I do not wish to be a doomsayer," Jack said, "but I fear the blockade of Southern ports has had a serious, negative effect on the commerce necessary for the South to conduct the war."

The first dish in a procession of ten courses had suddenly appeared. Unspeakably agitated, she dropped her soupspoon to the floor, splashing droplets of green asparagus soup on the white linen tablecloth.

"I find your opinions untenable, sir." She was exasperated with this pompous Englishman now. She didn't care what he thought, or the whole room for that matter.

They moved at the same moment to retrieve the wayward utensil and collided. The resounding thwack centered everyone's attention on them.

"Is there a problem with the soup?" Lady Caroline raised her head, dabbed at the corners of her mouth with her napkin, and looked toward Jack.

"Madam, this is the finest asparagus soup I have enjoyed in many a year. I would beg the pardon of the entire table for the interruption. We seem to have lost a spoon."

His stepmother turned to the footman behind her chair and gestured toward Lillie, who now sat in disgrace, heat spreading from her face down to her neck. The man moved quickly down the side of the long table, and deposited another silver spoon at the precisely correct position next to her soup course.

Hot shame spread throughout Jack's body. How had he managed to foul up the dinner conversation with Lillie before he'd barely tucked into his soup?

Terrified to say anything else lest he descend into total blithering, he glanced at Edward some distance down the table. The madman was staring back at him with a smirk on his face. He would smash his friend's head into the card table this very night and take every last farthing he had at Commerce.

He looked covertly at Lillie. Dangerous, sparks flashed from her eyes.

"You must tell me all you know of the state of the war in the South." She fairly hissed at him in a low whisper.

Jack tried to think of a suitable answer, but all he could do was stare at her lips. They were dark red and puffy from her incessant chewing on them. Maybe he could calm her if he lifted a finger and gently touched her swollen—.

"Jack?" His stepmother angled for his attention. "I asked you a question, dear."

He had no idea what she had asked. Once again, Letitia came to his rescue with a sharp jab of her elbow. He was lost. Should he beg forgiveness of the entire party and excuse himself, or should he just bluff his way through?

"Yes, yes, of course," he said.

"I knew you would agree with me," Caroline said, and gave him a mysterious smile before continuing her conversation with Lord St. James.

What in the devil had he agreed to now? He turned a questioning look at his sister. She hid her laughter beneath a napkin.

Jack turned back to Lillie and said, "The South cannot win this war." He leaned close and spoke in low tones. "The conditions for civilians are deplorable and deteriorating more each time I return. I cannot imagine how much longer Southern ports will remain open."

"Sir, you must be mistaken. Our cause is just, our troops are honorable, and far better trained than the Northern aggressors."

"Miss Coulbourne, we must cease this unpleasant dinner conversation," Jack said, his tone insistent. "If you remain calm until the end of dinner, I promise to reveal what I know of the situation."

"No. I must know now." She clutched her spoon so tightly, her knuckles whitened. Didn't he understand? This was her very life he spoke of so casually.

"Lillie, neither you nor I can do anything about the war this evening." He put his hand gently over hers and turned her back to the soup.

She gritted her teeth and tried harder to bring her raging emotions under control.

He filled her glass with sherry, and she numbly lifted it to her mouth. The liquid seared her throat and spread heat to her limbs.

"Good girl," Jack said, and sat back with a sigh. "Some things cannot be helped, no matter how hard we try. Nothing like a bit of spirits to steady yourself."

She longed to wipe the condescending look off his pompous face. No matter. Her resolve strengthened even more. Soon she would see for herself. How could a sea captain possibly know anything about how the war was going on the ground? He was merely delivering goods and lining his own pockets.

He filled her wine glass with a fine German hock when the soup was removed and replaced with baked Dover sole. She downed the wine without stopping and smacked the glass back onto the table. *Maman* craned her head around the Reverend Walker to her right and gave her an odd look.

Damn, she was tired of doing what these English penguins expected of her. She would show them how things were done back home.

"Are you quite sure you want another glass of wine?" he asked.

"Of course. American women can hold their spirits. We're not mewling, sickly things who faint at the sight of our own shadows."

He sighed and carefully poured a small amount into her glass. When she attempted to quaff the entire lot again, he moved the goblet out of her reach. She gave him a furious look and snatched at the drink, but he only grasped the glass more tightly.

"I will not reveal anything to you about what I know of the state of the war," Jack said, "if you do not cease this infantile display. Immediately."

She turned away from his look of censure and took a bite of fish.

The rapid ingestion of alcohol had a strange effect on her ability to remain angry. She was suddenly exhausted and required her entire force of will not to lean into his broad shoulders.

"Lillie – for heaven's sakes, where are your manners?" Her mother's sharp tone brought her up short. "You are monopolizing poor Lord Jack. Why not tell Reverend Walker about your adventures at the French court?"

She looked to her right. The elderly man glanced nervously between her and her mother.

"Lillie served as an interpreter to Napoleon's ministers," her mother said, with a smug look.

"An interpreter?" Jack interrupted, not giving Lillie a chance to direct her comments to the minister. "Whatever would possess a young woman to dabble in affairs of state?"

"Not that it's any of your concern, but I offered my services after we were presented to the Empress. Eugenie is very sympathetic to our cause."

Jack shook his head and returned his attention to the fish.

Never had such conflicting feelings roiled about Jack. He tried to ignore Lillie, but he couldn't. Would she never tire of shocking everyone around her?

He slid a surreptitious look to his right, only to be assaulted by a view of the top of her generous bosom straining out of a low neckline. She was turned toward the poor pastor who was forced to look directly down into a creamy field of warm woman. Lucky sod.

Heat crept up his neck and rushed to his face. He attempted to rearrange his now tight trousers but couldn't help responding to her in spite of his best intentions. Was there no end to the pain to which this woman could subject him?

His sister intruded into his discomfort. "Jack, tell us a tale of your latest adventures," she said, and gave him a look of encouragement.

Thank God for Letitia. He would never again complain of her interfering ways.

"Actually, Edward and I did get up to a bit of excitement on one of our last deliveries into Wilmington, in the Carolinas." Grateful for the distraction, Jack shifted uncomfortably on his chair and began his story.

"We took our jackets and boots off for cleaning by the hotel staff and set them in the hallway. After hurrying downstairs in stocking feet to get the last serving of food for the day, we returned to find an impudent young fellow trying on my boots. His accomplice had already made off with Edward's belongings.

"When we demanded he desist, the man turned an indignant face on the matter. He insisted any right-thinking gentleman would understand clothing left in a hallway is fair game in time of war.

"After pummeling him to regain my boots, we had to return to our ships the next day in nothing but our shirtsleeves and trousers. Poor Edward was reduced to climbing back aboard his vessel in bare feet."

Some polite chuckles came from dinner guests at the end of his story.

"Now, we keep all of our belongings with us when ashore, especially our medicinal flask of brandy," Edward added with a wink.

Lillie seethed with anger. How could Jack speak so casually of the deprivations suffered by her countrymen?

With each new callous remark out of his mouth, she became more determined to complete her mission.

She tried a bit of each succeeding course and then discreetly arranged the remaining food to look as though she had consumed a fair portion. She did not want to insult the countess's hospitality on top of all her other transgressions.

She kept her eyes focused on the fragile china plates, ringed with a profusion of roses similar to the real flowers overrunning the estate wherever one looked. She could not resist sneaking a few stolen looks at Jack when he was conversing with his sister.

"I say, Miss Coulbourne." He turned toward her, catching her mid-stare. "Is there something you require?"

"I wonder," Lillie said, "if Sarah and I might challenge you and Mr. Harken to a game of cards this evening?"

"Are you quite sure you're alert enough to take us on after all the spirits you've imbibed?" Jack leaned close and cautioned her in low tones.

"Is that an attempt to avoid a trouncing?" Lillie asked, and downed the rest of her wine.

CHAPTER NINE

Friday Night, May 1, 1863
Clarendon
Wiltonshire, England
51°43'0"N, 0°45'0"W

"I have never shirked a challenge on land or sea, young woman." Jack couldn't tamp down the anger burning across his face. "I was trouncing sailors twice my age when you were still learning to read.

"Do you think our meager talents will not stand up to your superior grasp of the game?" Lillie asked.

The silly child acted as though she couldn't see the warning signs. Most of his friends and acquaintances would have backed down by now.

"Besides," Jack continued, hating the peevish tone in his voice, "aren't you a bit young for late-night games of chance?"

Irritation buzzed around him like a swarm of bees. Once again, this annoying young woman challenged him. But for the life of him, he couldn't figure a way out of the game with his self-respect intact.

"I'm sure Edward is exhausted from his travels today. Perhaps we should beg off."

At the mention of his name, Edward half-rose from his seat. "A card game with these two gracious young women?" Edward said. "How could we pass up such an opportunity?"

Lillie favored Edward with a wide smile.

If Jack hadn't saved his friend's life so many times at sea, he would have shot him dead.

"Very well," Jack conceded. "As soon as we finish with cigars and brandy, we'll meet in the game room. We should be able to finish you off within one or two games."

"I would not be so certain, Lord Jack." Martha leaned around the rector's back and delivered a warning. "Lillie is an expert."

"We'll see," he said.

Lillie flushed, anticipating how good she would feel when she trounced Jack. If he thought he could belittle her, she would show him a thing or two with a deck of cards.

Right after dessert, that is. Tiered trays of sweets were brought to the table — elegantly iced cakes, an array of fruit-flavored ices, and three kinds of ice cream. Heaven.

Dainty crystal finger bowls appeared in front of her with slivers of lemon floating in warm water signaling the end of dinner.

When Lady Caroline nodded to Sarah's Aunt Louisa, they stood and gestured to the other women to follow them.

Lillie followed stiffly down the hallway to the drawing room. Her legs were numb from long entrapment in a chair with voluminous petticoats that allowed only limited movement. After she'd adjusted her skirts at dinner so they didn't spill over onto neighboring chairs, she didn't dare tempt fate by moving.

The drawing room was not quite so overwhelming as the cavernous dining hall, but the appointments were luxurious. Crystal candelabra gleamed atop a pianoforte in the corner, and heavy wine-colored brocade drapery covered the full-length windows.

Lillie took a cup of tea and joined Sarah so they could retire to a quiet corner. They collapsed onto a plump sofa in a far reach of the room.

"You gave a great performance tonight of ignoring the captain," Sarah said, and plucked at Lillie's sleeve. "You showed him. You certainly did."

"Sarcasm does not become you," Lillie said with a hiss and motioned for Sarah to keep quiet.

"There was not a single person in the room who did not see how hard the two of you were trying to pretend you didn't care."

"You're making that up just to torture me," Lillie said.

"If you don't believe me, ask your mother. She'll tell you the same thing. I'm surprised she hasn't come over here to give you a piece of her mind."

"Please don't leave me, whatever you do," Lillie begged, when she saw her mother move casually, but steadily, in their direction.

Sarah stood and walked toward the tea service with a dark backward look at Lillie.

She expected the worst, but the expression on her mother's face was unexpectedly soft.

"Your Lord Jack is quite the gentleman," *Maman* said. "He remained calm despite your unsettling behavior." Her smile was self-satisfied, like a cat finishing a bowl of cream. "He must have nerves of steel."

"He is not 'my' Lord Jack, nor is he even a lord. Why must you constantly mock the poor man?"

"Believe me, my treatment of the 'poor man' is nothing compared to yours. He is doomed. He just doesn't know it."

"Please keep your voice down," Lillie pleaded, with a quick glance around the room.

Unfazed, her mother continued, "His family would love to find an heiress with a fortune like yours."

"Stop." Lillie covered her ears. "You know the real reason we're here." She held up her hand to forestall any further comment from her mother. "You've met the man I will have to serve under to complete my mission. I've kept my part of the bargain. What do you say?"

"I'll leave it up to you. He is a good man — God knows, he must be to have suffered your moods this evening without putting you over his knee for a spanking.

"Furthermore, Lord St. James spoke highly of Jack's valor at sea when he was in the service. You could not have chosen a better champion to see you through the gauntlet. In fact, he was decorated twice by the queen."

Lillie breathed a sigh of relief and reached out to embrace her mother. "Thank you."

"However," her mother continued, "Let's hope your father doesn't find out about this outrageous plan. He would be paralyzed with fear."

"Papa has never been 'paralyzed,' let alone fearful." She nearly laughed at the thought of her tall, battle-seasoned father immobilized by panic.

"You don't remember all the times you brought him to his knees with your perilous adventures as a child. Thank heaven he's a physician."

A servant opened the door and walked to Lady Caroline's side with a message. After unfolding and reading the note, she rose and walked toward them.

"Miss Coulbourne," she said, "your card game victims await you. Woodward will take you there."

Jack sat across from Edward, legs stretched in front of him, facing the fireplace. He studied the flames. Perhaps inspiration would jump out at him if he stared long enough. He dreaded having to face Lillie again.

"For heaven's sakes, Edward," Jack said. "Wipe the insipid smile from your face before those foolish women get here. They'll think you're an idiot."

"If I'm an idiot, what does that make you? You're the one who let the spitfire bait you into a game of cards."

"And you're the one who sealed our fate, if you recall." Jack started to chuckle, and then Edward joined him, doubled over in laughter.

"We've been in battles where we looked at each other across decks running with blood," Edward said. "And you're terrified of a nineteen-year-old?"

"I'll show you real bravery. Let's pummel them into submission at cards." Jack stood and motioned toward the game table.

"There's something I still don't understand," Edward said, and rose to join him. "If you are immune to her wiles, and she means nothing to you, then what were the two of you up to at dinner?"

"She is very difficult to manage in conversation."

"Go on."

"I made a few thoughtless comments about the war between the states."

"You violated the first rule of polite company," his fellow officer said. "Never discuss anything remotely controversial. If this gets out, you'll be banished from all the best dinner parties."

Jack glared at his comrade and then began pacing between the hearth and the card table.

"This woman has you totally flummoxed," Edward said, surprise in his voice.

"Lillie is hardly a woman. I'd say she's more like a spoiled child who lets whatever flits into her head tumble out of her mouth," Jack said. "Her dinner conversation was inappropriate. I had to settle her down."

"And just how did you 'settle her'?" his friend asked. "It looked pretty damned interesting from where I sat."

Heat raced from Jack's temple to his neck where his white, pleated shirt sagged open at the loosened top button. He discarded his uniform jacket and sifted through a deck of playing cards from the game table. He held the queen of hearts in his hand for a moment and then replaced it into the deck.

"I need to get through this weekend and away from here before I cause someone bodily harm," Jack said. "Who knows?" he added. "It might be you."

At that moment, Lillie and Sarah burst through the double doors, unannounced. Jack and Edward hurriedly shrugged back into their jackets.

"Miss Coulbourne, why didn't you let a servant accompany you?" Jack asked. His temper began to build like steam in one of his boilers before a run at sea.

"Well, why didn't you come to get us? Poor Woodward was going to bring us here, but we made him go back down to the kitchen. He looked really tired. Didn't he, Sarah?"

Her friend nodded, glancing nervously at Jack, and then quickly away.

"Well then, we should get on with it." Jack motioned toward a table laden with fresh stacks of cards and crystal water tumblers.

As they moved toward their chairs, he became painfully aware of Lillie's disheveled state. The early spring heat, along with her unwise intake of spirits, had taken their toll. Her dark, heavy curls defied all semblance of restraint under the assault of humidity, morphing her earlier hairstyle into a wild, springy mass. Her already rosy skin darkened from a hot flush spreading from her cheeks down to her neck and beyond. And she couldn't stop licking her lips.

He had to exercise restraint to resist reaching out to touch her. How would her thick hair feel in his hands, or spread out on a white linen pillow?

"Jack, are you there? What game would you like to play? Miss Coulbourne has asked twice now. It is your choice, since she challenged you." Edward's voice took on a querulous tinge.

"What kind of game? Oh, yes, quite. Commerce, of course." He winced when he realized he'd lost all sense of what was going on around him.

"Commerce?" Lillie asked. "It's similar to our game of poker, isn't it, Sarah?"

"Yes, but only three cards are drawn at a time, not five. And trades and discards are among fellow players as well as out of the common pile," Sarah replied.

"If it would be easier for you, we certainly could play your version," Jack offered.

"No. I want to beat you fair and square. I don't want any sniveling later."

"Miss Coulbourne, you impugn me with your insinuation I would disparage whatever the outcome of this game."

"Please, Jack, ladies." Edward held up his hands in a mock cease-fire. "Let us take the field of competition and may the best player prevail. Each of us takes one hundred chips. Whoever has the most chips after two rounds wins." He looked pointedly at Lillie and Jack.

"Agreed," they said in unison.

Sarah let out a weary sigh and took her place next to Edward. Lillie and Jack settled into the remaining two chairs.

Lillie struggled to keep her rage in check. In order to beat Jack at his own game, she would have to maintain absolute concentration while interfering with his.

They each drew one card from the deck to decide who would serve as dealer. She settled back against the chair with her draw – the three of hearts. Edward won the deal with a two of diamonds. He quickly shuffled the cards, dealt each of them just three, and then placed the "widow" stack in the center of the table.

Jack stretched his legs to her side of the table and crossed his boots at the ankles. He considered her for a moment, took a sip of water, and then picked up his hand of cards.

"Miss Coulbourne," Jack said, "you challenged us to this game, but you haven't named the stakes."

She bent to the table and anted a chip before lifting her head to reply.

"I should think your honor as an Englishman would be stakes enough. I will have satisfaction in merely seeing you brought to task in a game of chance."

"Very well," he snapped back. "If you win, I shall apologize in front of the entire company tomorrow at breakfast for my boorish comments of this evening, and you may work whatever magic it is you do with Nelson, the beast. However, if I win, what should the payment be? Edward, what do you think?"

Edward pulled uncomfortably at his collar and ignored the question.

"Miss Devereaux?" Jack asked, moving to the next opponent. She kept her head down and examined her cards.

"Right, then. I will decide. If I win, you two young ladies will have to endure our company for a ride in the park tomorrow morning. Fair enough?"

Lillie was incensed. He was turning her challenge into a joke. "How dare you? I cannot let you off with such a frivolous wager."

"Fine. Then not only will you have to endure my company, you must appear to enjoy it, comport yourself as a well-behaved young Englishwoman, and remain quiet throughout," Jack insisted. "What do you think, Edward? Is my proposal fair?"

"I think you are in dangerous waters, my friend. I also know we should finish this blasted game before I collapse onto the table from too much food and too little sleep."

"Absolutely," Jack said. "May the best player win."

She kept her head bowed, studied her cards, and seethed. He had no idea the formidable adversary she could be. She tried to visualize him being thrown from his horse and groveling in the dust. When she ventured a glance to her left, his icy blue eyes bore into her.

"Miss Coulbourne, I believe it is your turn. I'm advancing in age awaiting your pleasure, and I fear I haven't many years left."

Jack nearly bit his tongue at the sound of the condescending words coming from his mouth. How did Lillie manage to reduce him to schoolboy antics? Why did he have to bait her?

He regained his concentration with a start. Lillie had exchanged one card with the widow pile while he wasn't paying attention.

She said nothing, but looked at him expectantly, a hint of a smile on her face. Her eyes had changed to a light, hazy shade, and seemed to see through him. He could almost smell the fragrance of a walk through the garden on a summer evening. Why was everyone looking at him? It was his turn.

He was making a fool of himself. He was going to lose this game, if not his mind. Edward would never let him forget.

Jack quickly exchanged two of his cards for hers. He would show her. He checked his new hand and nearly groaned. Now he was stuck with an ace of clubs, a four of diamonds and a queen of spades. In exchange, he had just turned over a two and a four of hearts to the bothersome wench. What if she had another heart in her hand? What was he thinking?

"Are you quite finished?" Sarah asked while she studied her hand and discarded the entire lot in the center of the table before sweeping up all three cards in the widow hand.

Edward raised his head and nodded to Jack with a smirk before rapping sharply on the table. His signal meant he did not need to improve his hand, and the bidding could begin.

"I'm just lucky. At love, at cards—," he said.

Jack feared he might smash his friend's head into something before the night was over.

"I doubt you have a perfect hand this early in the game. He will bear watching, ladies," Jack warned.

"Why must you always be the arbiter of fairness and order?" Lillie asked, and deposited ten chips in the pile.

It was his turn again, and suddenly the weariness of the day dropped away. He rallied his senses and debated whether to pass or bluff his way through. It was only the first round.

"Pass."

He sneaked a glance to the side. She looked like a satisfied cat, one that had just polished off an unwary mouse in the stables.

And speaking of mice, something was moving stealthily across his boot. He turned sideways and chanced a look below the table. She had removed a shoe and was absent-mindedly massaging the arch of a small, stocking-clad foot across the top of one of his boots. And then she suddenly pushed her foot higher, inside his knee.

Concentration was impossible in such a state. He doubted he could even stand up and walk away from the table.

At the sound of the heavy door opening, Lillie and Jack, Sarah and Edward · all looked up from their hands.

Martha and Lady Caroline eased into the room and settled onto a corner settee.

Irritated, Lillie turned away and contemplated her next move. Why must her mother dog her every waking moment? She was just getting to the good part of destroying Jack's concentration.

Sarah sat across the table, with her tongue stuck outside her upper lip. She always did that when stumped at cards. Lillie settled her chin onto her fist and studied her hand.

With a look of defiance, Sarah surprised Lillie and matched her ten-chip bet. It was Edward's turn now, and he pushed another ten chips to the center of the table. He added a five-chip raise and smiled at Jack.

Lillie covered Edward's raise and bet another ten chips of her own. Both Jack and Sarah folded. Edward laid three kings on the table. Lillie turned up the two through four of hearts.

Edward raked the pile of chips toward his side of the table and began shuffling the stack of cards again.

When Lillie turned to check on *Maman*, she and Lady Caroline were deep in discussion, appearing to ignore the card players.

"Miss Coulbourne, would you do us the honor of making the first cut?" Edward asked.

"Of course." She bent forward toward the pile of cards and canted her head to the side to glance at Jack. She smiled innocently as her breasts strained perilously close to spilling out of her décolletage. She lifted a third of the stack to tuck under the pile.

"Here comes the second round," Edward said, and dealt the cards. He snickered at Jack's squirming under Lillie's blatant display.

She exulted at Jack's seeming lack of concentration, but then her confidence flagged when he discarded and traded cards in a flurry of moves.

He finally rapped on the table with a look of triumph to signal the beginning of betting. All Lillie had managed to accumulate were a four of diamonds and a pair of deuces.

Her only hope was to bluff. Both Edward and Sarah dropped out when fierce bidding raged between Jack and Lillie.

Lillie finally deposited all of her chips, and Jack produced a royal flush with a flourish and a cutting look directed at her.

"At last. I might have known you would win, Jack, no matter what. The old sailor's luck always kicks in for you. I for one am more than ready for bed." Edward rose and stretched his back before scooping cards and chips back into the rosewood box on the sideboard behind the game table.

Lillie sat immobile, fuming at the way Jack rolled over all of them in the last hand after lulling her into complacency with the first one. He sat next to her, silently staring.

"Miss Coulbourne?"

"Yes?"

"Are you ready to admit defeat and gather strength before our morning ride? I rather suspect paying off your debt may be the hardest part of the weekend for you."

"Lillie, let's be good sports and congratulate Mr. Finch-Barton on his luck. Then we can make our way back to our rooms. I'm really tired." Sarah stood and laid a hand on Lillie's shoulder.

"Don't bother yourself. I'll walk back with *Maman* and Lady Caroline."

After Sarah left, she glanced at the sofa in the corner where the two women had chatted during the game. They were gone.

"Let me call for someone to escort you back to your room." Jack walked to a bell pull in the corner.

"Not so fast," Lillie said. "Do you think just two hands of a game I've never played should settle our bet?"

He turned and stared at her as if he thought she'd lost her mind.

"I beg your pardon," Jack said slowly. "Are you accusing me of unfairness?"

"You heard me. You deliberately took advantage of the situation."

"Really?" Jack walked over to a wall cabinet and retrieved a decanter of a dark amber liquid. He returned with the bottle as well as two small glasses and placed them on the game table.

He took a seat, this time directly across from her, and opened another sealed deck of cards.

"Very well, Miss Coulbourne," he said in low, measured tones. "Do you think you could sufficiently understand a simple one-card draw?"

"How many draws?" she asked.

"Oh, say four out of five — how does that sound to you? Fair enough?"

"Fair enough." She assented with a nod.

"And there is one more stipulation to this game," he added. "Each time you get the high card, you have to have a shot of whisky."

"You're on," she said, and took the clean deck to shuffle. She pushed the stack to him when she finished, and he made the first cut.

"Shall I deal," Jack asked, "or would that be an unfair advantage?"

"No — please deal," Lillie insisted.

She won the first round and pride compelled her to down the fiery liquid as quickly as possible. Her wits appeared to ebb, but she refused to show any sign of weakness. Unfortunately, Jack won the next two but seemed to remain clear-headed in spite of the obligatory accompanying drinks.

She began to panic and tried an earlier tactic, slipping off one shoe and massaging her way up his ankle. This time Jack grasped her foot hard and pulled her closer under the table. He said nothing, but laughter bubbled up out of his throat when she tried to wrench her foot out of his grip.

"Miss Coulbourne, you are a skilled manipulator," he said, "but I think you've met your match this time. Shall we say this little side game is a draw and call it a night?"

He dropped her foot, and she quickly pushed away from him.

"Let's see, it's two to one now," Lillie said. "Didn't you say four out of five?" She was having difficulty reasoning. Could one tumbler of spirits have clouded her judgment that quickly? "I can't have you saying there were exshtenuating circumstances."

"Come on," he said. "You should give up and retire."

"No." She nearly shouted in answer.

"Right." Jack dealt two more hands; she won each, and downed two more drinks. "Now, neither one of us can win four out of five. Let's call this game a draw." He spread his hands, palms toward her.

Anger coursed through Lillie, but she felt as though she were down in a well and couldn't reason. She stood to leave and batted his hands away when he offered to help. Suddenly, her brain ceased to communicate with her feet and legs, and she leaned hard against him.

One moment she was slumped against Jack's unyielding shoulder and the next he somehow turned and brushed her lips with his. When he jerked away as if burned, she pulled him back and deepened the kiss. He tasted of smoky alcohol and something more.

He pulled her more tightly into his arms and claimed her lips while burying his hand in her out-of-control hair.

Abruptly, he pulled away and gave her a slow smile. "More's the pity, but you won't remember any of this when you wake tomorrow."

After pushing through the game room door, Jack trod down one hallway after another with Lillie's limp form cradled in his arms. When the danger of his predicament began to sink in, he ignored the warning bells clanging in his head by telling himself tomorrow was another day. He would smooth all the feelings he had ruffled thus far, exact his due from the stubborn Miss Coulbourne when she was sober, and then go back to Portsmouth.

He turned at the juncture of two hallways near Lillie's room and rapped sharply on the door.

Giselle answered his knock and frowned at Lillie's inebriated state. She helped Jack duck-walk her boneless charge to the bed while they each held an arm.

As soon as he escaped, Jack leaned against a wall in the hallway. He shook his head and gathered his bearings before moving again. There was a certain fair innkeeper in Portsmouth he trusted would cure the yearnings racing through him. Then he would return to the most important woman in his life for the next few months – his ship, *The Kate.*

CHAPTER TEN

Saturday Morning, May 2, 1863
Clarendon
Wiltonshire, England
51°43'0"N, 0°45'0"W

Lillie followed the pebbled path to the stables, taking care not to scuff her riding boots while she went over the events of the previous evening. She could remember nothing after the nonsensical one-card draw game. But worse, she had no idea how she got back to her room, and Giselle refused to tell her.

She'd risen early that morning with a headache so intense, she was surprised her scalp hadn't burst open. She tried to avoid Jack at breakfast, but he fell into step beside her when she headed toward the cavernous morning room.

The sideboard was loaded with eggs, ham and crisp sausages. Fluffy breads piled high in baskets accompanied by fruit jams rivaled the treats their own cook prepared back home, but she could not manage to choke down a single bite. Her misery had only heightened when Jack rose and apologized to all present for his "boorish actions" toward Miss Coulbourne.

Now she was honor-bound to fulfill her payment of the stakes in the card game she'd lost so ignominiously the night before.

Jack, Sarah, and Edward stood outside the stable courtyard, talking with one of the grooms.

"There you are," Sarah said, and skipped toward her. "We thought you were ill this morning."

"Jack and I had a small open carriage readied for our ride this morning," Edward said, and turned toward Lillie with a teasing twinkle in his eye. "You do remember the terms of defeat at cards last night?"

"How could I forget? I am more than ready to eat humble pie and behave as any well-bred English lady. However, I must apologize in advance if my knowledge is lacking in what your notion of proper behavior might be," Lillie said.

"I would be happy to instruct you," Jack said.

She frowned and wrinkled her nose when what she really wanted to do was stick her tongue out at the unbearable man.

Sarah snatched Lillie's arm and pulled her aside. "Listen to me. This is not the time to irritate Mr. Finch-Barton. We are almost at the end of this dreadful weekend." When Lillie tried to jerk her arm away, Sarah pinched her. "You should concentrate on getting by with as few memorable incidents as possible. If you will recall, you will be disguised as a man in his presence in a few weeks."

Sarah was right. From now on, she would avoid tormenting the odious one. But baiting him did get his attention, and she craved the feelings aroused by his icy blue stare.

Jack's entire body ached with fatigue. Day two with the spitfire, and still they sparred. The woman's verbal jabs had worn him down as much as if he had fought off a ship full of Russians.

But he was determined to do his duty and put his best foot forward. In order to get the excursion around the park behind him, he promised himself he would not, under any circumstances, let her bait him. Then he would be on his way back to Portsmouth. He joined the two women while his friend helped one of the grooms harnessing the ponies to the carriage.

Sarah turned to him with a sunny smile. Since Lillie's face was somewhat less welcoming, he steeled himself for yet another verbal bout. If they got under way soon enough, he might be able to muffle her acid tongue.

"Sir, we are ready to settle our gambling debt," Lillie said. Her facial expression seemed less than eager, but not exactly a pout.

"I, for one, am ready to get outdoors and enjoy the beautiful park," Sarah said with determination.

"And enjoy it you shall," Jack assured her. "I'll take you to my favorite places and share some of the local history. Parts of the manor hall have been here since before the Norman Conquest. However, the Clarendons' direct line died out a generation ago, and my father, a distant cousin, assumed the title of Earl of Wiltonshire."

"You're not really Mr. Clarendon, then?" Lillie asked.

"No, I'm not."

"You've deliberately been letting me make a fool of myself. Why?"

He sighed and turned to lift her up onto the front seat. He moved to the other side, took the reins from the groom, and nodded to Edward to help Miss Devereaux onto the rear seat with him.

"Answer my question, sir," Lillie demanded. "A lady can't be expected to ride out with a gentleman when she doesn't even know his name."

"Since we probably will never cross paths again, perhaps we could overlook formalities for the next hour or so. Could I possibly prevail upon your good will to call me simply Jack?"

Lillie smiled unexpectedly, and while he still reeled from the shock of her sudden warming, she reached over and took the reins. She gave the groom a look, and he released the ponies after an uneasy glance at Jack. They trotted off through the park, into a sky-blue day.

Jack counted to ten in silence and then scanned the sky for weather signs. Solitary puffy clouds drifted slowly across the clear expanse, but the feathered, striated textures of higher formations warned of big wind later that evening.

The few times he was back in port and allowed himself the luxury of returning to his family home, he would store memories of the land to last through long days and nights of nothing but expanses of water and rolling waves.

They moved through a narrow avenue of grand beeches lining the long approach to his family home with the manicured green of the park stretching beyond. An occasional deer and fawn wandered close to the roadway, only to flee in fear of the gaudily painted carriage rolling by.

Beyond the park, an occasional ancient oak studded the thick forest. Only the light bark of beeches interrupted the full late spring greenery. The woods were shrouded in privacy, partially hiding some of the walking paths of his childhood.

No matter how many visions of land he soaked up during the day, he still dreamed of the ocean at night. After a few days back at sea, however, he would dream of land. The sights and sounds he absorbed hungrily would have to last him for many a month.

"What an odd assortment of colors for a carriage," Sarah said. "Red, ochre, shades of blue, and even purple," She tapped Edward on the shoulder and leaned toward him. "Looks as though it were painted by a band of gypsies as a caravan."

"It was, in a way," Edward said. "Jack and his siblings played with the wagon when they were children. It's been in the family ever since. The only changes seem to be the cushioned seats and springs for adult comfort."

"I hate to bring up an unhappy possibility, but do you think there may be an explosion coming soon from the front seat?" Sarah glanced toward their fellow riders.

Lillie still held the reins, but her companion remained silent. He sat stiff and unbending, clutching the side of his seat with a tight grip.

"No, not really," Edward said. "She has a fine touch with the ponies, which he probably senses. He'll leave her alone. He can be tyrannical at times with his crew at sea, but he appreciates talent and lets good people do their jobs without interference. It's one of his great strengths."

Lillie exulted in the wind whipping through her hair, extracting frizzes of curls to fly madly behind her when they picked up speed through the park. She had nearly forgotten Jack was beside her. It had been a while since she'd enjoyed access to such fine animals.

"Have you thought about possibly slowing down?" he asked, his tone clipped and sharp.

"Why? Are you having an attack of nerves at the thought of a mere woman in charge of the rig?"

"No, but a crossroad looms," Jack warned. "We can only hope you don't make the turn on two wheels. And then there are the ponies. They enjoy a good trot, but they do need a few respites too."

Lillie tried to tamp down the fury building inside her. Jack's easy tolerance had begun to feel like condescension, or a ruse to catch her off guard. She responded by bringing the pair to an abrupt stop.

"Now, once we reach the end of the hedge row directly ahead of us, you should gradually bear to the right." He pointed toward a dirt path diverging from the graveled lane.

"Where are we going?" she asked, tapping the reins to move them forward more slowly.

"I want to show you the Queen's Gap," Jack said.

They all turned at the cries of a red kite raptor swooping down on late morning thermals to snatch an unsuspecting field mouse. The bird had been drifting slowly, low over the fields. His reddish brown body, angled wings and forked tail were illuminated in the morning sun as he fled with his prize.

"His wing-span must be close to the height of a man," Lillie said, after several moments of observing the bird's flight. Her mouth fell open when she craned her neck to watch the raptor's progress across the field.

"He's lucky the local farmers haven't caught him. They blame the poor bird every time a predator snatches one of their sheep," he said.

She turned back toward Jack after the huge winged creature finally disappeared from sight. He'd moved next to her as the bird glided across the sky, and the closeness of his body caused heat to rise to her cheeks.

"What is the Queen's Gap?" Lillie asked, eager to change the subject and dilute the curious effect he had on her.

"A distant ancestor of ours wanted to make sure Queen Elizabeth's progress to Clarendon would not be impeded by the deep woods, so he had a gap cut through the middle. It also provided a great view of the estate while she progressed along the path with her party."

"And what did she do for him?"

"He was simply a great patriot. He was sheriff of this county for a time and served in Parliament in 1585."

She tried to read the look on his face, but a broad-brimmed straw hat shaded his expression.

"Jack?"

"Yes, Miss Coulbourne?"

"I would very much like to see the Queen's Gap." She handed him the reins, and they proceeded along the path at a more sedate pace.

"And, Jack?"

"Yes."

"I know I'm not acting like a proper young Englishwoman, but —"

"Go ahead."

His voice was so soft she could scarcely hear his reply, but she forged on.

"Since you requested I use your first name, can you not call me Lillie?"

He did not reply, but reached over and briefly covered her hand with his. Returning his attention to the ponies, he slowed the carriage for the turn onto a side path.

From the rear seat, sighs of relief issued from Sarah and Edward.

Jack had gone into what his friends and crew liked to refer to as full battle mode. He focused only on what he had to do to survive. He had to get back to his ship, with the mercurial Miss Coulbourne out of sight and out of mind.

The odd thing was, it was damned near impossible to force all thoughts of her from his mind. Everything about her confounded him.

She contrasted vividly with other women, much like an exotic hothouse flower. Instead of serviceable brown serge, her riding dress was blood red velvet with black lace peeping from inside the collar and cascading from the cuffs of the double-breasted jacket.

It also might have something to do with the heat she seemed to radiate. Her scent made him feel like a boy again on Christmas morning.

Just then they rounded a turn in the nearly impenetrable wood where the gap opened at a high vantage point. In the far distance, across a dry bottom, Clarendon nestled amongst the trees. The morning sun reflecting off the walls and towers washed the view in a pink-gold glow. At the edges of the wood, patches of early bluebells dotted the way to the manor house.

He reined in the ponies and pulled the carriage toward the side of the pathway.

"What does it feel like to have been born into all of this?" she asked.

"I may have been born into the family," Jack said, "but I'm not really part of all this. Although I spent a wonderful childhood here, it all ended when I entered the service at thirteen." He extended his arm to halt her forward momentum when he slowed the cart for a startled hare charging through the clearing, followed by two others.

"Clarendon has been here for so long, it's more like a trust. Our family has been in public service for centuries, serving in Parliament and as officers of the parish. But everything always passes to the eldest son, along with all the burdens and responsibilities."

"Do you ever wish it were yours?" She tilted her face toward him, and for a moment his breath caught in his throat. The color of her eyes echoed the shade of bluebells blanketing the edge of the forest.

"Absolutely not," he replied. "My brother deserves every boring meeting and smoky day in London he has coming to him." He softened his declaration with a smile quirking the corners of his mouth. "He was such a tormentor and tease when we were children, there aren't enough unpleasant duties to make up for all his transgressions."

"What about your other brothers?"

"They were always much better in school than I was. They're all barristers now, in London, except for young Teddy. I'm afraid he's a younger version of myself. His mother despairs of the boy ever completing his education. He'll probably end up in the service too.

"Of course, all of us are on annual stipends, and a commission will be purchased for Teddy if he chooses the military. Commercial ventures are not even thought of in our family, which is why I'm somewhat of a black sheep with my shipping business."

With a mischievous grin, he jumped from the cart and came around to her side, seizing her hand and pulling her along behind him up a short path into the woods. "I want to introduce you to a very old friend of mine."

Lillie's knees turned to jelly as if her bones had deserted her. She glanced back to check the progress of Sarah and Edward. If she couldn't trust her own heart in the middle of a crowded dinner party, then racing off into the woods alone with Jack was certainly a bad idea.

"Wait. Let them catch up with us. We should meet your friend together," she said breathlessly.

"No need," he said, and pulled her more deeply into the woods.

They tramped through a thick stand of beeches surrounding a circular clearing. She'd avoided facing him until then. When he turned to her with a smile, she was lost.

Morning sun filtered through the leaves, and shards of misty light framed an ancient oak anchored in the center.

"This is it," Jack said. "My old friend is over there." His boots crunched through dead leaves left over from winter and dry, exposed roots when he moved behind a massive oak. Light bathed the two of them as he pressed his palm against the tree. "This old fellow and I have solved many of the world's problems together. He's no doubt centuries old."

She exhaled sharply and cursed her fickle soul. Every time she resolved to dislike him, he made her care again. When he clutched her hand on the way into the clearing, she'd tried to extricate herself. But now she missed his touch and didn't want the moment to end.

"Sometimes, in battle, or weathering a storm at sea, I can reach out and feel this oak. Sometimes I fear this old tree is the only thing holding me to the earth," Jack said.

When he strode back and took her in his arms, it seemed like the most natural thing in the world to melt into him. He ran one of his hands through her hair, held her tightly, and kissed her thoroughly.

Lillie rose up on her toes to encircle his shoulders and cling to him while his hands moved lower to the swell of her breasts.

"Now I'll remember you too, Lillie," he said in a hoarse whisper, and released her just as their friends crashed into the clearing.

Edward and Sarah laughed and pelted them with pebbles picked up from the path. "Jack, you need to mind the time if you're leaving for Portsmouth." Edward pulled a pocket watch from his vest and fiddled with it. "It's nearly eleven."

Jack was confused. Now that he had made plans to leave early, he really didn't want to go. He'd lost his mind.

"Why leave so soon? Surely an early start tomorrow would be much better," Sarah said, a touch of regret in her voice.

Lillie crouched down, examining a bluebell. Her face was hidden, so he could not gauge her reaction. He yearned for a response from her. If only she would plead with him to stay. Instead, she bounced to her feet.

"Good. Let's go back," she insisted, "so I can help you gentle Nelson's mood before you ride out." Lillie gathered her skirts and became a bright blur of red flashing through the beeches, racing back to the cart.

The rest of the party followed more slowly. Jack climbed onto the front seat and gathered the reins, urging the ponies back onto the pathway. Beside him on the seat, Lillie cocked up a knee to support an elbow and leaned her chin into her hand. He stole a sideways look at the woman who had driven him mad all weekend.

Thoughts of a specific woman had never interfered with his resolve to return to life at sea. If he did not flee soon, he would be mooning over her as nonsensically as his friend did over his sweetheart. As soon as they returned to the house, he would find his stepmother and sister and make his apologies.

Lillie was silent when they emerged from the wood to the view of Clarendon spread out below. Painfully aware of her unruly hair, she clamped her hand to the top of her head to prevent her hat from flying off in the wind. They sped down through the park and Jack let the ponies go full tilt toward the stables.

She smiled in satisfaction at the thought that in a few weeks, no one would care about the state of her hair, or her wardrobe.

Jack slowed the horses when they entered the wide avenue of beeches, and she leaned back as far as she could to absorb the dizzying view of the leafy canopy above her head.

"Lillie," Jack shouted, "please mind your balance. We don't want to lose you overboard now."

"Why? Would you launch the jolly boat to come after me?" She challenged him with an impious grin and threw back her head again. Gripping one side of the seat and his arm tightly, she managed to maintain her precarious hold. She whooped and hollered like a naughty child.

Jack swung the carriage abruptly to the side of the path and pulled the ponies to a standstill.

The expression on his face turned stormy when she reached to straighten her hat, which had disappeared. The red velvet confection had blown away, the victim of her wild antics. Her hair defied all restraint. When she turned to her fellow passengers for support, Sarah ignored her and Edward handed her the wayward hat. The frivolous bit of fluff had fallen into his lap.

"Sarah —" She began.

"You've gone too far this time," her friend snapped back at her. "Apologize to our poor host, or I won't ever go riding with you again."

"I guess this means I've done something a well-behaved young Englishwoman wouldn't do?" Lillie plucked at Jack's sleeve, hoping for some reaction. "All right, I'm sorry. I'm sorry I've been a disappointment. I'm sorry my behavior has offended you. I'm sorry —." At his continued silence, she pleaded, "For heaven's sakes, Jack, say something."

He ignored her and picked up the reins before heading the cart back onto the path. When they gathered speed, he suddenly handed the reins to her.

She opened her mouth to protest and then watched, eyes wide, when he abruptly stood up. Leaning forward with the slightest hesitation, he leaped onto the back of one of the ponies. She brought the animals to a gradual halt, her heart pounding.

His shoulders shook, but his face was turned away from her. Jumping down from her seat, she raced to his side to find him overcome with laughter. Now he was hooting so loudly, tears formed in the corners of his eyes.

"Are you mad? You could have been killed," she said, and pushed him hard.

Their companions joined them, and Edward was laughing uncontrollably as well.

"Is this what you and your brothers used to do to frighten your sisters?" Edward clapped, approving his friend's performance.

"Every chance we got. We practiced this hundreds of times. I've often wondered if I could still do it." Jack pulled a handkerchief from his pocket and wiped the tears from his eyes.

Lillie slowly returned to the carriage. Jack slipped down from his perch and followed her, but she pushed him away when he tried to help her. After hauling herself up, she awaited his progress around the carriage to the driver's seat.

"Why did you do such a fool, crazy thing?" Her hair was now beyond redemption, but she still tried to smooth it out of her face while she berated him.

"I have no idea," Jack admitted. "I fear you bring out the worst in me. Your childish antics brought back fond memories of my own boyhood tricks."

She searched his face for a clue to his bizarre behavior. Laugh lines crinkled around his mouth, another unexpected quirk.

By the time they pulled into the stable yard, she regretted everything she'd done to irritate him. She didn't want their time together to end. He, of course, was itching to get away from her and back to his ship.

Jack confirmed her suspicions when they walked back to the hall. Turning first to Sarah and then to her, he apologized for the abruptness of his departure.

"Edward, I had better see you in Bermuda." He clapped his friend on the back. "And, Miss Devereaux, the pleasure of your gracious company is something I will treasure for many a lonely night at sea."

He turned to Lillie, hesitated, and then settled for no more than a light squeeze of her hand before disappearing down one of the cavernous hallways.

Edward moved to her side and put his arms around her while she laid her head on his shoulder. A few tears slid down her cheek onto his jacket.

"And that, ladies, was the honorable and mysterious Charles Augustus Clarendon, alias Captain Jack Roberts, moving on to his next adventure."

A shiver snaked through Lillie. Not only did Jack share the same spit-and-polish traits as her father, they both shared the same name.

She tamped down the growing attraction she felt for him and instead took comfort in the thought that the next time she saw Jack, she would be on more equal footing, as a man.

CHAPTER ELEVEN

Monday, May 04, 1863
London, England
51°30'62"N, 0°10'0"W

The Mayfair townhouse lay silent except for the front hallway clock chimes. Lillie counted twelve bells. She could have been a wraith creeping toward the back door to ease out through the garden to the mews. Thick Turkish carpeting absorbed the sound of her stocking-clad feet.

Black pants and a bulky wool sweater hid her identity and gender. A folded piece of blanket stuffed down into the waistband of her pants further altered her curves.

Hesitating at the door, she listened for any stirring in the household. Neither Sarah nor *Maman* knew about this latest adventure. She was going to rendezvous with her father's friend, Weatherby, in the alley outside the mews at precisely five minutes after midnight.

A suspicion niggled: Could she trust this man? On her way through the kitchen, she slid open a drawer and pocketed a small knife. As an afterthought, she snatched Cook's rolling pin and stuffed it down the back of her waistband.

She slipped out the kitchen door into the garden and retrieved a crude pair of men's shoes from beneath a bush. Quickly covering the distance to the stables, she tiptoed past the stalls. The groom snored loudly in the room above.

She hesitated before heading into the alley, to adjust the banding Sarah and Giselle had designed for her. Made of thick muslin, it was fairly easy to wrap from her back to front in several diagonals. Ending in front with a snug fit, the cloth was simple to button comfortably below her breasts. Gazing down at her now flattened chest, she smiled.

Her thick curls were still a problem. She had not worked up the courage to shorten the mass into something more manageable for a young sailor. That night, she stuffed her hair under a seaman's watch cap.

She crouched for a moment near the wide stable doors opening onto the alley, listening for signs of traffic. Nothing. The night was deadly still, and a sliver of moon did little to illuminate the area. She closed her eyes tightly, and then gradually opened them to adjust her night vision.

After a few minutes, she took a tentative step forward only to be yanked off her feet from behind. A gloved hand clapped over her mouth while she struggled to snatch the knife from her pocket.

"Ah, my brave little Miss Coulbourne, we have a lot of work to do," a low, rasping voice warned. "Weapons in your pocket, or stashed in your pants, are not going to do you any good." In one deft motion, he pulled the rolling pin from her waistband and slipped the knife from her pocket.

She didn't even miss her makeshift weapons until he set her back on her feet.

When she spun around to argue with her attacker, he swept her over his shoulder and trundled her to a waiting carriage. He lifted her up the steps and then pulled himself inside.

"Is this your idea of a lesson in self-defense, sir? I think not. I..." Lillie scrambled for words.

"Please stop talking and just listen. We don't have much time. Let's not waste it in debate."

The darkness was so thick she could not make out his face. She tried to stifle her fear while she listened to the disembodied voice.

"You have much to learn in very little time," he said, and settled back into the shadowed seat across from her. "I will ask you to do many things you may not want to do, but you have to trust me. We have only two more nights for you to learn to defend yourself."

"May I ask a question?" She leaned closer and tried to get a better view of her companion.

"Go ahead."

"Why are you being so mysterious?"

"In my profession, the less we know about each other, the more likely both of us will live to see morning." He eased back and stretched his booted feet across the enclosed compartment. "Anything else you need to know before we begin?"

She had many more questions but resigned herself to silence. They took off with a lurch, and the carriage turned out of the alley onto the circle around the square. They had not traveled more than a quarter of an hour when they came to a halt with a sudden turn. She guessed at the sound of large doors sliding open with a muffled creak before the carriage rolled forward again.

Softly glowing gas lanterns lit the interior of a large carriage house, their final destination she guessed. He handed her down, and after her eyes adjusted to the low light, she studied her companion. He stood barely an inch taller than her, but his muscular build and tightly coiled stance suggested a menacing aura. Moving catlike toward a staircase, he motioned for her to follow. They must be on the ground floor of a nearby townhouse.

An ivory-topped cane, the same one he carried when she first saw him at the cemetery in Paris, now swung from his hand.

They climbed past the entry, parlor, and kitchen levels before heading down a long hallway. Her breathing returned to normal after the endless climb, but he showed no sign of exertion. He ranged ahead of her on the staircase, springing from step to step on the balls of his feet.

Fishing a ring of keys from his pocket, he unlocked a door at the end of the hall. Standing aside as she entered, he locked it behind them. The warm study had book-lined walls and a crackling fire on the hearth. Her companion moved to a bookcase as if to select a volume, and one of the bookshelf bays swung aside to reveal another passageway.

She followed him through the portal and up a short flight of steps to another doorway that opened into a large airy room with padded mats on the floor and a wardrobe cabinet spanning an entire far wall.

Neither of them had spoken since leaving the carriage. He turned to her now with an impish grin, hinting at the boy behind the serious man. He too was dressed entirely in black, but unlike her cobbled-together outfit, his clothing was finely tailored. The only indication of the nature of their meeting was the soot smudging portions of his face not covered by his watch cap.

"So, the adventure begins." He whipped off his cap, and thick, wavy chestnut hair sprang loose.

This was the same shadow man who had dogged her moves since Paris. However, she had imagined a much older, more sinister looking creature than the warm, charming one before her. He had to be nearly as old as her father, but his only concession to age appeared to be a dash of silver at his temples.

"Come show me how you would defend your life," Weatherby said, his tone brooking no argument. He moved toward one of the mats and motioned for her to follow.

"Isn't your job to show me?" She stumbled forward in the ill-fitting men's shoes.

He said nothing, but smoothly whirled her around and pressed her to his chest with Cook's knife at her throat. She flailed instinctively, only to have her arms pinned to her sides.

After a moment of panic, memories of childhood street adventures streamed back. She kicked hard at one of his shins and encountered a thick padding over his lower leg. Her ankle ached from the power of her thrust into his immovable armor.

In response to her feeble attempt, he lifted her, her feet dangling uselessly a few inches above the mat.

"Come on, you're fighting for your life." His whisper was little more than a warm breath in her ear. "You can do better."

The knife pressed tightly to her neck. With one last burst of strength mixed with fear, she freed an arm and jabbed hard with her elbow. It was just enough to loosen his grip on the knife so she could drop to the mat and roll quickly away.

"That's my girl." He looked at her with approval, and she beamed. Within seconds, however, he flipped her and pinned her on her back. He had substituted the rolling pin for the knife and slowly pressed it into her neck, choking the breath out of her.

With her last effort, she pulled her right knee up sharply, slamming into his groin with as much force as she could muster. She was rewarded with an easing in the pressure on her neck. Of course, he was not much affected by the pain, considering the extent of his padding. Too bad he couldn't have extended her the same courtesy. Within seconds, she found herself face down on the mat, her left arm pinned painfully behind.

"You haven't committed your life force to this battle." He released her and rolled to his side on the mat, his elbow supporting his weight. "You have to be totally present during a struggle. If you let your thoughts wander, your father will be claiming your body from some battlefield morgue, or searching among unmarked graves," he said.

"Who are you to frighten me this way?" She brushed away angry tears and jumped to her feet.

"Never turn your back on an aggressor, and don't break eye contact, ever." He leapt up behind her and turned her to face him. "Be aware of your surroundings. What is within reach you could use as a weapon? Rocks, sticks, a handful of dirt, even a man's own neck cloth can be used against him.

"Choose your battles carefully. Bluffing your way through a confrontation is much better than taking on an unknown adversary."

He released her and ran his fingers through his thick hair. "Since time is short, our work today will focus on breathing and meditation." He slanted his head toward hers and grasped the nape of her neck, pulling her close. "First lesson: The essence of your attacker is here." He pointed to his own eyes. "Fear begins here." He reversed the direction of his fingers to her eyes.

"The object is survival." He released her and motioned her back toward the mat. "Forget what your mother taught you about polite young women. If you can disarm or disable your opponent, your first priority should be escape. Don't look back. There may come a time when you will have to kill or be killed."

"I am prepared to do whatever is necessary to complete my mission." In spite of her hope for a matter-of-fact tone, Lillie's declaration came out as an embarrassing squeak.

"I understand how hard this is for you." A faint smile tipped at the corners of his mouth. He took her by the arm and pulled her around to face him. Producing Cook's knife from his pocket, he put it into her right hand. "If you have your dagger in hand instead of in your pocket when attacked, you may have a chance." He placed the knife with the hilt outside the left side of her hand and the blade to the right.

"Make a fist and slash your assailant's jugular vein from left to right. I know it seems awkward, but you have to trust me. This angle lets you muster as much strength as you can, and you will need it."

"What if I miss?" she asked.

"Speed and intent are of the essence. You have one thing in your favor — you are a woman, and if your attacker is a man, he will be distracted." He stretched his neck cautiously away from her when she gripped the knife and leaned toward him. "Use your sex to your advantage. You should feint a slash toward his eyes first. When he throws his hands up to protect to his face, immediately go for his jugular. Don't hesitate. He won't expect an attack from you.

"Easy." He carefully took the knife from her clenched hand and led her to a corner. An effigy of a man stuffed with straw hung from the ceiling. The padded dummy approximated the height of a potential attacker.

"How can this, this scarecrow help me learn to defend myself?" She stifled a laugh at the sight of the lopsided grimace on the effigy's face.

"It's important to understand the anatomy of your attacker." He positioned the knife in her hand again and turned her to face her adversary. "Now, prove you're as good as any man, and send this devil to the hell he deserves."

She did not hesitate but focused all of her strength into a left-to-right slash across the pathetic beast's throat. Straw flew everywhere, bits of it settling into her hair. She sneezed.

"Excellent — for your first attempt."

How did he know her deepest desire, to be as good as any man? She bristled at the thought of this infuriating stranger and her father talking about her hopes and dreams.

She turned to accuse him, but he had returned to the mat, an expectant look in his eyes. He sat cross-legged, resting his hands at his knees.

"Come here for your most important lesson." He patted the space across from him. "And take off your shoes."

"What heinous torture do you have planned for me now?" She advanced cautiously, the embarrassing takedowns fresh in her memory.

"Just sit. Remember, you have to trust me."

"Why?" She snapped off, testy from his constant deviousness.

"Who else is going to help you?"

He had her there. The use of mulish tactics to get her way was not going to work with this persistent man. She settled onto the mat and looked directly into his eyes. They were an odd hazel color with golden flecks.

"Now what?"

"Breathe."

"I thought I was already breathing," she said.

"If that is the best you can do, you should give up now."

A nasty retort died in her throat, but she sighed and bowed her head in resignation. "Please begin your lesson, oh Great One. I sit here, your humble student."

"Good. Acceptance is the beginning of wisdom." He eased back, hands resting lightly on his opposing knees. "Watch me breathe. Let your breath come from down here, not up here." He first indicated his mid-torso area and then the high chest and throat areas. He took in a deep breath, paused, and expelled it fully. "Now, it's your turn."

She gulped in air, held it as long as she could, then let it out.

"No, you're not even close. Here..." He grasped one of her hands, pulling it tight to his stomach. "Feel this." He repeated the breathing exercise. Removing her palm, he placed it back on her own stomach. "Now, you try. Make your hand move with the force of air flowing in and out."

"Like this?" After focusing on her breathing, she was rewarded with a feeling of light in-and-out movement. She gazed across at him, excited.

"Good." His stern, tanned features lightened into a brief smile. "Now..."

"Wait. Let me try again." She interrupted him to repeat the exercise two or three more times.

"Now you're ready for the next step."

"I don't understand. What does this have to do with defending myself?" She leaned forward for his answer.

"Fair enough. Let's say you're creeping through an enemy camp at night. There is not a sound to be heard. Suddenly, out of nowhere, someone glides up behind you and wraps a garrote around your neck. If you manage to run away, how would you be breathing? You would be fleeing for your life and gasping for breath."

"I see what you mean." She nodded in agreement.

"But this is just the beginning," he said. "You must practice as often as possible before you go, and continue to do so while on your mission."

"How many breaths should I practice at a time?"

"The object is to center yourself and relax. You will know when you achieve inner calm, but for now you have to return to the palace, Princess," he said.

Reaching inside his pocket, he retrieved an ornate watch attached to a gold fob. In a catlike move, he leaped to his feet and pulled her with him. "I have no desire to run afoul of your mother."

"You know my mother?"

"There is much of her in you," he said, and lifted her chin, examining her eyes.

"Everyone else thinks I look like Papa's family," she insisted.

"There is more to the essence of a woman than outward appearance," Weatherby said.

While they retraced their path to the carriage house level, she mulled the lessons of the night. How could she possibly be ready with only one more night of instruction?

"Trust me. You will be ready." He helped her back into the carriage and squeezed her arm as if he had read her thoughts.

She looked back at him in the dim light while his two assistants harnessed the horses and rolled the conveyance into the alley. One of them clambered down to close the huge doors. He raised his arm in a farewell salute while the doors rolled shut.

Who was this man? And when had he crossed paths with *Maman*? After another night of this clandestine class, she would have to confide in her mother. She could hardly hide her exhaustion. Perhaps *Maman* could shed some light on the mysterious Mr. Weatherby.

The darkness was beginning to seep away, replaced by tinges of sunrise, when she crept back into the townhouse. In her stealthy trip across the kitchen, she paused to slip Cook's knife and rolling pin back into the drawers where she found them.

The sight of pans of dough set out to rise overnight stirred her to quicken her pace toward the front staircase. The kitchen maids would soon be coming down from their attic quarters to begin the day's baking.

She shut the door to the bedroom behind her and turned to glide across the rug to the comfort of the waiting bed.

"Where have you been?" Sarah voice snapped at her in the darkness. Sitting up in the bed they shared, her friend widened her eyes at the sight of Lillie clad in the crude men's clothing she had scrounged over the last few days.

Lillie nearly broke into a fit of nervous giggles. Her bedmate's hair was wreathed around her head in a crown of rags twisted among her long curls.

"I might as well confess. There is no way I can do this for another night without you and *Maman* knowing where I am." She knelt on the end of the bed and pushed at her friend's foot.

"You've been away from the house all night, haven't you?" In spite of Sarah's accusing tone, her face filled with incredulity. "What are you up to now?"

"I haven't told *Maman* yet. Promise you won't tell a soul until I have a chance to talk to her." Lillie crossed her heart and refused to continue until her friend returned the sign.

"Papa somehow got wind of my plans to run the blockade. The day I went to see the solicitor to make the arrangements, this strange man accosted me in the park. He said Papa sent him. He knew things only my father would know."

"Lillie — he could be a Union agent in disguise out to trap you."

"If he were a agent and suspected me of anything, he would have arrested me. And anyway, I've told him nothing of my plans."

"You still haven't explained why you sneaked out and spent the entire night God knows where."

"He's teaching me to defend myself."

"Noooo." Leaning back with her face as white as linen covering the down pillows, Sarah put her hand to her forehead and moaned piteously. "If my mother were here, we'd both be under lock and key with a guard outside the door. If she discovers what you're about, I'll spend the rest of my life in a convent."

"Sarah, please. There's no reason for your mother ever to know."

"How can you be so sure? What about your mother?" They had been keeping their voices low, but now her friend's words came out in a loud hiss.

"*Maman* is not going to cause a scene. It appears she also knows this man who is teaching me to fight." A chuckle escaped her lips. "I can hardly wait to hear her explain how Weatherby knows so much about her."

"When are you going to tell her?" Sarah pulled the sheets up to her chin and stared uneasily at Lillie.

"As soon as I fortify myself with a few hours of sleep." She shed the night's disguise and reached for her white cotton nightgown still lying across the chair where she had flung it hours earlier. "I'll need a clear head to handle her."

She crawled in next to her friend, and the two of them lay back, staring at the ceiling for a few minutes.

"Lillie?"

"Yes."

"Are you sure you want to go through with this madness?"

"Absolutely." She rolled to her side and lay there in silence, trying to calm her skittering thoughts. After pounding her pillow a few times, she pressed her palm to her stomach and began to practice Weatherby's exercises.

Tuesday Morning, May 5, 1863
London, England
51°30'62"N, 0°10'0"W

How odd, Lillie thought, to be talking to her mother again in the same garden, watching fat koi darting from one side of the ornamental pool to the other.

"*Maman*, I'm afraid I have another secret to reveal." She lifted her head and faced her mother. "I hope you hear me out before tearing apart my plans."

"I know what you're going to say." Her mother hesitated and studied her hands a few moments before she lifted her clear, blue eyes to Lillie and said, "James Weatherby is an old friend of mine, as well as your father's."

"You admit to knowing him?" She gaped at her mother in disbelief. "How long?"

"Almost as long as he and your father have been friends."

"How? Why?"

"It was during the Mexican conflict, in battles outside Vera Cruz. Jim, er, Mr. Weatherby, " she corrected herself, "was shot from his horse, and his right leg was badly mangled. The other battlefield surgeon wanted to amputate, but your father disagreed. He saved his leg, and quite possibly his life. They had known each other since West Point."

"But how were you involved?"

"Before you were born, I followed your father along on assignments. I helped him in his surgery." She stretched her fingers out in front of her and carefully examined them again.

"*Maman*?"

"While your father went ahead with the troops, I stayed with the seriously injured patients who could not be moved. Mr. Weatherby, of course, was one of those." Her mother paused and took a turn staring at the koi.

"I still don't understand. How did you know I've been working with him?"

"He sent a message to me to meet him shortly after he contacted you." Now her mother was fidgeting with the rings on her left hand.

"So you know what we've been doing?" Lillie asked. "And you approve?"

"If you're determined to fling yourself into this dangerous affair, then you should learn what you need to know from the best."

"What exactly does this man of shadows do?" She studied her mother's face carefully.

"He investigates and fixes things for certain countries."

"What kinds of things, and for what countries?"

"His loyalties are to whoever pays him." Her mother's face glowed with a slight flush when she shared the details. "He was born in Scotland and moved to New York City with his parents as a child. He spent a number of years in China before going to West Point."

"You still haven't told me what kinds of 'things' he does." Lillie wanted some real answers.

"He is a professional soldier." Her mother shrugged and added, "I can't tell you more."

"Why does he know so much about you?" she asked, and was startled by tears forming at the corners of her mother's eyes.

"I've already told you more than I should have. Please don't ask me again." Her mother pulled a handkerchief from her pocket, dabbed at her eyes, and then left the garden.

Tuesday Night, May 5, 1863
London, England
51°30'62"N, 0°10'0"W

Lillie watched Weatherby, fascinated. Since her mother had alluded to a relationship with the man, she was curious to know more about him. They were back at his townhouse, and he was demonstrating the next level in her instruction. Unfortunately, her concentration was off.

His unerring sense of the state of her mind had begun to annoy her. He pinned her to one of the mats, both of her arms rendered immovable.

"Why must I spend the lion's share of our time together groveling on the floor under your person?" This time, however, she was not gasping for air.

"You must learn to fight from the ground, where you will certainly land with your ever-wandering mind." He eased his tight hold on her arms and assumed his now-familiar meditative position on the mat.

When she scrambled up to face him, he continued his lesson.

"Constantly seek your opponent's weak moments. That will be your cue to strike. Oddly enough, those openings will tend to appear when he tries to punch or grab you. You will have only a split second to make your move. Do not hesitate, or all will be lost" he said.

"In our remaining time, we'll work on the most effective blows of all." He sprang to his feet, pulling her with him.

They moved to the corner where she had maimed the scarecrow the night before. The effigy had been replaced with a tightly stuffed dummy whose lifelike body was more rigid.

"Now, I want you to curl your fingers into a claw and thrust upward with the heel of your hand. The point on your attacker's face you want to strike with all of your strength is right here." He pointed to the dummy's upper lip area just below the nose. "Remember to muster all of your forces from the center of your body." He pointed to her mid-section.

She practiced a few thrusts before stopping in frustration. Most of her blows lost their force before smashing into her foe. He stood behind her and moved her arm in a sort of slow dance demonstrating how to smooth her jerky movements.

"Mr. Weatherby, do you have any children of your own?" Lillie asked.

"Yes." He stiffened a bit at her abrupt question, but answered easily.

"Well, how many?"

"Just one."

"A son or a daughter?"

"I really don't know." He paused for a bit too long before answering.

"Where is your child?"

"Some things are best left to the great unknown, Miss Snoop." He pulled her around until their faces were close together. "In the here and now, you must use your time to focus on what will bring you safely back to your family."

"What do you mean?"

"This —" He gently pressed his thumb to her forehead. "And this —" He moved his hand lower to rest it over her chest.

In a split second, she moved smoothly out of his grasp, positioned her right foot behind his left leg and pushed sharply against his shoulders. He suddenly looked up at her from the floor, and she was pushing her wooden practice knife against his throat.

"Well done." He rewarded her with a rare, devilish grin before reaching out in a flash, pulling her down to roll over his shoulder while her weapon clattered uselessly to the floor. "But you still have a long way to go."

Wednesday Night, May 6, 1863
London, England
51°30'62"N, 0°10'0"W

Lillie's third night of what Sarah called her "School for Thugs" had arrived. She made her bleary-eyed way to the mews in high spirits for having survived reasonably intact after the first two nights of Weatherby's lessons.

He waited outside the carriage and quickly handed her up through the open door before hauling himself after her. With a word to his driver, they sped off, but headed in a direction other than their usual route.

Without preliminaries, he turned to her and warned, "We're being followed."

"Why?"

"Do not ask questions. We're on our way to an alternate safe house."

"Who would follow us?"

"No questions," he repeated. She could imagine the boyish grin spreading across his face in the dark gloom of the carriage in spite of his stern tone.

Swaying with the motion of the carriage while they raced down side alleys, she braced herself to keep from sliding onto the floor.

Wednesday Night, May 6, 1863
Portsmouth, England
50°49'00"N, 1°05'00"W

Jack sat on an ottoman in a small cheery bedroom on the top floor of an inn with windows overlooking the coast. Waves crashed below with a dull intensity similar to his mood.

He studied the lush curves of his old friend, Elizabeth, while she sat at the edge of her bed and slowly pulled her stockings back on. Stretching like a cat, she pushed her feet forward while keeping her head down. Her rich caramel-colored hair hung in a curtain across her face, hiding her expression from him. He bent to take her foot in his hands and gently rubbed the calloused pads at the base of her toes.

"What are you doing?" She looked up with a start and jerked her foot from his grasp.

"It's the least I can do." He could not bring himself to face her directly, but kept his head lowered while he recaptured her foot and continued the massage.

"Jack, it happens to the best of men. You must have a lot on your mind." She leaned forward and lifted his chin. "You have to leave in a few days, don't you?"

He nodded in mute affirmation.

"Come back to me when you're done with this round of blockade running. Bring me something pretty. I'll wear it just for you." She moved her mouth to close over his and leaned into a kiss.

His usual response would have been to pull her close and explore her lips and tongue with his. Instead, he merely brushed her lips.

He stood abruptly, pulling her up with him. "You've hit the heart of the matter, of course. My mind is on *The Kate*. We've made so many adjustments to her, I've been driving everyone to test as much as possible before we head out to sea." Egad, he was rambling now. "I guess I've forgotten how to be just a man," he ended lamely.

"Don't tell me." The corners of her generous mouth spread into a sly smile. "Who is the clever, lucky woman?"

He stared at her, mouth agape, as if she had grown an extra head.

"Jack, it's written all over your face." She crossed her legs on the bed and patted the space next to her. "Come here and tell me all about her. I've wondered if this would ever happen." She paused and pressed a hand to her forehead. "Oh, my God. The stoic Captain Jack Roberts is in love."

"You, madam, are mistaken." He attempted his best intimidating tone, but she just giggled at him.

"There is no one. I cannot afford to let myself be distracted, as you well know."

"Love is like the mumps or the measles." She tipped her head and continued, her tone mock serious. "There is no quick fix. Your only choice is to ride it out."

He wanted to argue the point, but the sinking feeling in his stomach warned him he was in dangerous waters.

"I just spent the most painful weekend of my life at Clarendon." Exhaling a weary sigh, he came to a decision. He had to unburden his feelings. "I've never had much experience dealing with women, and I really don't want more of this one." He heaved himself down next to her and began to vent.

"First of all, she's an American. Secondly, she is an incredibly spoiled child who can't keep any of her thoughts to herself. Thirdly, and might I add the worst of all, she has this bizarre need to keep insisting she is 'as good as any man.' Why, she even had the audacity to re·train Nelson."

His companion burst into laughter and could not stop. Tears flowed down her cheeks.

"What could you possibly find so humorous in such a situation?" he asked.

"This is much worse than I first thought." She finally calmed down to just hiccups and dabbed at her eyes with a handkerchief. "You are besotted. Where is this woman?"

"I have no idea, and come to that, have no intention of finding out." He tried to remain stern.

"I'm not afraid of you. You know that." She refused to back down from his look of censure. "But, if you do not finish what has obviously begun between the two of you, you should be afraid."

"Me?"

"Yes, you. You should be quaking in your sea boots."

"I'm not going to stay here and listen to your wild imaginings—."

"Has Edward met this woman?" She interrupted his indignant speech.

"Yes."

"And—?"

"He is simply not to be trusted in this matter. He has far too many of his own domestic sins to manage."

"What are you talking about?"

"He's managed to get the young daughter of our former landlady in the family way."

"Edward?" Amazement registered in her expressive hazel eyes. "Have the two of you gone mad at the same time?"

"I suppose we have." He paused for a second or two and then shook his head slowly. "I suspect the only cure for what ails us is the sea, which is where I am headed forthwith." He stood and pulled her into a warm embrace. After a long moment he gave her a brotherly kiss and reached for his broad-brimmed hat hanging on the chair next to the bed.

"When I return, things will be different. You'll see."

"I'll be counting the moments." After flashing him a saucy smile, her look turned serious. "God go with you, and Edward, too."

He left then without a backward glance.

Wednesday Night, May 6, 1863
London, England
51°30'62"N, 0°10'0"W

Lillie sat at a table in the safe house where she and Weatherby had ended the night's long chase. He sat across from her and produced two cases, placing them in the middle of the table.

"What are those?" She reached toward the cases only to have him grasp her hand tightly.

"These cases contain the keys to your survival." He eased his grip and leaned back. "Guard them as you would your life."

She opened one of the cases. The velvet-lined box cradled two pistols with elaborate engraving on the brass frames. The smooth metal bores would accommodate only single shots, but the diminutive firearms would fit perfectly in a hidden pocket or in her hand.

"Do you know how to shoot and care for a gun?" His question was half hesitant, as if he already knew the answer.

"I learned from the best."

"Yes, I'm sure you did." He leaned closer and lowered his voice. "If you take time each day to care for your weapons, they will take care of you." He switched gears abruptly. "Show me how you would take aim if you are threatened."

She carefully lifted one of the guns from the case, expertly opened the chamber, and sighted down the barrel to assure it was not loaded. Assuming a firing stance with the gun held out in front of her and supported by her other hand, she looked up in surprise when he snatched it out of her grasp.

"You're not going to be on a practice range with your enemies lined up like ducks at a carnival." He took the gun and held it close to his chest, the pin cocked. "You will have but one chance, and it has to be at close range. These derringers have a range of only a few feet. Don't forfeit your chances by waving the gun about. Your attacker will seize the weapon."

"All right, all right," she agreed, exasperated. "What's in the other box?" She could not contain her curiosity.

"There you are, letting your scattered mind rule again." He moved the second box out of range of her impatient grasp and opened it slowly.

She sucked in a breath. Never would she use the words lethal and beautiful together, but the two thin gleaming daggers nestled in the dark velvet grooves demanded such description.

"Where did you find these?" She could not tear her gaze away from the perfectly crafted twin blades.

"Feel the balance of their weight in your hand." He transferred both weapons to her grasp.

"But they're deadly sharp. How am I supposed to conceal them without injury?"

Weatherby produced two leather sheaths with thongs. "Safe, secure carriers," he said.

The knives felt like extensions of her hands when she gingerly hefted and turned them over.

"Tie one of these to your ankle and get used to the feel of the knives against your skin."

She looked up with a start and nearly laughed at her own trepidation. She'd been surrounded for the last several years by excruciatingly polite gentlemen who would never refer to the feel of her skin in conversation. The path she had lately chosen twisted and turned so much she could never go back. Straight forward was her only option.

"And where is your jittery mind leading you now?" He rudely interrupted her thoughts. "Put the weapons down. Come with me." He led her to a pile of cushions in the corner of the room. "Sit."

He was right. Her mind raced.

"Close your eyes." He assumed a meditative position and waited. "I said close them." He sent her a withering look, and she grudgingly complied.

"Your thoughts are flitting from tree to tree, from limb to limb, like a chattering monkey. And what is the word you hear over and over? Me, me, me." A ghost of a smile passed across his face when she cracked one eyelid to sneak a look. "You're not concentrating.

"Breathe in and out. Empty your mind. Push your selfish 'me' into a corner. Make her stay there until we're ready to call her back."

Minutes passed, but she couldn't be sure. She felt as if she were floating. She was back in the woods at Clarendon with Jack. He was touching the old oak and turned to her with his other hand outstretched. She returned to awareness with a start.

"Our time together is over, Princess. You're on your own now," Weatherby said, and extended his hand.

The ride home was uneventful, and when he climbed from the carriage behind the mews, he squeezed her shoulders before sending her on her way with the two diminutive velvet-lined cases tucked inside her clothes.

She stood in the stables for a few moments, listening to the carriage roll away until the sound of the wheels was a faint rumbling. As her last contact with Weatherby faded, the horses stirred in the stable making chuffing noises. Only then did she turn to find her way back to her bed.

The last time desolation had overcome her this completely had been three years earlier, on the day she bid her father farewell.

CHAPTER TWELVE

Thursday, May 07, 1863
London, England
51°30'62"N, 0°10'0"W

"No, no, no — that one will never do," Lillie said, and rejected a creamy white linen shirt by tossing it into a corner. Giselle gave her a dark look and retrieved the discarded item.

Lillie had closeted herself in the bedroom with Sarah for the better part of the day with strict instructions to the servants to make sure they were not disturbed.

"It's not too late, you know," Sarah pleaded, while Lillie stuffed clothing into a crude oiled sea bag. "You could tell the solicitor you've changed your mind."

"How well do you know me?" Lillie asked. "I can't back down now. Our boys need this money and support to continue fighting."

"I still can't imagine you bunking in a smelly, dark place below decks — and with all those dirty sailors."

"Sarah, Sarah — this ship is different. It's a brand new steamship. The stakes are so high, successful captains are provided every luxury." She paused and sifted the ends of her long curls between her fingers. "I'll be his cabin boy, next to his quarters, not in with the rest of the crew."

They spent most of the morning assembling a simple set of clothing suitable for a young man going to sea for the first time — warm woolen pants, a heavy pea coat, and two well-worn shirts. Their maids, Giselle and Annette, had acquired the set of slops in a harrowing trip to the London waterfront. Boy's long underwear purchased on Fleet Street and an assortment of rags completed her kit. Her courses had finished the day before, and she prayed they would not reappear before she was on land again.

"You must not pack those clothes before we have a chance to boil them in hot water." Giselle stood in the middle of the room, hands on hips, glaring at her. "Those men on the waterfront were a rough lot. I don't know how we could have survived without Monsieur Thomas at our side.

"After driving us down there, he refused to let us wander the docks alone." She pressed a hand over her chest and gazed dramatically toward the ceiling. "He left young Andrew in charge of the carriage and followed us." She fell silent and made the sign of the cross. "*Mon dieu*. Who knows what would have happened to us otherwise." She turned a scathing look at Lillie. "The very idea — to offer such men money for their clothes."

"Giselle, calm yourself. You're safely back home. No one hurt you," Lillie said, trying to reassure her.

"Yes — in spite of your wild scheming." Her maid gathered the soiled laundry and stalked from the room.

"You haven't said a word about Mr. Finch-Barton since we got back from the weekend. It's not like you, Lillie, not like you at all." Sarah climbed upon the large four-poster they shared and lay on her stomach with her chin propped up, an expectant look on her face.

"What a strange observation." Lillie crouched in the middle of the room, sorting through a pile of essentials for the trip, still clad in just a linen shift. "What do you expect me to say?"

"There was a spark between you and Jack. Don't deny it. Edward saw it too."

"Oh, so now it's not just you who is an expert on my feelings. Edward's opinion makes it unanimous." In spite of her protestations, a hot flush crept up her neck. She lifted her head and impatiently swept back her heavy hair. "It's time."

"Don't change the subject."

"It's time, Sarah, to get rid of this." She gathered her thick mass of curls at the nape of her neck and pointed to the scissors on the table by the bed.

No." Her friend's face filled with anguish. "There must be another way." Sarah slid from the bed and knelt beside her. "Maybe we could twist it up into a knot on top of your head, and—"

"Get the scissors, Sarah." She turned to her with determination in her eyes. "Let's get it over with."

"All right. Come here." Sarah pulled a chair to the center of the room. Tears pooled in her eyes.

"I will tell you exactly how I feel about him if you come over here, quit your whining, and finish this nasty task." Lillie added, firmly, "This is a minor sacrifice compared to what others give up every day. I'm ashamed of myself."

Her friend ripped a sheet from the bed and spread it under the chair. "I'll hide the evidence as soon as possible so your mother doesn't faint dead away when she sees the carnage."

"She'll be fine once she realizes this is the safest way to ensure no one sees through my disguise."

"Now, you have to reveal all the feelings you harbor for Jack, or I may be tempted to plunge these into your neck." The scissors sliced through the first section of lush raven curls, and they fluttered like exotic birds to the floor.

"We did kiss, several times, actually, and he held me so close I thought my heart would hammer out of my chest." She turned her head and flashed an impish smile.

"Have a care," Sarah warned. "I nearly dropped the scissors. He kissed you? When did that happen?"

"After everyone else left the game room."

"Lillie — Sarah said, her mouth gaping open. "You were alone with him without a chaperone?"

"Oh, yes, and then in the woods before you and Edward caught up." She smiled at her friend's discomfiture.

"So what else happened? Tell me." Sarah's earlier mood of censure turned to fascination.

"Nothing else." Lillie sadly turned to her friend. "Nothing at all." Regret swept through her, taking her by surprise. She missed him with a heavy ache.

Sarah gave Lillie a mirror, and reality returned with a shock. Even she didn't recognize the vision staring back at her. Thankfully, the short bob had curbed some of the runaway curliness of her hair. It would be easier to stuff the entire mess under a hat for the duration of the trip.

"Come help me decide which of Mr. Weatherby's disguises are most believable." Lillie turned to her friend and grabbed her hand to pull her over to the haphazard piles near her sea bag on the floor.

Friday, May 8, 1863
Portsmouth, England
50°49'00"N, 1°05'00"W

Martha stood on the quay in Portsmouth, dabbing her eyes with a lace handkerchief. Lillie awaited a shore boat rowing toward them from *The Kate* and quivered with excitement

She stood on one foot and then the other in the cool, early morning mist. She'd been unable to contain herself since the first sight of the sleek ship bobbing at anchor the night before.

"Why must you constantly deprive me of what little peace life affords me?" Her mother blew her nose with a noisy honk and continued weeping into a now sodden lace square. "How could you do this to me? Your hair was your best feature. It was glorious. What will I tell your precious father?"

She observed her mother as if she were seeing her for the first time. "*Maman*—" she said, choosing her words carefully. "I cannot imagine why you are mourning the loss of my hair, of all things, at a moment like this. Papa knows what I must do. He even sent Mr. Weatherby to help me. He certainly would not expect me to run the blockade dressed as a man with long hair flowing down my back."

"How dare you contradict me? You've always wanted to steal his affections."

"*Maman*, the boat is nearly here. Please don't talk to me as if I were a woman." She leaned toward her mother and placed a kiss on her forehead. Pulling back in sudden terror, Lillie reached up to touch the skin between her upper lip and nose to make sure her false mustache was still firmly in place.

A black eye starting to yellow a bit as if in the final stages of healing had been a last-minute inspiration of Sarah's. Oh, how she wished her friend had come along to see her off. They'd made their tearful good-byes at the train station in London the day before.

An earlier quick glance in the mirror of the room in the boarding house had boosted her confidence in the final effect of her hard work. She looked the part. Now if only she could focus all her powers of concentration on walking and talking like a young sailor.

Affecting too gruff a voice might make matters worse. Actually, she planned to say as little as possible until she had a chance to listen to the other crewmen. Her talent as a mimic would serve her well.

Sarah and Giselle had helped her sew the French documents and gold into the seams of her clothing the night before. She patted the French dispatches inside a leg of her pants and felt the bonds and gold sovereigns whip-stitched inside the seams.

As the boat neared the dock, she scrambled down the steps to help the crew tie off. Returning to heft her sea bag over her shoulder, she gave her mother one last quick peck on the cheek before hurrying to embark, ignoring the woman's final dramatic wail when she flung her bag into the boat.

Friday, May 8, 1863
Aboard *The Kate*
Portsmouth Harbour, England
50°49'00"N, 1°05'00"W

Jack wiped the sweat from his forehead while he and Algernon Summer monitored the inventory of uniforms and guns in *The Kate*'s forward hold. The count had been going on for hours.

"You, down there — crack open another box." He periodically instructed his crew to open the wooden cases containing Enfield rifles to double-check the number stamped on the outside of the box. "I've had my fill of owners blaming me for suppliers shorting the goods." Jack turned to the solicitor and motioned for him to follow him up to the deck.

"Do you find many boxes short of the count?" Summer asked.

"I used to." He turned to his companion with a wry smile. "The suppliers know better now. They've incurred the wrath of the syndicate too many times."

"So, why do you keep doing the count?"

"To keep them honest." He clapped him on the shoulder, and they both laughed. "Come along to my cabin. Let's have a toast to another successful voyage."

Friday, May 8, 1863
Aboard *The Kate*
Portsmouth Harbour, England
50°49'00"N, 1°05'00"W

Lillie pulled her scratchy woolen shirt away from her skin where sweat trickled down the inside of her arms.

"You're a soft excuse for crew on a runner, lad. You're lucky your pa is a friend of the cap'n's." Martin Fitzwilliams, or Mr. Fitz, as the crew called him, was *The Kate*'s first mate.

She grunted an acknowledgement and lowered her head under a cap slanted low over her eyes. Lillie had been following him around the ship for hours. All she could think about was ripping off her clothes and sinking into a cool tub of water. How did sailors work day in and day out in these heavy slops?

She'd finally realized her fondest dream. She wasn't merely as good as any man, she *was* a man. And it wasn't all it was cracked up to be.

She drew a sharp breath when he grabbed her hands and turned her palms over to inspect them. She silently prayed the dirt she had rubbed into them would hide the softness.

"These hands haven't seen much hard work," he said. "Why are you here? You'll be lucky to make it to Bermuda, lad." The stern expression on his face softened then. "How old are you?"

His line of questioning was interrupted by one of the crew rushing up with another problem to be solved. Fortunately for her — a reprieve.

"Tomorrow morning at eight bells you'll begin your lessons on the sextant." He turned sharply away from the young crewman to address her. "Navigation chores should suit till you've toughened up a bit," he said, and added almost as an afterthought, "You don't carry much weight. Just remember when the weather gets up, mind you keep one hand for the ship and one for yourself." He walked away then, after instructing the other crewman to take her back to her quarters.

"What should I call you?" Lillie asked and turned to the young man waiting to guide her back to her cabin. With her cap still slanted low over her face, she used a soft, low tone of voice. She estimated her guide was not much older than twenty. Soft brown eyes watched her from under a thatch of thick dark hair he seemed obliged to keep pushing off his forehead.

"Abe Wilkinson, but everyone calls me Abe. What would your name be?"

"Rafe." After having used the name all day, she was getting used to the sound of it. Her choice had been an inspiration off the top of her head, since she had not even considered such a detail. Solicitor Summer had specified merely to board the blockade-runner as a Mr. Horlock, the son of a friend of Captain Roberts.

A first name had come to her out of thin air when the crew on the boat making for the ship had asked the same question. She remembered her faithful old dog, Rafael, and the name slipped out naturally.

"Could you explain some things for me on the way back? I don't want to take up too much of your time, but this is my first time on a blockade runner."

"Be sure to stay away from some of the other crew who like to bully. As short as you are, there's some who'd take advantage." Abe turned to her with a smile and added, "Cap'n Roberts don't tolerate bullying on his ships, but he can't be everywhere." He ended his warning with a conspiratorial wink.

She froze at his assessment of her size and vulnerability. Her calculations hadn't taken that into consideration. After a moment's hesitation, she seized upon her only option.

"I've got ways. No one takes advantage of Rafe, ever." To further emphasize her roughness, she grabbed his shirt and pulled him hard around, pressing a fist into his neck. "If I had a knife with me now, you'd be beggin' what for, you would." She'd never been devout, but she sent up another short prayer, this time one of thanksgiving for her intense three nights with Weatherby.

Abe scrabbled for his balance and jumped away when she relaxed her hold.

"You're a little scrapper, you are." There was new respect in his eyes. "You'll do fine." A frown crossed his face. "But don't let ol' Fitz catch you scrappin'. There's no fighting on this ship, ever." He assessed her again and added, "Now that ugly eye of yours makes sense."

His cautionary words were lost on her when she caught sight of Jack on the other side of the ship, his long-legged stride and silver-blond hair impossible to miss in the late afternoon sun slanting across the decks. Damn her fickle heart. She had to force herself to remember to breathe, and not stare.

She spun around to avoid being seen by him, or Solicitor Summer who was close on his heels, racing to keep up. Eventually, she'd have to face Jack as a man, but for now, she wasn't ready. With any luck, she could delay meeting him until the sun had gone down.

"Now, what can I show you? I know *The Kate* like me own mum after all these weeks workin' to get her ready," Abe said.

"I was wonderin' where they store all the coal for the runs." Lillie asked and turned to look around. "It must take up a lot of space."

"Come with me." He gave her a wide grin. "You won't believe it," he said. "She's two-hundred-thirty feet from bow to stern. Why, she can carry over a thousand bales of cotton back out, and thousands of feet of coal keep us ready to fire up top speed."

"Where do they get so much coal?"

"We been loadin' it for weeks. It's some kind of fancy grade — can't remember what they call it. Comes from Scotland." He shook his head. "It don't burn like normal coal. Hardly gives off any smoke, but what does come out of those big funnels is the lightest grey. Those Union boys on the blockaders will think we're a ghost ship slippin' through the water."

She could imagine the effect the light cloud-colored paint covering the steel hull of the huge ship would have at sea, like an illusionist's trick.

"Sounds like you've been on a lot of runs."

"I have, but never with anyone but the cap'n. He's pure luck, he is." It seemed as if Abe might say more, but he simply added, "You'll see."

She followed close on his heels and drew up short behind him when he stopped abruptly at the edge of a chasm dropping down below decks. The coal was stacked at least six feet high in the deep bunker. There were four such bunkers fore and aft of the two boilers. A large cluster of crewmen transferred coal from a huge barge rafted next to them.

"With all this fuel, why does she need those masts fore and aft?"

"It takes a fearful amount of fuel to outrun the blockaders. We try to save as much as possible for emergencies. There's plenty of wind out there. Might as well use it."

"I hate to keep you from your duties, but could I ask just one more question?" She nearly groaned out loud. She was beginning to sound as if she were flirting with him.

"You're not keeping me from anything. Mr. Fitz said to help you learn the ship particularly."

Hallelujah · her gender slip had gone unnoticed.

"Where are all the guns?" She peered around to either side of the beam of the ship and rose up on her tiptoes to check the far reaches.

"The only arms you'll see on *The Kate* are the two swivel signal guns on the bow." He gave her a smug look.

"How do you defend yourselves from the blockaders?"

"Cunning and luck," he said, adding, "Our Cap'n Jack, he can out-fox the best."

"I'm afraid I just don't know how such a strategy would work." She shook her head slowly and moved toward one of the two huge paddle wheels to either side of the boilers. "How fast can the ship go if we're being chased?"

"If we push her, somewhere between sixteen and seventeen knots." A tone of pride crept into his voice. "Of course, most of the time if we're just cruising toward port, we'll keep her down to eight or ten knots." He moved on toward the stern of the ship and motioned for her to follow.

"But I thought this was just her maiden cruise after coming down from Liverpool." She tried to prolong their conversation as long as possible to give her time to practice getting just the right inflection in her voice before she encountered Jack.

"Oh, we've been testing her in the waters around here for weeks." Much like all the other crew on board *The Kate*, her companion lengthened his stride and moved quickly toward the far end of the ship.

Walking as fast as she could to follow, she forced herself not to run. Doubting her ability to move rapidly and still be perceived as a young man, she tapped him on the shoulder to slow his forward motion.

"Mr. Fitz said I would have to learn navigation duties. What does that involve?"

"You'll work back there." He stopped and pointed in the direction of the binnacle where the helmsman would stand at the wheel once they were under way. "Mr. Fitz is a good teacher. It's an honor to be trained in navigation. He must like you."

"How long do you think it will take me to learn?" The sight of officers peering through the mysterious sextant had fascinated her over the years, even as a little girl on voyages with her mother.

"Oh, I don't know. It all depends on how much you want to learn and get ahead." He ran his hand through his wind-tossed hair and stared for a bit out toward the horizon. "It's not easy. There's lots of tables you have to use, and you have to have a real steady hand when the sea is trying to roll you about." He stared directly into her eyes then. "You'll do just fine, Rafe. I'm sure of it."

A frisson of anxiety seized her. In the excitement of leaving the dock, she forgot to don the clear glasses Weatherby had given her. There was nothing at all masculine about her eyes. She wished she could hide the unusual shade of lavender and the long, silken lashes.

They stopped at the rail to watch the falling sun near the horizon. The fiery orb's lazy descent appeared to speed up at the very last just before it dropped precipitously and disappeared, leaving only intense bands of orange and pink.

"Tomorrow will be perfect for weighing anchor. We leave on the morning tide." Abe turned to her and warned, "You'd best stow your gear and get your rest. Mr. Fitz likes to get an early start with his students."

There was an awkward silence between them before she remembered to seize his hand and pump it energetically. She paused for a minute before opening the door to her cabin. When Abe strolled away, she

nearly smacked her hand against her head in
frustration. She would have to concentrate more on
reacting as a man.

The Irish whisky Algernon Summer had brought to
celebrate the maiden voyage of *The Kate* slid down
Jack's throat smoothly. Too smoothly. He pushed away
a third offering of the rich, amber liquid when Summer
leaned across the chart table to pour him another
generous shot.

They had spent the entire day going over last-
minute concerns when the solicitor had suggested
toasts for luck before he headed back to shore.

Summer was more than just his legal
representative; he was married to his sister, Miranda.
During Jack's years of leave from the British Navy the
man had become a trusted advisor in his wide-ranging,
lucrative affairs. The thing about family was they
could get one into and out of all manner of
predicaments. He was glad his solicitor was both
family and friend.

"Have I exceeded the legendary Captain Jack
Roberts' capacity for spirits?" Summer drew back the
bottle and gave him a quizzical look, half joking but
half serious.

"You know me as well as anyone." Jack leaned back
in his swivel chair attached to the floor of the cabin
and put his feet on the supports beneath the table. "I
developed a bad habit of using spirits to come down
from the high of preparing for battle the night before.
But it's stood me in good stead over the years. I relax
enough to fall into a deep sleep and then awaken
refreshed the day of engagement. I can nap on
command throughout the day to snatch a few hours of
rest, but the nights are hard." He brought his feet back
down to the floor with a sigh. "There is a fine line,
though, between calming and detrimental. Let's just

say there's too much at stake for me to cross over tonight."

"By the way, you haven't said anything about your new cabin boy," Summer said. "Have you met him yet?"

"Blast it. Forgot all about him. I gave instructions to have him installed in the spare cabin down the passageway from here. Wouldn't do for the rest of the crew to suspect there is a courier on board. I'll have to check with Fitz to see if he's been settled in and given a tour of the ship." He stared across the table at his friend. "Should I have any reason to be concerned about the young man?"

"Not as far as I know." Summer bent his head to pick at some invisible lint on his lapel. "I met him a few weeks ago when we made arrangements for his passage." The solicitor leaned forward then and added in a low tone, "For an extra thousand pounds, I think you can put up with him until you reach Charleston Harbor. You are to rendezvous with a fishing boat off Sullivan Island after which he will be out of your way. Arrangements for his exit back out of Charleston are entirely between you two, and at your discretion."

"Does this courier have any experience as a seaman?"

"Well — he has been on many sea voyages." Summer spoke hesitantly and avoided Jack's questioning gaze.

"Never mind. Fitz will keep him busy and out of my way." He threw back the remaining whisky in his glass and stood to end their discussion. "I need my bed, and you need to get back to shore."

The solicitor's departure was interrupted by a knock on the cabin door. Fitz pushed his lean muscular frame through the opening.

"The boat is waiting, Mr. Summer, any time you're ready to head back." He nodded to Jack, and his solicitor hurried up to the deck after a fast farewell.

Jack motioned his first mate to stay behind. "Have you taken care of the new cabin boy, Fitz?"

"Yes, sir. I showed him the ropes before I turned him over to Abe this afternoon to answer any questions he might have. I think he might do well helping out with navigation duties. I'll start his training first thing in the morning."

"I suppose I should have a few words with him, welcome him aboard, make sure he's sorted." Jack turned wistfully toward his comfortable bunk. "That will be all. Go turn over to the next watch. Get yourself a good night's rest. Tomorrow begins another adventure." He moved toward the door and clapped his mate on the back.

He followed the man out and detoured down the short hallway between his quarters and the cabin of his newest crewman.

He pounded on the door and waited for an answer. Nothing. After a short pause, he pounded again, this time much louder. The worthless little swab was probably bedded down already for the night.

Lillie crouched in her bunk, debating whether or not she should feign sleep. When the pounding became wilder, she jumped up, hastily pulling on her woolen pants and shirt. Fortunately, she had decided to keep her muslin banding on when she climbed into bed.

She'd left the mustache on as well in case of just such an emergency. Jamming her hair under her cap and putting the glasses on, she hastened to swing open the door. She caught him mid-pound and he stared vacantly at her for a moment.

"Did you already retire for the evening? I apologize for disturbing you, but I've not had a chance to welcome you aboard."

She mumbled a few words and kept her head down.

"For God's sakes, speak up, lad, and take off your cap. You may be serving on a blockade runner, but do not presume for one moment we will dispense with formalities at sea. After all, we fly the Union Jack. I'll not have any of my crew showing disrespect."She was terrified but whipped off her hat. Her curls, dampened by the sea air, sprang free. Once again, she was praying to whatever deity would listen to be delivered from her predicament.

"Aren't you a trifle young to place yourself in such danger?" Jack asked. He lit the oil lamp by the doorway and studied her.

"I'm older than I seem." Lillie turned from the shadows to give him a full view of her battered eye. "I've been on my own for some time now, and I know my way around Charleston like the back of my hand. I'm just a courier, not a spy."

"Right. I trust you have the sense to do your job as long as you are on my ship." He turned to leave, then wheeled around with one last warning. "If your activities at any time put my ship in danger, I will personally see you turned over to the authorities, and hanged."

He ended his dire warning by slamming out of her cabin. What a tyrant he was now that he was on board his ship. She turned back to her bunk with a weary sigh and stooped to shed the heavy woolen pants. At the last minute she decided against undressing and simply crawled under the rough blanket. She was asleep almost as soon as she stretched out on the hard mattress.

Jack settled into his spacious bunk, but sleep escaped him even after another few sips of the whisky Summer thankfully left behind. He punched his pillow in frustration a few times and then lay there staring into the darkness of the enclosed bed. Something was not right. He was also trying to ignore twinges of guilt over his earlier harsh words to the young man in the adjoining cabin.

Drat. He swung his long legs over the edge of his bunk and groped in the dark to find his pants hanging over the back of a chair. He sat down to pull on his boots and determine his next move.

Once again he stood outside the lad's door. This time he tapped tentatively for a few moments before resorting to pounding. Lord, what a sound sleeper the boy was.

Finally, Lillie opened the door, her head bare, but with the glasses jammed firmly on her nose. She stared up and over the bothersome lenses, blinking against the light of the lantern.

"I say, do you always sleep so soundly?" Jack stepped forward and placed the lantern on a chest in the corner of the room.

"When there is no one to pound on the door throughout the night, yes, I do sleep quite well."

Ignoring the young man's impertinence, he sat down with a thump on the bunk, his eyelids heavy with exhaustion. He even leaned back a bit with the pillow behind his back and...

"To what do I owe the pleasure of your company this evening, sir?" She broke the prolonged silence. "I'm afraid I'm not familiar with ship protocol."

"Nothing really important, but I just wanted to come back and clarify a few things. I thought perhaps we got off on a bit of a wrong foot earlier." He trailed off for a moment, and tilted his head a bit to study her.

She turned away, not wanting to give him too close a look.

"No one could ever know the hardships endured by the captain of a ship such as this," he said. "I alone am responsible for *The Kate*, her costly cargo and all forty-five souls under my command. The starboard aft cabin can be a lonely place. Every decision has to be made by me. Every mistake by even the lowliest crewman is my responsibility."

He quieted again and lengthy silence ensued. She could not help herself and opened her mouth to rebut his smug speech. Surely he was not the omniscient god he believed himself to be. Should she be appalled by his overblown ego, or should she just take the poor man in her arms and...? Wait a minute. She came to her senses just in time. She was a man.

"An agent put the lives of my crew as well as my ship in the way of hazard a year ago." He shifted his weight on the bunk and pulled the pillow behind his head. "I vowed then never again to take a spy aboard one of my ships."

"Then why did you agree to my passage?"

"The reward was too generous to refuse." He sat up straight again, staring intently into her face. "I cannot imagine how a slip of a boy could warrant the exchange of so much gold."

"Sir, I'm sorry, but I cannot discuss my mission with anyone. Many lives are at stake."

"Take care, young man. You are playing the deadliest of games."

Unable to remain silent any longer, she had to assure him she knew what she was doing in spite of her apparent youth.

"Sir, I..."

Loud snoring interrupted her small speech. Was there no end to the embarrassments she would have to suffer from this pompous man?

With a sigh, she moved to her sea bag in the corner and pulled out a woolen blanket. Rolling a spare pair of pants to serve as a pillow for her head, she dropped down in a corner and fell asleep.

Shouting this time interrupted her sleep, and she sat up abruptly, thinking she was still in the midst of a disturbing dream. She nearly smacked her head on the top of the bunk before she realized where she was. Something else was not quite right. The ship was moving. They must have weighed anchor with the early outgoing tide.

"Rafe — it's me, Abe. You have five minutes to get on deck for your first lesson. Don't be late, or Mr. Fitz will dog you the rest of the trip."

Panic struck. She'd slept through the early seven bells.

Leaping from her bunk, she bent over the chest in the corner and dipped her head in a basin of water. Sucking in a breath in shock from the coldness, she glanced around the cabin. A sickening realization struck her. How had she gotten back in her bunk?

Jack must have put her there. She was mortified. Had he noticed anything unusual? But then as captain, he probably had risen before daylight to oversee their exit from Portsmouth Harbour. With any luck, he probably had been a bit fuzzy from the night before, and very little light illuminated her cabin in the morning. She emptied her mind and breathed, forcing her anxiety to recede.

After running a comb through her wet hair and jamming her cap on her head, she swung out the door to race to her lesson.

In her headlong rush, she tripped over a swarthy sailor scrubbing the deck.

"Sorry, mate," she mumbled.

He didn't reply, but she could feel him following her with his eyes.

CHAPTER THIRTEEN

Saturday, May 9, 1863
Aboard *The Kate*
Portsmouth Harbour, England
50°30'30"N, 1°45'15"W

"Mr. Horlock — At what times of the day must we log a fix?"

Lillie snapped to attention and locked eye contact with Mr. Fitz, hoping to buy time to remember what the devil he'd been talking about. Lack of sleep the night before had left her fuzzy around the edges.

Steady vibrations from the boiler shook the deck beneath her feet while the ship sliced through the channel separating the Isle of Wight from the southern coast of England.

A freshening breeze filled *The Kate's* two sails, and they made steady progress toward the open Atlantic to the west.

"At the end of each watch and at noon each day," she replied, just in time. He continued the lesson after giving her a stern, thin-lipped look.

Tonight, she would seek the comfort of her bunk as early as possible and, with any luck, the captain would stay in his cabin too. She was startled out of her thoughts when she realized the two other trainees had moved to follow their teacher.

"Where are we going now?" she asked, and stepped closer to Abe to find out what she'd missed.

"You'd better start paying attention, or they'll put you ashore in Bermuda and make you find your own way home." The concerned look in the young man's dark eyes belied the sharp tone of his warning. "You've never served on any ship, have you?"

A jolt of fear coursed down her spine. She'd been found out already.

"Please don't tell the others," she pleaded. "I have to get back to Charleston. Ma's ailing, and there's no one to take care of her. Captain Roberts —"

"All right," he said. "I'll help you, but promise me you'll do the work and get your rest. The cap'n won't tolerate overdoing the spirits. He don't like crew falling about. Even if he knows your da, it won't make a difference."

She stared at him in confusion for a moment, and then recognition dawned.

"You can count on me. I won't let you, or him, down. I'll do better."

The first mate and the other recruits halted abruptly at the raised deck behind the binnacle where the helmsman stood. Fitz climbed the short set of steps and motioned for the students to follow him.

She fell in behind the others and adjusted her stance to the rolling swells accompanying their sail through the narrow channel between the coast and the island. The first mate opened a black leather case and pulled out a beautiful brass instrument made of elegant arcs.

She had watched with rapt attention while crewmen on other ships used the sextant during ocean trips with her mother. Busy sailors had always turned away her childish, eager questions about the mysterious instrument. She could not believe her luck. For a moment she almost forgot her worries.

In the morning light, the faint outline of the not quite set moon was visible above the far horizon. The first mate raised the eyepiece for sighting and began to fiddle with one of the arcs, all the while fixing his view on the waning moon.

"You need a gentle touch with the sextant, lads," Fitz said. He adjusted his stance by setting his feet wider on the deck beneath him and bending a bit at the knees. "We need accurate sights in good or bad weather, as long as the moon, the sun or the stars can be seen."

He handed the instrument to one of the young sailors and then stood behind him.

"First, you must know the correct time." He pointed to the chronometer gently swinging from gimbals mounted on a brass stand near the helmsman. "Rock the sextant — easy, until the lower or upper limb of the moon just hovers at the horizon."

He again checked the hour, minutes, and seconds. "Ideally, this is a job for two. One of you can help by recording times and readings while the other minds the sextant. In foul weather, you may have only a few moments to get a sight. You may have to memorize the numbers until you get inside the wheelhouse."

So far, what he said made sense. Memorization was her strength.

"May I try?" she asked, and stepped to his side.

"Of course." He moved back a few steps to make room and motioned her forward. Abe stood behind her at the chronometer, and they spent the next several hours practicing sights.

Mr. Fitz stowed the sextant back in the wheelhouse and then beckoned them on to the boilers.

She stood behind the others, giving herself as much distance from the monstrous machines as she could. She and *Maman* had been on a ship off Panama when one of the boilers caught fire. The deck turned deadly hot under their feet before the crew brought the blaze under control. Several of the firemen tending the boiler died in the blaze.

"Are there always so many new crew on a crossing?" she asked Abe in a low voice, diverting her attention from the fiery furnace. Her cheeks burned hotly, and sweat trickled down the inside of her arms. She moved her fingers to her mustache to make sure it wasn't sliding off.

"No." His frown turned into a grimace. "The fever in the islands has taken down so many experienced crew, we were forced to take on green recruits."

"I don't have to worry about the fever." She swallowed hard. "I went through a mild siege as a child."

"You're lucky. Many a sailor doesn't live to tell the tale."

"Have you ever had the fever?"

"No, but the cap'n succumbed on a run last year. He nearly died." He made a brief sign of the cross before continuing. "We had to change course for Halifax, lost over a third of the crew before the clean air saved us."

"What do we do now?" she asked, eager to change the morbid turn of conversation. Her heart hiccupped a beat when he told her of Jack's close brush with death.

Once they were on deck again, she coughed to clear the suffocating heat from her lungs.

"Now," Abe said, when he fell into step beside her, "we clean the ship till it seems like she'll never need to be cleaned again."

"And then what?"

"We clean her again."

Jack shook his head at the endless details of setting off to sea on a ship's maiden voyage. After all the sea trials he put *The Kate* through, she still surprised him with a few minor malfunctions.

He turned from the rail to see Fitz double stepping toward him.

"Captain — a blockader frigate is dogging us."

"How close?"

"A quarter mile and steady, two points to starboard off the stern."

"Keep to course and speed." Jack clenched his jaw and tightened his grip on one hand still clutching the rail. With his other hand he pulled a small spyglass from his pocket.

"Anything else?"

"Yes. Give the orders to start building the pressure in the boilers."

"Aye."

Jack raised the glass. Even though *The Kate* flew a British flag, blockaders were not above trying to stop suspected blockade runners offshore. The pursuit ship had all her canvas flying. They could be in for a long night.

On top of all his other niggling problems, he was haunted by the memory of a pair of eyes deviling him through a cloud of vanilla scent. The soft, curvaceous imp had even invaded his dreams the night before. This confounded weakness had to end. He ticked off the miles between *The Kate* and Portsmouth, and prayed some rational thought would come with distance.

"Captain?"

He'd done it again · woolgathering instead of paying attention.

"I'm sorry, Fitz. What did you say?" He turned from his study of the receding shoreline and faced his first mate.

"What are your thoughts about the frigate?" Fitz asked.

"Have the watch notify me if he starts to shorten the distance between us. I don't want to push the boilers to full speed yet if I don't have to." Jack tilted his head and studied the sky. "Some weather is about to roll in. When the wind freshens, he'll probably come up close."

"Sir? Do you have any other orders for me?"

"No — wait. I do have a question. How is my new cabin boy faring? Is he going to be decent crew?"

"Well, he's a bit slight for his age, but he seems sharp, very quick. I think he'll do fine at navigation chores." As if re-thinking his earlier assessment, he added, "He certainly doesn't seem to have much experience as a seaman, though."

"That's all right. I'm sure you'll bring him through."

Jack moved into the wheelhouse and picked up the hinged parallel rulers. Twirling a pair of sharp-ended metal dividers, he smoothed a large chart with his other hand and checked their course. Some time later he went outside to give the helmsman new instructions for the next compass heading.

Jack stood for a few minutes behind the man while he made the course correction and then walked on toward the boiler rooms.

Lillie fell into her bunk and curled into an exhausted heap. The darkness of blessed sleep had barely overtaken her when sharp rapping on the door awakened her.

In her groggy state, she thought she might be reliving the disastrous previous evening. Thank God she'd decided to sleep in her clothes and mustache.

She swung open the cabin door to be greeted by Abe, who was pounding loudly by now.

"All hands on deck, Rafe. American ship's chasing us."

She trembled when his words sank in. Just then the entire ship rocked with the muffled whump and a cannon ball splashed short of the stern. At the same time, the deck beneath her feet vibrated with an urgency unlike the earlier slow, steady sound.

"Stay low," Abe shouted at her, before he dashed off to join the rest of the crew.

Since she had just begun her training the day before, she wasn't sure of where to go, but decided to follow the crew headed toward the boilers.

A burly sailor extended a muscled arm to stop her headlong flight and nearly knocked the wind out of her.

"You there — help those lads if a fire breaks out." He pointed to a sea pump station surrounded by stacks of buckets. Two sailors already manned the pump while others filled pails, sloshing water across the deck.

Lillie struggled to maintain her footing while racing to take her place in line. She'd ceased to care about being recognized as a woman. Hell, she didn't even worry about performing "as well as any man."

A rush of courage cleared her mind and after several calming breaths, she grabbed a bucket of water.

The wind howled across the deck and blew her short, unkempt hair into her eyes. She set down the bucket for a few seconds and resettled her cap more firmly on her head. In the mad dash from her cabin she forgot to bring the glasses to complete her disguise. No matter. They would have been smashed in the confusion. Besides, Jack would be glued to the helm or the wheelhouse with his officers until he resolved the blockader threat.

Huge grey, rumbling clouds scudded past at an alarming rate, and swords of lightning stabbed through breaks in the thick cover. In the distance, a strike hit the ocean's surface and turned into a green‐white ball of fire and rolled toward them.

A glance toward the stern revealed the blockader had all her sails unfurled and was flying toward them. She was closing in, fast. Every few minutes, a warning shot fell just short of the *The Kate's* hull with an accompanying shudder and blow. How could Jack prevail against so much firepower? She stifled a curse for having entrusted the odious one with her life.

The other ship dogged their stern, angling to come alongside, when *The Kate* suddenly shot forward, nearly surfing the huge, rolling waves at an angle. The helmsman had turned sharply, directly into the wind, so they were meeting the huge waves head-on.

When the force of the turn pushed Lillie to her knees, she jumped to her feet and reached for a side rail. The blockader fired several more shots, but began to fall behind in the distance. The closest her captain could come to following their course was a slight angle to the wind, which still put them hopelessly off the line *The Kate* now flew along.

In seconds, both ships slipped into a thick blanket of fog covering the ocean surface.

She set the bucket down with a thud, and her whole body slumped. Exhaustion claimed her, and the thought of a warm, dry bunk beckoned.

Conversation was impossible above the wild keening of the wind, so she followed her fellow crewmen when they slipped away to their various stations, or bunks.

Once back in her cabin, she stared longingly at her blanket and pillow. Should she be prudent and keep her sodden clothes on in case of another late-night emergency, or should she just strip down to nothing but the restraining cloth around her breasts?

She would compromise. When she bent to pull a spare shirt out of her sea bag, her stomach took a sick roll. Someone had pawed through her possessions. Maintaining careful alignment of the items in her sea bag was a trick Weatherby taught her.

Thank heaven she'd sewn the gold sovereigns and documents into the clothes she wore at all times.

She fell into her bunk and closed her eyes with a sigh. Tomorrow she would figure out who had snooped through her things. Tonight she would sleep. She settled her wet curls onto the rough pillow and sank into dreamless slumber.

Sunday, May 10, 1863
Aboard *The Kate*
At the West End of the English Channel
49°20'20"N, 6°00'00"W

"What course, sir?" The Welsh helmsman stood firm on the rolling deck, covered in oilskins, protection against the torrents of rain behind the storm.

"Let's take one our Yankee friends would not expect. What do you think?" Jack drifted into easy conversation with the man while he settled against the binnacle and took the measure of the weather gusting across the night sky.

"Make 'em think we're headed for Halifax?" The helmsman peered around the side of the wheel with a broad grin.

"Why not?" Jack shrugged and headed back to his quarters. "Have Fitz adjust the course on the chart, and tell him to raise me immediately if anything changes — anything." He had not rested since they first sighted the frigate earlier in the day.

He was nearly asleep on his feet by the time he reached his cabin. The niggling mystery of his young spy crewman briefly fluttered through his mind before he crawled into bed. As soon as he stretched out his long frame, he was sleep.

After a few hours, he shot upright in his bunk, nearly knocking himself out when he slid out past the top trim.

"Damn her." He yanked on his pants in a fury before slamming through his cabin entry to pad down the passageway to the adjoining quarters. He lifted a fist to pound on the door but burst through instead. He lit the wick of an oil lamp swinging from its gimbal on the wall near the bunk.

Without hesitation, he hauled the small, sleeping figure out of the bunk. As soon as Lillie's eyes fluttered slowly awake, she began flailing and kicking.

She stilled as soon as her eyes opened fully. Her damp, bedraggled short hair was standing up in corkscrews all over her head.

"Captain — is there something you need?"

"You can just stow the bloody lies," Jack bellowed. "I know who you are. The only other information I require is just why you dared come here and endanger my ship." He fairly sputtered in his anger. "Do you have any idea what could have happened to you if we'd been boarded?" He shot a quick glance around the cabin. "God knows what you're carrying with you."

He held her away from him with a firm grip on one of her arms and gave her a sharp shake with each point he made.

"I have no idea to what you refer, sir," Lillie insisted, and stuck out her chin.

Jack jerked her to him by the front of her shirt and popped loose the buttons. Nothing covered her but the muslin banding she had contrived to flatten her breasts. Propelled by blind rage, he ripped the banding loose.

"See — you're not a man. You've been lying to me from the beginning," he finished lamely.

"I can explain—."

"It's over." He interrupted her with a sneer. "The lying, the scheming. Somehow, I have to clean up the mess you've created before my crew discovers your secret." This silly woman-child had reduced him to a shouting maniac. Soon, the whole ship would be roused.

He had to calm down, but his rage began to build again in spite of his resolve. Heat rose in waves from somewhere low on his body. The pants he had hastily thrown on in his rush to confront her did little to hide his growing dilemma. He nearly groaned at his earlier assumption about his inability to function with Elizabeth.

She moved closer and raised her hand to his cheek. The burn where her palm lay was worse than the inferno of the boilers during the chase. He closed his arms around her and surrendered to what he'd wanted since he first touched her arm at the damned dinner party. He grabbed a blanket and wrapped her in it before picking her up and treading back toward his cabin.

"Where are we going?" She clung to him in alarm.

"To my bed. I can't possibly fit in your bunk."

"Do you think this is wise?"

"Absolutely not." Jack kicked open the cabin door and dumped Lillie onto his bed.

"We should talk about this." Lillie's voice took on a pleading tone and she licked her lips.

"Right." He closed the door then returned to the bed and drew her to him. "The only words I want to hear from you are whether or not you want me. And you have to use my name, not 'Mr. Finch-Barton,' not 'my lord,' and not 'Captain Roberts.'"

"My name is Jack." When he took her face into his hands, her eyes widened. They were a light plum, still hazy from sleep. When she closed her eyes, he leaned in and kissed each eyelid.

"I do want you, Jack." A tear slid down her cheek and she moved her mouth across his in a feather-soft kiss.

In one jerk he pulled the rough blanket from her body and claimed her mouth. When he bent to trail kisses down her neck and shoulders, he shook like a frightened schoolboy when he reached the soft mounds of her breasts.

Jack lost count of all the laws of God and man he was breaking, but he didn't care. He moved his hand across her soft belly and then much lower. She moaned when he suckled her lush breasts and then returned to take her mouth in a lingering kiss.

His resolve shattered. He could not ignore the feelings she awoke in him. When he claimed her tongue and moved more deeply into her soft, welcoming mouth, he fell past the point of no return.

If only Lillie could turn back the clock. How she had come to be in Jack's bed welcoming his gentle touch, she could not say. Her feckless heart and body would ruin everything.

She wrenched away from him and began to sob bitter tears into his pillow. He sat up and pulled her into his lap, rocking gently and rubbing her back.

"Don't cry, love. I would never hurt you." He bent his head to plant a soft kiss in the mass of short curls covering her head. His tenderness brought on another siege of tears.

"I can't be as good as any man and help my country if I end up as nothing more than your lover." Her sobs subsided into hiccups.

"You don't need to be as good as any man." Jack patiently turned her face to his with a thumb beneath her chin. "You're already head and shoulders above most men I know. And you've given the sailor's life your best effort. Even Fitz commented on how quickly you learned to use the sextant." A wry grin broke out on his face. "And praise from him is rare.

"But we cannot sit in the middle of my bed all night. I may be needed on deck or at the helm before morning." He gave her a questioning look. "What will it be?"

She did not answer, but simply wrapped her arms around his neck. He lowered her back on his bunk and peeled out of his trousers.

A strange sensation passed through her, as if she were in two places at once. A part of her wanted to run back to her cabin while the rest of her continued to press as closely as possible to Jack. All of her mother's dire warnings about men flew right out of her head.

She couldn't concentrate on all the "should not's" when his hands were moving across the planes and curves of her body. He pleasured her in ways she would never have thought possible.

His steady caresses brought her to a point where she wanted to beg him to stop. She opened her mouth only to have him cover it again with his own. He moved away for a moment to pull a pillow from the head of the bed and tucked it just below the small of her back. When he moved between her thighs and lifted her hips, she started at a steady pressure followed by a moment of pain.

Jack realized too late she was not the experienced woman he'd assumed based on her unconventional lifestyle. He could almost feel the hurt her sharp intake of breath revealed.

He muffled her whimper with his mouth. He could no longer deny his need and gradually filled her completely. Her heat nearly undid him as she sheathed him tightly.

He moved gently at first and then the thrusts became intense. She fell into a place of pure sensation where no doubts intruded. Reason failed her. She surrendered and moved with him. For a few seconds she lost herself so completely, she couldn't breathe.

Cold air hit her flushed body when he suddenly withdrew and moved away. He returned after a few minutes and pulled her to him. She faced him squarely and feared what she saw in his eyes. This was more than just a mutually pleasurable experience. He had laid claim to her very soul.

"Why did you leave?" Lillie wanted to cry and pound his chest but instead kept her voice calm and steady.

"We cannot risk the possibility of a child," Jack said, and reached up to push a wet tendril of hair from her forehead. He claimed another kiss and said, "You have to return to your cabin, and we both need to get some rest tonight." He kissed her again. "Tomorrow, we'll decide what to do."

"What do you mean?"

"I mean," he said, his voice stern, "the captain of a ship cannot share a bed with his cabin boy." He ran a hand through his disheveled hair and added, "Secondly, women are strictly forbidden on my ship. There will be hell to pay if you're found out. He bent his head in thought. "We'll have to make up a tale of some sort to explain your being confined to quarters."

"Nooooo," she said, with a wail.

"Right." In a swift series of movements, he swept her blanket from his bed, wrapped her in it, and swung her up into his arms. "Off to bed with you ... be a good gel."

"Why can't I stay here with you?" she asked with a pout onto his shoulder while he strode back to her own tiny cabin.

"Did I not make myself clear?" He gave her an awkward pat on the back and added, "This cannot happen again. The sea is my life. You have yours. We were lucky tonight. None of my men disturbed us."

"But why can't we stay together?" She lifted her head and stared into his icy blue eyes.

"You are a wealthy, bright young woman with a wonderful life ahead of you, as long as you don't get yourself killed on this misbegotten mission." He continued with a heavy sigh. "I'm an old sea dragon with my best years behind me. You deserve a home and family." He turned away so that she could not see his face and added, "I simply can't give you those things."

Jack delivered her back to her bunk while Lillie's eyes, heavy with sleep, closed in spite of her protests. Her cheeks were still flushed when he tucked the blanket around her and stood back for a moment.

He'd told her the truth for her own good, but the heaviness in his heart mocked his rock hard certainty.

She rolled over suddenly, burying her face in her pillow with unintelligible mutterings.

He doused the oil lamp and turned on his heel, firmly shutting the door behind him. He closed the portal on what might have been. His life stretched ahead of him, out on the open seas.

CHAPTER FOURTEEN

Monday Morning, May 11, 1863
Aboard *The Kate*
Southwest Course, North Atlantic

In the early morning light, Lillie sat cross-legged on the cabin floor and wielded the needle and thread Sarah had thrown into her sea bag at the last minute. Too bad her clever friend hadn't crawled in along with the sewing supplies. Lillie's stitches were crude, but she was getting the job done.

Searching along the edges of the cabin floor, she managed to retrieve her shirt buttons from all corners of the room where they had flown the night before, victims of Jack's fit of anger.

More importantly, she had to repair the cotton muslin binding for her breasts. She was determined to escape confinement soon and resume her tasks along with the rest of the crew. She had to find a way around his stubborn insistence that she stay out of sight. Besides, someone had tampered with her belongings, and she intended to find out who, and why.

Strange. She had expected to be overcome by remorse and horror at the memory of their lovemaking the night before. Instead, part of her felt nothing but a warm, comfortable glow.

Her other part had been busy, scheming at ways to get around her confinement to the cabin for the duration of the run into Charleston. She considered

sneaking off the ship when they made port in
Bermuda, but discarded the idea as unworkable. She
would not find another blockade-runner captain who
would take her on, let alone one who would be as kind,
and brave, and warm, and—.

Damn, she couldn't fall under his spell. She bit off
the last of the thread with a savage jerk of her teeth
then searched the cabin for a tool to pick the lock.
Hands on hips, she turned full circle and inspected the
tiny space. When she felt around the edges of the cabin
entry, the lock turned with a snick from the other side.

Probably Abe. Maybe she could sweet-talk him into
letting her out.

The door swung open suddenly, smacking her on the
shoulder. The crewman she'd seen swabbing the deck
the day before stood in the doorway. Before she could
dash out, he blocked her exit and pinned her arms to
her sides.

"Sorry, Miss, but you and me, we got some business
together."

"Who are you?" She gritted her teeth and tried to
stamp down on his foot.

"Oh, I may not be a gentleman like the cap'n, but
you'll like me just fine." He sidestepped and pulled her
tighter to his chest so she had to breathe in his hot,
foul odor.

She took in two slow breaths and then smacked his
head with hers with as much strength as she could
muster. When his grip on her arms loosened
momentarily, she thrust her fingers into his Adam's
apple and shoved her knee up hard into his groin.

As soon as he bent over in pain, she fled from the
cabin into the passageway only to collide with Abe.
Her relief changed to chagrin when she remembered
her bare legs peeked from beneath the long linen shirt
she'd just repaired.

He ignored her state of undress and shoved around
her into the cabin. After slamming the breakfast tray

onto the floor, he plunged a knife into her attacker's neck, replacing his bellows of pain with a gurgle.

For a moment, she didn't know who terrified her more – the frightening brute who broke into her cabin or Abe, who was not what he seemed.

Whipping the blanket off her bunk, he covered Lillie's attacker and stanched the flow of blood onto the floor.

"You've really botched this, you know." He turned to her before leaving with his gruesome bundle. "I'll be back with some water and rags to clean this mess."

After he left, a cold shiver moved up her spine. She reeled at the impassive way Abe dispatched the intruder. Unless the man was a stowaway, someone would have to notice the ship was short a crewman.

She hurried to pull on her pants and cap and reached for the bedraggled mustache lying next to the washbasin. Somehow, she didn't have the heart to glue it back on. Why should she bother when Abe already had seen her in nothing but a shirt?

At the sound of a muffled click, she whirled but relaxed when Abe stepped in and raised his hands in the universal sign of peace.

"I was afraid this would happen," he said with a shake of his head. "Have you managed to lose the dispatches and the gold too?"

"I'm not telling you anything until I know who you are." She lifted her chin and waited in angry silence.

"I can see this mission is a lark for you, a spoiled woman who doesn't even live in the South. You can't possibly know the deprivations our soldiers suffer."

Lillie refused to be baited and waited him out.

He stood and glared at her for a moment before grudgingly admitting, "At least someone trained you well."

She still wouldn't speak, so he gave in first. "All right, you win – I'm an able-bodied seaman and I've made a lot of runs with Captain Roberts, but my loyalties are to the Confederacy. I was assigned to watch you to guarantee you get through the blockade."

"Do they think I'm a child?" she demanded, anger creeping into her voice. "Who hired you?"

"You don't need to know. Now eat your breakfast." He turned and motioned toward the tray. "You'll need your strength." He reached out and touched her hand with a smile while pressing a key into her palm.

"Whoever that thug was, he had a copy of your cabin key in his pocket," Abe said. "Hang on to this key for emergencies, but don't tell anyone.

"And don't worry. I won't reveal your little masquerade." When he turned to leave, he added with a grin, "I'm sure the cap'n enjoyed unwrapping your secret much more than I did." He glided out as quietly as he came, locking the cabin door behind him.

She collapsed against the door, and her legs began to tremble. Probably everyone on the blasted ship knew what happened last night. She searched for something heavy to shove against the door but gave up after a few minutes. Instead, she pulled one of the derringers out of her sea bag.

Jamming the gun down the back of her trousers beneath the flannel padding, she vowed to be more vigilant. Assuming she was safe on the ship was a mistake she could not afford to repeat. She smoothed her hand down the inside pocket containing the sealed dispatches, relieved to feel the thick packet still in place.

Monday Afternoon, May 11, 1863
Aboard *The Kate*
Southwest Course, North Atlantic

Jack had been anxious all day. How could one small woman wreak so much havoc? And on the very deck of his ship. He had no one to blame but himself. He sat at the table in his dining quarters and poured himself a steadying glass of brandy.

"I say, Jack, what the devil is whittling away at you now?" his surgeon, Fergus, asked.

"Nothing, except we're a little over forty-eight hours out of Portsmouth, and already we've been attacked by a blockader. And then Fitz tells me we've got a missing crewman who didn't show for his watch this morning. Searched the whole damned ship for him – nowhere to be found."

His long-time friend, Fergus MacDonald, tipped back in his chair, hands clasped behind his head.

Although his surgeon was a good six years older, the two had been fast friends since childhood. Fergus's father was a merchant sea captain who had lost his heart to a dusky Hawaiian beauty.

Shortly after Fergus's birth in England, she died of smallpox. His father never recovered from his grief, and Fergus had been sent to live at Clarendon while his father dealt with his sorrow in long voyages at sea. Jack's father had been a stern taskmaster with his own sons, but had always had a soft place in his heart for the son of his old friend.

"Now, about your unfortunate young cabin boy. Who is she, Jack?" Fergus frowned at him from across the table.

"What? Have you gone mad?" The unexpected change in direction of the conversation caught Jack off-guard.

"No, I haven't, but I'm beginning to believe you have."

"I suppose there's nothing for it but to come clean." Considering his options and possible explanations, Jack sighed and plunged ahead. "How did you guess?"

"I'm a physician." Fergus fairly snorted at him, peering above the glasses perched low on his long, thin nose. "Come on. Confess. After all these years, what made you decide to stow a woman on board?"

"I hate to ask this," Jack said, "but as an old friend, could you suspend your usual cynicism and hear me out?"

"Aye." Surprise registered on the doctor's craggy face. "Go on."

"I'm afraid the situation with the young woman in question has careened out of control," he said. "Even now I don't understand the whole unfortunate business. She is a young American heiress, living abroad with her mother until the accursed Yanks resolve their differences with the Confederates."

Jack poured himself a finger of brandy and settled back into his tale. "She's on a bizarre quest to go back into the South and somehow help the cause. Unfortunately, she seems to be drawing from a bottomless well of funds to accomplish this quixotic venture. My solicitor fell victim to her wiles and, incidentally, her access to funds.

"Wade Devereaux, that blasted double agent, proposed I allow a spy on this passage, posing as my cabin boy. He made the arrangements with my solicitor." Jack paused for emphasis. "I had a nasty experience with a woman spy a year ago on one of my runs into Wilmington and have vowed since then never to allow one on board again.

"Suffice it to say her wealth won over my solicitor, and the two of them schemed to bypass my prohibition." When he glanced up, he caught an odd look crossing the doctor's face.

"Jack, you're rambling. You never ramble," Fergus said, and broke into a chuckle. "This young woman appears to have upset your usual aplomb."

"Right." He glared at his grinning surgeon. "To make short work of this tale, she put forth a very convincing disguise. In all the confusion of getting under way, I neglected to spend much time with the supposed spy. When the truth finally hit me, I confronted her." He stopped then and fiddled with a saltcellar on the table.

"What?" Fergus leaned forward. "Look at me, Jack. What happened then?" As if another thought had occurred to him, he added, "How do you happen to know so much about her?"

Jack remained mute, his head bent over, closely examining the spilled salt. "She and her mother somehow obtained an invitation to my stepmother's weekend house party. Unfortunately, I happened to be there and—. Fergus, I've never behaved like such a cad as last night," Jack admitted. "She is so young, and I took advantage of her."

Fergus said nothing for quite a while, then a slow smile spread across his tanned face. He suddenly threw his head back, hooting in laughter.

"The great lion of the sea has been brought to harness." He paused to wipe a tear from the corner of his eye. "You're in love."

"No, I'm the worst sort of reprobate." He hung his head in his hands and rubbed savagely at his forehead.

"It happens to the best of us. Don't be so hard on yourself. You've led a lonely life. Why not give yourself over to a late-life love?"

"Because I can't." He rose brusquely, shoving his chair back and nodding to Fergus. "I have to leave now."

"Wait a minute." His friend rocked the chair back to the floor with a thud. He stood and moved forward until his face was close to Jack's. "You haven't told me the rest of the story."

"That is the end of the story. We'll put her on the first mail ship back to England when we make landfall in Bermuda."

"Since you're already in a foul mood," Fergus said, "I suppose it won't hurt to throw another concern on the table." Fergus rose and bent forward, his fingertips resting on the table. "A thief slipped into my surgery and helped himself to our entire supply of laudanum and quinine."

Jack's usual high tolerance for problems encountered at sea evaporated. "We have a whole ocean ahead of us to cross and then God knows what we'll have to face in run-ins with blockaders." He rose and moved to one of the surgery portholes. The dark grey-green waves were just starting to froth a bit at the edges with a freshening wind.

"Looks like we'll be making a side trip to Horta in the Azores to replenish your supplies," Jack said. "Might top up the coal and water too."

"Exactly," Fergus added. "Someone wants to sabotage the ship, and we have to stop them."

Lillie dreaded the cleanup task ahead of her but knelt down anyway and began scrubbing her cabin floor.

She was still on her knees, near the cabin entry, when the sound of a key turning in the lock again caused her to jump to her feet, throw her shirt back on, and grab her derringer.

The tall shadow filling the entryway was unmistakable. If he meant to do her harm, she probably would be at his mercy. He was just too damned big. She stuffed the gun back under her bunk mattress and hung her head. There would be hell to pay if he suspected she had weapons aboard his ship.

"What are you doing back there?" Jack demanded and craned his head around the door.

She fisted her hands at her sides, knuckles whitened. It was all she could do to keep from throwing her arms around him. To add insult to injury, he didn't show any evidence of acknowledging the love they'd made the night before. His lack of emotion galled her.

"I have to be careful. I appear to be at the mercy of whoever happens to have access to my cabin," Lillie said with a sniff.

"Who?" he demanded. "Has someone threatened you?" His voice boomed in frustration. "By God, there'll be no skullduggery on my ship, or I'll throw the lot of you spies overboard."

Anger bubbled up and she snatched at his arm. "Do you care about nothing but your ship?" she spat out.

He turned away from her and for the first time appeared to notice the faint, pink stain on the floor. He wheeled around, his face darkening in anger. "What happened here?" He moved forward and gripped her arm tightly. "Are you hurt?" When she remained mute, he shook her hard. "For God's sake, woman. Speak to me."

"I'm not hurt," she said, and pushed out of his grasp.

"I am the captain of this ship," Jack said, slowly gritting out his words. "Your life, as well as that of the other forty odd souls on board, depends on the decisions I make. You'd damned well better believe I make it my business to know everything that happens on this ship."

Lillie continued her stubborn silence and refused to give in to his bullying.

"Very well then. Have it your way. I'll find out eventually, and then you will pay the price."

Suddenly, his hard demeanor softened, and he pulled her to him. "I know you must think me the worst bounder, but my personal feelings have to remain on hold until I've completed my deliveries and I'm back in England." He let her go and paced across the room, taking a seat on the edge of her bunk. His legs stretched in front of him, braced by the heels of his boots. "But for now, Miss Coulbourne, we must decide what's to be done about you."

"Why not let me go back to my duties, as if nothing has happened?" she asked. "After all, there's no reason any of the rest of the crew would suspect I'm a woman. No one guessed all day yesterday when I worked beside them." She gulped in a breath. She prayed he could be coaxed around to her cause.

Straightening in defiance, she added, "If I don't return to work my watch, you'll be short a crewman."

"I'm already short a crewman, thanks to whatever is afoot on my ship. What's one more? Perhaps I'll just tie you to your bunk and return each night to ravage you."

"You're not that kind of man," she said, and then stopped, frustrated. The beginnings of a grin quirked at the corners of his mouth. He was enjoying a joke at her expense. A slow, hot flush started at the swell of her breasts and crept up to her cheeks.

"Before you overwork your devious little mind, I will tell you what we're going to do." A faint smile softened his face again. "According to my first mate, Mr. Fitz, you are extraordinarily adept at navigation. You will continue with your lessons each day.

"When you are not working with the sextant and charts, you will apply yourself to maintenance duties, which should keep you sufficiently engaged and out of the way of the working crew. Then when we reach Bermuda, I will personally arrange your safe passage back to London aboard a mail ship."

"No. You mustn't," Fear tugged at Lillie's gut.

"Oh, but I can - your fate is entirely in my hands." A smug smile crossed his face. "You have to do whatever I tell you to do."

"But..." She was determined to circumvent his decision.

"Or would you like to sample the brig? I would be happy to arrange your confinement there. You could spend the rest of the voyage in a dark cell."

"But your own solicitor arranged my passage."

"He also knew my strict policy concerning women passengers. I assume my prohibition is what prompted your bizarre disguise," Jack added. "He'll pay dearly for his deceit."

"For heaven's sakes, can you not at least arrange passage for me on another ship running into Charleston?" she pleaded. "What about Edward? Surely he would take me."

"Yes, I'm sure the fool would jump at the chance to go around me and consort with you. However, as luck would have it, you will have no opportunity to cross his path."

Lillie refused to concede defeat.

"You don't understand, do you?" he asked with a tired sigh. "I do care for you. There is no way I would let you sail off into danger on your own."

"Then let me sail off with you." Her heart nearly leapt out of her chest at finally hearing some encouragement.

"And the nonsensical weekend at Clarendon?" His eyes narrowed. "Nothing more than a ruse," he said, recognition dawning in his eyes. "Your mother had to meet me before giving her consent, didn't she?"

She nodded mutely.

"What kind of family lets a young woman dash off on a cockeyed mission like this?" he asked.

"My family is every bit as respectable as yours, and a lot more loving and warm," she said, her voice indignant. "What kind of people send a thirteen-year-old away to serve on a British Man-of-War for years at a time?" she countered.

Good. Lillie gloated to see his pompous look finally disappear. But then he grabbed her by the arm and shook her like a small dog. Although her teeth rattled, she refused to back down; she would never give him the satisfaction.

"All right. You can put me on a mail ship," Lillie conceded. "I don't care, but I'll still find a way to escape and seek passage on another blockade runner."

Jack's only reply was to pull her close and bury his face in her cropped curls. He released her so quickly she nearly fell to her knees.

"Mr. Wilkinson will be here soon to escort you to your lessons."

"Does he know?" Lillie asked, pretending innocence.

"Absolutely not, and it's your job to make sure he doesn't find out."

Lillie could tell by Jack's face he didn't entirely believe Abe was oblivious to her identity. She'd had too much experience at the poker table.

"Does this mean you'll let me go with you to Charleston?" She hesitated a moment and then added, "Sir?"

"You don't get to ask questions," Jack said. Without a backward look, he stormed into the passageway, locking the door behind him.

She couldn't decide whether to rejoice or slump into a tearful heap in the corner. Within a few short minutes the infuriating man had swept her along on a breathless ride of emotions. Now he'd left her alone with nothing but unanswered questions. Then again, he didn't know she had a key.

Jack moved along the companionway to the upper deck on his way to re-chart a more southerly course toward the Portuguese Azores.

He still had no idea whether or not Lillie would go along with his plans for her, but did not for the life of him know what else to do. She was the only person who could make him feel so out of control. He had to survive this run with his ship and crew intact while still retaining a little of his sanity.

CHAPTER FIFTEEN

Thursday, Morning, May 14, 1863
Aboard *The Kate*
Three Hours Northeast of Horta, Azores

Lillie closed the ship's log with a thump and leaned back in the wheelhouse chart table chair to stare out at the sea for a few minutes.

"Worn out?" Fitz asked.

"Yes, sir," she replied.

"Why don't you go see if cook could warm something for you? You missed supper. I'll finish off the coal entries."

"You think he would, just for me?" she asked, unbelieving. Lillie still dressed as a young man and performed work with the rest of the crew, but there were times when she sensed a subtle, protective attitude in some of the officers' dealings with her. She hoped none of them had guessed her secret.

"Everyone knows you're working hard to learn navigation. I think he might help you out this one time," Fitz said. "Just don't make a habit of expecting special treatment," he added in a gruff tone.

Jack slipped inside the wheelhouse after waiting for Lillie to leave and confronted his first mate. "You're spoiling that boy," he said.

Fitz put on his stubborn Scot act. "And what if I do? He's a good, hard-working lad, and you treat him like he's dirt. Someone has to go easy on him."

Jack had a feeling his first mate suspected his young apprentice was not what he seemed. Beyond that, he had no idea how much his officer really knew.

He sat at the table and pulled the ship's log along with the charts toward him. "We'll just see how 'hard-working' the little weasel is." Fitz frowned, and Jack laughed. "I see he's become 'teacher's pet.'"

"According to the log, and my reckoning, we're about three hours northeast of Horta. Do you think we could get some help taking on supplies there tonight if we pass out a few bribes?"

"I don't see why not," his first officer said. "There's not a lot of traffic in and out of those islands this time in the season. They'll be glad for our trade."

After Lillie left the wheelhouse, she idled along the way before going to the galley. Her head on her arms, she leaned against the side rail while they sliced through the waves. At the sound of loud splashing and clicking noises, she lifted her eyes to a scene similar to a circus on dry land.

A large pod of Orcas jumped in and out of the waves in groups, some of them seeming to balance on their tails. The noise they made sounded like a combination of human chuckles and squeaking.

When one jumped near her at the side of ship, she extended her hand in a gesture of greeting, only to set off a frenzy of leaping among the bold performers.

"A sure sign of landfall soon."

She turned at the sound of Jack's voice close behind her. "Sorry, sir. I was headed to the galley and stopped to rest for a minute. Didn't mean to waste time."

"It's all right, Lillie," Jack said, and wrapped his arm around her. "You don't have to pretend you're afraid of me. I don't think we're fooling anyone."

Thursday Night, May 14, 1863
Aboard *The Kate*
Port of Horta, Azores
38°31'59"N, 28°37'59"W

Jack took over the helm when they glided into the port of Horta under steam power alone with just the light of the stars and moon to guide them.

The night was heavy with moisture and not a zephyr of cool air was to be had inside the harbor. He swatted at an insect on his neck and signaled for the crew to shut down the power. The capstan chains rattled in the stillness when the two anchors slid down from the bow. He and Fergus stepped quickly to the side of the ship while the crew lowered the shore boat.

Once ashore, Jack and his crew lit whale oil lanterns and headed toward one of several large warehouses flanking the customs house. Fergus set out with a small party to find the port physician to beg for replacement medications. He didn't envy his friend that task. Not many medical men were eager to relinquish any of their supplies of quinine and laudanum. They would probably have to give up a large sum of cash to persuade the man.

He'd made sure Lillie was securely locked in her cabin before they left the ship. The last thing he needed was for her to decide to sneak ashore. Horta was not the sort of place where a woman would be safe on her own.

Just the thought of her tucked in her bunk in the cabin next to his made his mind wander in an unfortunate direction. The sooner he could get her to a safe haven in Bermuda and onto a mail ship back to England, the sooner he could return to sanity.

Jack concentrated on climbing the uneven cobblestone street in the dark to the first warehouse where he pounded on the door. He hoped to God someone was still there at nine at night to take his bribe to load coal and water.

Hours later, close to dawn, he gave the order to raise anchor and then returned the wheel to his helmsman once they cleared the harbor.

He moved quietly down the short corridor past Lillie's cabin but couldn't resist doubling back just to listen and press his palm against her door.

"Jack, is that you?" Lillie asked from the other side of the door.

Convinced he detected a tremor of fear in her voice, he answered "Yes." She opened the door and jerked him inside, then down to her level for a searing kiss.

He wavered in indecision for a second or two before kicking the door shut.

Sunday, May 17, 1863
Six Days Out of Bermuda

Fergus walked into the wheelhouse and motioned for Jack to follow him outside. He leaned his head close and said, "One of the firemen may be taken with the fever."

"No – that can't be," Jack said. "We're in the middle of the Atlantic Ocean. How is an outbreak possible?"

"You recall there were those few hours in the port of Horta when we provisioned. It's possible one of the dock laborers loading coal was sick. Nobody really knows how the fever spreads."

Jack's shoulders slumped. The last time fever stalked his ship, a full half of his crew fell victim. He'd been forced to bury many of them at sea. Firemen were key to keeping the huge ship's boilers ready for rapid flight, and he needed every one of them. Now the lot of them could be infected. During the previous siege, the disease had claimed crew almost hourly until it ran its course.

Shuddering at the memory of his own bout with the fever, he recalled days of complete breakdown when he was too weak to stand, let alone manage the ship. Fortunately, his battle with the dread disease had left him immune to new outbreaks. However, he periodically succumbed to recurrent fever for which there was little to do but rest and recruit his health.

"I know what must be going through your mind, but I assure you, I've taken every precaution." Fergus squeezed Jack's shoulder before heading back to the sickbay.

Lillie was still awake when Jack's steady tread passed, heading toward his cabin down the passageway. She strained to listen, hoping for at least a pause at the midway point outside her door. The sound moved relentlessly on, with the far door opening softly and then clicking shut.

Swallowing bitter bile, she forced herself to concentrate on Weatherby's exercises. An hour of kicking and lunging left her exhausted and ready to drop into her bunk. She slept soundly in a place without dreams.

She awakened with a jolt sometime after midnight when soft tapping at the door down the passageway brought her to her feet. Creeping to the adjoining wall, she pressed her ear to the bulkhead between the cabins. The voices were too muted to understand, but within minutes, footsteps of two men swept past her door.

Monday Morning, May 18, 1863
Five Days Out of Bermuda

When Abe came to deliver Lillie's breakfast the next morning, the expression on his face was bleak.

"As soon as you finish this, we need to head to the surgery."

"Why?" she asked.

"Remember when you told me about having the fever as a child?"

"Yes?" A frisson of fear rippled down her spine.

"We have an outbreak onboard, and the surgeon and the cap'n need all the help they can get. I had to tell them you're immune."

Fergus rubbed his tired shoulders and sighed with relief at the sound of footsteps in the passageway outside his surgery. Feverish sailors filled four of the ten or so cots in the sickbay.

After Abe left to return to the upper deck, Lillie walked into the surgery and observed the doctor warily.

"Miss Coulbourne, please make yourself comfortable. You don't need to maintain appearances just for my sake."

"How long have you known?" she asked.

"Trust me on this. You are much too beautiful to pass for a young man, even with your hair chopped abominably short."

"Does anyone else know?" She pulled off her cap and self-consciously raked her unruly mop with her fingers.

"With the exception of our love-struck captain, probably not." At the pained look in her eyes, he added, "Come on over here. We have our work cut out for us if we're going to keep pace with the fever and stay a few steps ahead of the yellow death." He took off his glasses and held them up to the light to polish them with a corner of his shirt.

She opened her mouth as if a question hovered on her lips.

"Yes," he said in anticipation of her unspoken fear. "Jack is in love with you, but dinna expect him to admit his feelings, ever." He gave her one last hard look and added, "Now, get to work. You can tear sheets for cold compresses and then check the galley to see if the cook has a pot of broth ready."

Tuesday Morning, May 19, 1863
Four Days Out of Bermuda

Lillie fell into her bunk with a thud after working all night with Fergus while the fever casualties grew until they had to bring in extra cots. Out of forty-five members of the crew, thirteen men now lay in the ship's surgery. Abe came to relieve her at midnight after promising to wake her in three hours.

Sleep eluded her, so she focused on the underside of the top bunk, ticking off regrets. She must have closed her eyes because she awoke from a dreamless slumber to the feeling of Abe shaking her.

This time when she stumbled into the surgery, Jack was there, next to Fergus. The two talked softly while she counted the cots and sighed with relief when the tally did not go beyond thirteen.

Jack's face showed signs of fatigue. How long had it been since he'd slept? He must have given Fergus a short respite during the night.

"Are you sure you're up to this? This is not your battle." Jack crossed the room and covered her hand with his.

"Working here makes more sense than sitting alone in my cabin. Fortunately, nursing the sick appears to be one thing a woman can do without upsetting the natural progression of things," she said with a sneer.

He said nothing, but simply pressed her hand to his lips before turning and moving back toward the upper deck. Of all the things he could have said to her, his simple touch nearly undid her.

She hurried across the surgery to query Fergus on priorities for the rest of the night into morning. Her irritation with Jack faded when she bent to endless rounds of applying cold rags to foreheads and urging fever victims to drink water.

Wednesday Morning, May 20, 1863
Three Days Out of Bermuda

A light rap on Lillie's cabin door awakened her on the third day of the fever vigil. She rolled to her feet, expecting Abe to appear. Instead, Jack quietly let himself in and stood near the door as if awaiting permission to approach. His face was haggard and pale, most likely from another night of helping Fergus.

She sat back on her bunk and motioned for him to come closer. Extending her hand with a sigh, she pulled him to her. He knelt in front of her and gently pulled her face to his, covering her mouth and exploring her warmth with his tongue. She impatiently pushed him away. In response, he dragged her off the bunk onto the floor of the cabin with him.

"No," she insisted stubbornly.

"Shhh."

"Please, don't—"

"Could we just declare a short armistice?" Jack hugged her tightly and rocked back and forth, smoothing his hand over her hair and laying her head on his chest.

"Jack, what's wrong?"

"We lost three during the night—" he said, and the words seemed to stick in his throat.

"Who?"

"Two of the firemen and the navigator's assistant."

Her stomach lurched, and her insides turned cold. She had come to know the men during the nights of nursing them. They talked not only of their hopes and dreams, but also of their families, while she and the others fought to keep their fevers down.

"I need your help up on deck," he said finally.

"Of course, anything. What can I do?"

"I want you to take the assistant's place to help plot our course until we get to Bermuda. Then I'll try to replace him before I send you back to your mother."

"How can you use me so?" She jerked away from him in anger. "I'm happy to help, but you have to give me something in return."

"I'm your captain. You don't have any choice."

"I have lots of choices, and I'm not going to do what you ask without your assurance as a gentleman of two things."

"Two things?"

"Yes. You must promise you will take me along to Charleston, and—" she trailed off.

"What?"

"I must have your solemn word you will treat me as any other male member of your crew," she insisted, "in every way."

"You have my word on everything save the last," he said, and gathered her into his arms again.

"I have no intention of treating you like one of my crew." He planted a soft kiss on top of her head and then moved lower to her mouth, smothering her arguments. She half-heartedly tried to push him away but finally succumbed to his caresses.

Jack could not fight the fire racing through his body. He knew he should stop, but the annoying, beautiful Lillie felt so good in his arms. For the first time in his life a force greater than his own had taken over his will. He could neither rein in his desire, nor deny her what she asked. He should have surrendered the key to her cabin to Fitz, or Fergus, and confessed all in the very beginning.

He abruptly stood and pulled her to her feet. Her flushed face was a bright canvas for her eyes. Disappointment reflected back at him from the dark pools when he moved away to the door. He needed distance from the pull this strange child-woman exerted over him.

"Where are you going?"

"If I stay here a moment longer, there will be no turning back."

"Then go, but take me with you." A shy smile curved at her lips. "Isn't a cabin boy supposed to tend to the captain's needs?"

Hours later Jack lay in his bunk with an arm encircling Lillie. She slept on her side facing him, her face and lips still flushed. The fear he had experienced during fierce sea battles faded in comparison to what raced through his heart now. He extended his finger to brush lightly across the silky lashes resting on her soft cheek.

He kissed her forehead one last time before carrying her back to her cabin. She stirred once against his chest, mumbling in her sleep.

He deposited her in her bunk and then moved away with resolve. If her eyes opened again and locked onto him, he would be lost. Sometime during the night he had come to his senses and formulated a plan to save them both.

Back in his cabin, he threw on a fresh shirt and pants before splashing icy water onto his face. The trip back down the passageway past her door was one of the longest of his life. He moved with a heavy heart, up to the deck and back down into the surgery.

Fergus turned his weary face toward him. "You should rest while you can." The doctor bent over one of the cots and gave some quinine to one of the stricken sailors.

Abe ladled broth out of a large pot in the corner.

"The good doctor and I require a few moments' privacy," Jack said, and nodded toward the doorway.

Abe moved out into the passageway.

Jack turned back to Fergus. Concern now also etched the tired lines of his friend's face.

"I must ask a difficult favor of you," Jack said. "Take this key and promise me you'll make sure no one has access to her cabin." He faltered and hung his head, unable to face his old friend. "I will have Fitz retrieve the key from you for delivery of her meals and to collect her for navigation duties. Now I have to explain this whole mess to him."

"Don't do this, Jack," Fergus said. He took off his glasses and slammed them down on his desk. "Someday, on a far ocean, you will die an embittered old man with no one to care but a passel of nephews and nieces." He softened his voice then. "It doesn't have to be this way."

Jack gazed one last time at the small key that seemed to burn his hand and then thrust it toward Fergus. Turning to duck through the doorway, he motioned Abe back to his duties before returning to the deck to search for Fitz.

CHAPTER SIXTEEN

Friday, May 22, 1863
40°00'N, 55°00'W
Final Bermuda Waypoint

Lillie flattened a metal straight edge to the large chart and plotted their progress over the previous eight hours. She finished the calculations to pinpoint their coordinates as well as the amount of water and fuel consumed. The final notation she entered into the ship's log with a dip pen.

She checked her numbers twice in fear of another blistering condemnation. Jack had berated her unmercifully the day before at the end of the second watch when she made an error placing *The Kate* some one-hundred miles north and two points west of their actual position.

"We'd sail right through the reef off Bermuda if we were to follow your line of reasoning," he said, his voice thundering.

Her cheeks still burned at the memory of her own weak reaction to him. She didn't mind his anger. He had at least finally noticed her and stood close enough to make her silly heart leap.

"Sir, I promise," Lillie had assured him, "this will never happen again."

He'd turned away and stormed out of the wheelhouse without a backward glance.

As of the end of the current watch, her calculations put them about a half-day sail from St. George's Harbour. She prayed Jack would not deny her passage into Charleston after their stopover at the British island outpost.

She closed the heavy ship's log and moved to the deck to find Mr. Fitz. After she told him her findings, he gave her a broad grin. "I think you'll make a passable navigator yet," he said and clapped her on the back.

"How do you know without reviewing the charts?"

"An old sailor like me doesn't need fancy figuring to know we're close to land." He laughed at the questioning frown on her face. "See the bird up there?"

She leaned back and tilted her head, shading her eyes against the blinding sunlight. Brilliant shades of magenta and blue swept the tail of a majestic bird swooping and diving through the rigging.

"See — a Bermuda long-tail. He wouldn't stray far from home." When she turned to face Mr. Fitz again, he added, "Just sniff the air. Land has a different smell than the open sea. And watch the waves. They have a certain shape and rhythm when we get closer to shore."

She sucked in the sea smells and wrinkled her nose, trying to sense the difference.

"After another fifty or so crossings, you'll smell it just fine," he said, with a broad grin.

"So, will we go in to the harbor tonight after midnight?"

"Absolutely not." He shook his head vigorously. "The reef would have us. We'll wait till daylight so a pilot can come out and guide us in."

Jack stood at the rail while Lillie chattered with Fitz. He had observed her earlier when she stood at the chronometer and gathered the numbers for her calculations. The wind had whipped off her cap, and when she dove for it, the sunlight danced through her hair. The curls he ached to smooth with his hands had grown rapidly in just the few weeks they'd been at sea.

A vision of an earlier time flashed before him. Once again he was at Clarendon when she crossed the drawing room. She appeared as a pale, rose apparition in yards and yards of shimmering tulle with soft breasts straining at the low neckline.

He came to a decision. She would hate him for the rest of her life, but it couldn't be helped. He refused to lose her in the hellish war raging beyond the peace of the ocean. It would be better for her to despise him forever than to have to imagine her trapped in the horrors beyond Charleston.

Fergus crossed his leg and bent over the surgery table to enter his latest treatments of *The Kate's* crew — the usual assorted burns among the firemen and occasional dosing of sailors who had been unwise enough to indulge in seedy waterfront brothels before they sailed from Portsmouth. An assortment of jars lined the table, and he occasionally picked one up to squint at the writing on the label.

A steady, heavy tread moving down the companionway toward the surgery alerted him to Jack's progress. He placed both feet on the floor with a sigh and closed his log.

"Now what?" He removed his glasses and placed them in front of him on the table when his friend burst through the door. Leaning his elbows squarely on the table to support his chin, he glanced up expectantly.

Jack hesitated and then dragged a chair from a corner of the surgery and swung it close to Fergus, wrapping his long arms around the back and tilting forward.

"Come on, Jack. Out with it," Fergus said. "This endless drama begins to wear thin."

"I can't let her go through with this mad plan." Jack rocked the chair back with a thud and jumped up to pace the small surgery.

"You know the answer is simple, if only you weren't so pig-headed."

"What?" Jack demanded.

"The right thing to do is to marry her when we reach Bermuda and set her up in a safe household there until you're done with this series of runs. You can more than afford it, and each time you return for more supplies and cargo, it will be like another honeymoon." He smiled at Jack's discomfort.

"Have you taken leave of your senses?"

"No, and I wish you would quit insisting I have," Fergus replied in sharp tones. "The frustration swirling through your thick head is no different from what any other man suffers."

"And I suppose you believe she would go along with this preposterous plan of yours?" Jack said with a huff. "Have you not noticed her blatant disrespect for all authority and reason?"

"Yes, but I have also observed a young woman very much in love." He placed his hands flat on the table. "Since you've stormed in here for advice, marriage is what I would suggest. Beyond my solution, there is nothing but madness. The memory of this woman could devil you forever."

"She's not really a woman — she's a spoiled, unpredictable child," Jack said, continuing his pacing.

"Since when have you become a despoiler of children?" Fergus took perverse satisfaction in the telling, ruddy burn that rose from Jack's neck and spread to his face. "And what if she already carries your child? Will you send her packing back to England in disgrace?"

"I've taken care."

"Do you know what they call a man who 'takes care'?" Fergus asked with a laugh.

"What?"

"A father."

"I thought you, of all people, could be counted on to understand." Jack said.

"You'll not find any sympathy here." Fergus pulled a handkerchief from his pocket and wiped tears of laughter from the corners of his eyes. "Go find Fitz. Maybe he'll sympathize with your ravings."

Jack abruptly stopped pacing, turned on his heel, and left.

Jack seethed with anger at Fergus's biting analysis of his predicament. There had to be another way to keep Lillie safe and send her back to her family. When the solution hit him, he nearly stopped dead in his tracks in the midst of a mad rush past the boilers in search of Fitz. Why had he not thought of it before?

He had attacked the problem from the wrong angle. Lillie would never be convinced to give up her mission, but he could change the outcome from the other end. Wade had to know something about this murky affair, and he knew exactly where to find the soulless blackguard in Bermuda.

Hailing his first mate just as Fitz was securing Lillie in her cabin, he motioned him down the passageway to his quarters. Jack shut the door and turned to face him.

"When we get to St. George, I will leave the ship immediately, with the first shore party." Moving toward the table, he pointed toward the chair opposite him. "I need you to take charge of the ship for a few hours while I find Edward, and together we can bring the agent, Devereaux, to ground."

"Why?" Fitz's normally calm demeanor turned into something bordering on alarm. "Do you think he plans

to sabotage the ship?" Even his first mate seemed
aware of Wade's shady dealings straddling both sides
of the conflict.

"No, nothing so drastic." He put his hands on the
table between them and returned his first mate's
stare. "I met with him in Portsmouth before we left, so
he is already aware of our purpose." He paused and
added as an afterthought, "But he has no idea of our
capabilities or the extent of our cargo this trip."

"It's the lass, isn't it?" Fitz peered down at the table
and fiddled with a simple gold band on his left hand.
"Do I have permission to speak frankly, sir?"

"Of course."

"I've served you many years, and it's been a
privilege." Fitz said, and then paused before
continuing. "It's just — I've never seen you so
distracted, by a woman."

Jack peered off through one of the portholes and
studied the huge rolling waves. The wind was
building.

"I realize you have little reason to trust me," Jack
said, "but I would ask you to consider my dilemma."
He turned from the porthole and gave his full
attention to his trusted mate. "First of all, I swear to
you on all we have been through I had no idea she
would sneak aboard the ship in disguise. Secondly, I
never met the woman prior to being introduced to her
and her mother the weekend before we sailed. I had no
idea what she was plotting."

"And just what might that be, if I may ask, sir?" A
note of anxiety resurfaced in Fitz's voice.

"I've told you all I know at this point." He rose from
the chair and paced the cabin. "She refuses to reveal
the details of her rattle-brained scheme to me. The
sum total of my knowledge is this: My solicitor,
Algernon Summer, negotiated with an agent of the
Confederacy for us to carry a spy into Charleston. He
— I was led to believe the passenger would be a young

man — is to be transferred to a fishing boat near Sullivan Island before we make our run into Charleston Harbor. Otherwise, my only information was Summer's suggestion for him to serve as my cabin boy during the passage."

"Do you love her?"

Jack halted his pacing, stopped dead in his tracks by the blunt question. The concern on Fitz's face took him by surprise.

"Do I love her? I don't know." He considered the dilemma even as he formed an answer. "Would my personal feelings change my priorities? Absolutely not. I have to send her back to England on the first mail ship out of Bermuda." He sat down and pulled the chair close to the table. "But it has to be done so she believes leaving is her only choice. God knows she's already wreaked enough havoc on this trip. I cannot allow her scheming to undermine the safety of the ship."

"So, you think Devereaux is the key to whatever her mission might be in Charleston?"

"Yes." Jack set his jaw in determination. "I would not be surprised if the slimy bastard were behind this entire affair. He probably has some scheme to get his hands on her fortune."

"What will you do when you find him?"

"I will wring the truth out of his worthless hide, and then I'll make damned sure he calls off this nonsense."

"Nonsense indeed." Lillie gasped after eavesdropping on Jack's plans and nearly fell off the chair she stood on. The bigger shock, however, was that Wade was her mysterious "benefactor."

She had discovered some days earlier the ease with which she could make out faint voices coming from Jack's cabin. All she had to do was reach on tiptoes and lean toward the ventilation pipe between the two cabins.

As far as she was concerned, Wade was not the only slimy bastard in this affair. She refused to allow Jack to dismiss her and her mission as if she were nothing more than a helpless child.

But she was also suspicious of her childhood friend's involvement. She almost chuckled at how easy Jack was going to make it for her to get to the bottom of her own dilemma. All she had to do was sneak into St. George and shadow him to his meeting with Wade.

The only catch was, she had no idea how to accomplish such a plan. Details. She would figure something out tomorrow. In fact, Abe had a huge stake in the mission. He had to help her.

She jumped back down from the chair and resumed her self-defense exercises.

Saturday Morning, May 23, 1863
On *The Kate* at Anchor
St. George Harbour, Bermuda
32°22'46"N, 64°40'40"W

Later, after the noises of arrival and anchoring had subsided, she heard Jack tread down the passageway toward the top deck, she retrieved the key to the cabin door from its hiding place in her shoe — Abe had given her the copy for emergencies, and this surely qualified as one. She had to follow Jack into St. George.

After setting herself free, she peered to each side down the passageway and ventured out toward Jack's cabin. She pressed her ear close to his door for a few minutes to make sure no one was inside.

Creeping back to her cabin, she gathered a dagger and one of the pistols, and then stooped to her sea bag in the corner and gathered all of her spare clothes to stuff under the blanket on her bed to resemble a sleeping form.

After locking the cabin from the outside, she gained the upper deck and stopped to gather her thoughts. Fitz was right. The smell of land after weeks at sea was like nothing else. Fortunately, the flurry of activity on deck covered her progress toward one of the boats being lowered for sailors to take shore leave and procure supplies for the final leg of the journey.

Suddenly, her arms were pinned from behind, and she was nearly lifted from her feet in her rush toward the boat. Her heart plummeted.

"I'm tired of hauling you out of all your predicaments," Abe's voice whispered low in her ear. He whipped her worn cap off her head and replaced it with an equally disreputable straw hat with a brim to bar the sun, and suspicious eyes, from her face. "Whatever your mad plan, don't mess up this time. You've run out of options."

"I have to follow Jack. He plans to sniff out our mission from a Confederate agent and then bully him into calling it off."

"Is there no other reason you want to follow the cap'n?" He stared down at her with a smirk. "Don't be surprised if he leads you somewhere you don't want to be."

"What are you getting at?" Her pent-up anger simmered dangerously close to the surface.

"Only, well, you being on board the ship probably has driven him crazy." He smiled at her restless fidgeting. "Knowing you're just down the hallway and he can't touch you," he added. "If it were me, I'd head for the first sympathetic female I could find in port."

"Oh—." She stuttered and then made a vicious stab to his chest with her finger. "That is the least of my worries" She jerked her other arm away from his grip and moved toward the ladder down to the shore boat.

He hauled her back close to his face again and warned, "If you're caught out, your story is you're after supplies for the doc."

He released her abruptly and turned with a wave to motion for the shore crew to wait for her while she scrambled down the ladder and swung easily into the boat before they shoved off from *The Kate*. Focusing her attention on their progress toward shore, she forced herself not to glance back, although she was sure Abe still stared at her from the rail.

"Where will you be spendin' your shore leave, lad?" One of the ship's firemen sat next to Lillie in the stern of the boat. "I know a place where the rum is the best and the women are willin'."

"I'm to find some supplies for the doc, and then I have to return to the ship." She shuddered at a sudden vision of Jack in another woman's arms.

"Not even the cap'n would deny you a little fun after all those weeks at sea." The sailor smirked at her then. "Come with us, lad. We'll show you the sights."

"If he sees me carousing with the likes of you when I've a job to do, he'll punish me for sure." After a moment's thought, an inspiration hit. "So, where would a man like the cap'n head in St. George?"

"Well, normally, he would go in to conduct ship's business, but this time, he was in such an all-fire hurry, my guess would be the nearest fancy establishment. He does have a way with the ladies."

She leaned closer to him and struggled to contain her anger while she jammed her hat lower over her eyes.

"I've never seen a fancy establishment before." She sent up a silent prayer of thanks to Abe for the broad-brimmed straw hat. "I want to take a look before taking care of the doc's errands."

"You can't afford the likes of them ladies, lad."

"I don't need to sample, I just want a glimpse."

"All right. It's your shore leave. It just seems a waste to spend it starin' at somethin' you can't have." He pointed to a row of pink houses with gleaming white shell roofs along the waterfront.

When they finally tied off at the high stone quay, she scrambled up behind the rest of the crew and looked all around to get her bearings. She struck off to the left toward the cottages along Water Street.

Once again, she cursed the heavy, scratchy sailor's clothing she had to wear. Steady easterly breezes had not tempered the island's balmy temperatures. She feared she might faint from the confining heat inside her woolen jacket and pants.

Lillie had no idea what she would do if she were to encounter Jack in the "fancy" district. Surely, he would eventually get down to business and go in search of Wade. She would lay low, wait for him to finish whatever he was up to, and then follow him. Her plan seemed simple enough when she went over it in her mind. However, a lump lodged in her throat when she considered what he might be doing in one of those houses.

Recalling too late Weatherby's warnings about her wandering mind, she darted down an alley and was knocked on the back of the head. She sank blindly to the ground.

Jack sat back in his chair with a sigh in the third waterfront tavern he'd searched for Wade. He came up empty-handed each time he followed another lead.

He rose to investigate a disturbance near the front entrance of the current establishment and was greeted by a shout.

"Jack — where have you been? I've searched everywhere for you." His friend, Edward, made his way through a crowd of fellow blockade-runner crewmen.

"I have a table in the back." Jack turned and led his friend toward a quiet corner of the popular inn. Dropping wearily onto a battered wooden chair, he turned to Edward and said, "We have to talk."

"What's happened?"

"I have no idea where to start, but first, I have a puzzle for you."

"Of course." Edward's manner sobered at the serious tone in Jack's voice.

Jack's gaze swept the room again, searching for Wade, and made sure no one was close enough to eavesdrop.

"An odd thing happened during the passage over."

"So then there's a good reason it's taken so long for you to make port?" Edward sat back in relief. "What sort of 'odd thing'?"

"First of all, the minute we cleared the channel, a blockader came up in hot pursuit."

"Did you suffer any damage?"

"Thankfully, no. He was entirely under sail, and I lost him in a squall." He paused for a moment and then added, "We had to alter course for a day to throw him off the scent."

"So that would explain the delay." Edward ticked off the days required for passage, holding up fingers. "But the attack wasn't really the 'odd thing,' was it?"

"No —," Jack said with a groan, "it wasn't." He faltered moment and then continued. "Do you remember the young American women at my stepmother's weekend house party?"

"Of course." A broad grin broke out on his friend's face. "You were really taken with the little fiery one, weren't you?"

"That is neither here nor there." He stared at Edward, annoyance clouding his thoughts. "The problem is, she followed me on board *The Kate* disguised as a young man."

"How on earth did she manage such a masquerade?" Edward asked, alarm in his voice.

"She apparently is on a spy mission for the Confederacy, the details of which she refuses to reveal."

"How did you unmask her?"

"Therein lies the crux of the problem." He tugged at his collar, but heat rose from his neck in spite of his best efforts.

"Don't tell me you've bedded the poor girl." Surprise registered on his friend's face, and then Edward grasped his wrist across the table and twisted tightly.

"Who is calling the kettle black now?" He wrenched his hand away and began to laugh. "What a hopeless couple of sods we are."

"So how can I help?" Edward asked.

"For the short term, I have to find Wade Devereaux and discover what he knows about her so-called mission." He turned and motioned to the serving girl to come to their table. "Do you have any idea where the scoundrel might have gone to ground this time?"

"He's not in Bermuda, Jack." Edward pulled out a pipe and tamped a bit of tobacco into the bowl. "He was in and out of here a few days ago."

"Where is he headed?"

"Charleston."

"If he is behind this misbegotten game, why would he give her an assignment and then dog her every step?"

"You know Devereaux. He will stop at nothing to line his own pockets, no matter which side he has to fleece."

"What if there is no mission?" Jack said, and gave the young woman an irritated glance when she placed two tumblers of rum on the battered table. After she finally left, he continued, "What if this is merely an elaborate ruse to extort funds from her family?"

"Wait — let's just slow down here," Edward interrupted. "No need to jump to conclusions." He reached out and put a restraining hand on Jack's arm. "What does Lillie say?"

"Nothing — I can't pry it out of her. How can I protect her if she refuses to confide in me? I've never encountered such a mule-headed woman." He wearily dropped his head into his hands.

They sat in silence for a few minutes before there was another commotion near the front of the tavern.

"Captain," Abe charged through the crowd searching for him. "I hate to interrupt your evening, but we have a problem." Disheveled as if he had been running, his young officer stopped short at their table, his face red from exertion.

"Go ahead."

"It's the young crewman, Rafe, sir."

"What?"

"He's gone — must have somehow managed to break the lock on his door."

"Gone?" Jack gazed stupidly at the young man. "How long?"

"We're not sure." Abe began to breathe normally again. "When Fitz took his noon meal to him, he wasn't there, and we've searched ever since."

Jack jumped to his feet so quickly he overturned his chair.

"Blast it." He turned and kicked the chair, sending it spinning. "Blast it."

"I'm coming with you." Edward moved quietly to his side and righted the chair.

"This is not your problem," Jack said, gritting his teeth.

"I'm coming with you," Edward said, grasping him firmly by the arm and propelling him toward the door.

"Why in the devil did no one inform me before now?"

"Well," Abe stepped back fearfully. "We thought the lad had just gone ashore to see the sights. We checked all the obvious places —." The young officer's voice trailed off, his face bright red. "But you should know there have been some rumors of other ships' crew being shanghaied in town."

Lillie awoke slowly and tried to focus on her surroundings. There was something she had to remember, but couldn't figure out for the life of her what it was. She lifted her head, but fell back, moaning in pain.

She rolled onto her stomach and moved her hands around, to try to figure out where she was by touch alone. This was definitely not her rough bunk on *The Kate*. The sheets were silk, and the size of the mattress was so luxurious she could not reach the edges by tentative, exploratory sweeps with her toes.

Awareness returned with a shock. Her clothes were gone. She sat upright in a sudden fury only to have to lie back down until the pain and nausea subsided. At the sound of the door clicking open, she scooted back to a pile of pillows and pulled the sheets tightly around her. Recalling Weatherby's warnings about fighting from a prone position, she steadied herself for an upward lunge.

Attempting to keep the nausea under control, she slowly began to make out the features of a figure at the foot of the bed.

"Mademoiselle, you have slept all day," the blurry apparition said. He moved closer to her side. "I've been worried about you."

She refused to give in to panic and remained silent for a few moments. When he bent nervously to feel her pulse, she turned savagely and leapt out of the bed onto the floor on the other side, clutching the sheets to her.

The self-satisfied, placid look on his face changed to wary and guarded.

His face was tanned, and the pale, grey eyes that assessed her were startling in contrast. Dark hair fell thick and full to his shoulders. A bushy mustache covered his upper lip, and the chin beneath was smooth and strong.

"I wonder if poor Jack suspects what a tart little nymph was stowed away on his ship," he said, and exploded into laughter. His voice rumbled and filled the room.

"Why am I here, sir? What do you want?" Lillie demanded.

His insolent look shifted and gave her a searching one-over.

"We were simply seeking more crew to replace the ones who've been felled by fever." He slowly smoothed the hair above his upper lip with one slender finger. "It's a common enough practice in the islands, but you are not what you seemed. My deepest apologies, Mademoiselle. My men handled you so roughly they loosened your ingenious binding device."

"How did I get here?" she asked, ignoring his attempt to appear a gentleman. "And where are my clothes?"

"You are allowed only one question at a time, and then I get to ask one." He moved to one of the floor-to-ceiling windows, pulled aside the gauzy curtains and stared outside. Turning back to her, he continued, "Fortunately for you, my first mate was there when you were taken, and he knows my taste in exquisite women. He would not allow the rest of the crew to sample you."

Lillie had an overwhelming urge to retch but forced herself to stay focused on her dangerous jailer.

"You said you get to ask one question. What could you possibly care to know about me?"

"I want to know," he said, moving close, "whom you work for." He grasped a handful of her hair, forcing her toward him in pain. "And you will tell me."

"Captain Jack Roberts — I'm his cabin boy." In spite of her best intentions, Lillie's voice quavered. The speed at which his voice had changed from cajoling to cold and deadly unnerved her.

"Cabin boys do not saunter about St. George with gold sewn into their clothing. And, furthermore, they do not hide lush, young womanly bodies under their sailing slops." He pulled the sheet from her and jerked it down to her waist. "I think you're lying, and I will take great pleasure in forcing you to tell the truth."

He reached out to touch one of her breasts when hard pounding on the door made him leave her with a curse. She pulled the sheet back up over her breasts and edged closer to the window.

He opened the door to one of his crewman. They conferred in urgent whispers before he turned to her with a warning glare and closed the door behind him. When a key clicked on the other side, she wasted no time but moved to the blowing curtains.

The casement was open to the island breezes with only slats covering the hinged shutters. She swept the room with one last glance, searching for her wayward clothes. More importantly, she sought some sign of her pistol and dagger.

Assessing the courtyard below, she estimated a drop of only ten feet or so. She assumed the strange man's house must be terraced along a hillside leading down to the harbor. Extending one foot, she tested the strength of the latticework along which clung masses of blue and purple blossoms.

Lillie knotted her sheet above one shoulder and then stripped the bed of the remaining sheet. The only thing approximating a weapon was a knife-like letter opener on a dainty writing desk in one corner. She sighed and moved to fashion a rope she could use to shimmy down into the courtyard.

Jack was livid, but refused to show anger in front of the conniving Armand Villieu Hollis. He might have known the smuggler would prey upon *The Kate's* crew to replace one of his ailing sailors. He forced himself to listen without comment to the lies flowing from the man's mouth.

"It's true. We've had a bit of bad luck down island. Fever took quite a few of the men on my ships."

"Your bad luck is no excuse to shanghai one of my sailors."

"Come now, Jack. We both know one crew is as good as another. Let me give you one of the men who serve me here. Unfortunately, your man already left on one of my short-handed ships."

"If you do not return him immediately, there will be nowhere on this island you can hide. You could not have sent him away this quickly."

"Very well, then — let me compensate you for the loss of his services." The little weasel paused and then went on. "Very young and frail — should not be worth much more than a pound or two."

Heat rose from Jack's neck while he struggled to keep the other man from sensing his desperation. He fidgeted with his shirt collar.

"Return him, now," he exploded, "or face the consequences."

"Come now. I'm sure we could work something out—," Edward said, and stepped between them, "a mutually agreeable understanding.

"What would it take for you to give the boy up?" His friend faced Hollis, his face grim. "Jack is not thinking clearly. The young man is the son of an old friend. To give him over to hard labor on one of your ships would be unthinkable."

Hollis suddenly broke into hearty gales of laughter.

"How often I've wondered when we two would come to a day of reckoning. And here we are." Hollis turned to Jack. "I have something you want." A slow smile spread across his face.

"She is a pretty little piece. I had no idea the great Captain Jack Roberts would stoop to smuggle a woman aboard ship disguised as a man. Where is your sense of *joie de vivre*? Weren't you even going to share her with your fellow officers? A pity — what a waste. She will be a prime jewel in my collection of Water Street girls."

"Where is she?" Jack's control broke. He interrupted Hollis's taunting speech by pressing a pistol to his neck. "Enough. Bring the girl to me." He pushed the pistol harder into the Hollis's jugular vein. "If one hair on her head is harmed, you will regret the day you were born."

"She should be outside about now trying to escape from the courtyard," Hollis said, with another hard laugh. The object of Jack's ire tried to inch his body out of harm's way and gestured toward a window. "She certainly is a feisty little thing. However, it does appear as though I've had more luck than you in hanging on to her."

Jack loosened the tension on the firing pin just long enough to confirm she was safe. Lillie seemed oblivious to the drama inside the drawing room. She inched her way around the perimeter of the walled courtyard, searching for a way out.

He held his breath and stared while she gathered the sheet up to her knees, exposing a length of curved, bare leg. She ran one of her hands over the courtyard walls and searched for chinks in the surface, no doubt looking for a way to escape.

Without warning, he drew back the pistol and cracked it alongside Hollis's head. His enemy fell to the floor before the pirate's men could react. Jack handed the pistol to Edward and burst through the entry into the courtyard.

When Jack came up behind her and placed his hand on her shoulder, Lillie whirled and went for his groin with her knee.

Thank God for long arms to hold the spitfire at length. She continued to fight and flail away at him for a bit and then finally quieted. He gathered her into his arms and adjusted the sheet to cover her. How often had he taken this unmanageable woman into his arms? He couldn't recall a time when he didn't know what she felt like with her head against his shoulder, the weight of her warm body resting in his arms.

"Jack?" Lillie asked, as she nestled against his chest.

"Yes?"

"We can't go without my clothes. Make him return my clothes."

"For the love of God," he exploded again, only this time out of relief, and tilted her chin to stare into her face. "Can you not for one moment stop your headlong flight into perdition? You're lucky you've survived this escapade with your person intact. Let's leave before more of his men appear. I'll buy you new clothes in town, anything you like — something pretty."

"But you don't understand," she pleaded. The gold and documents for the Confederacy are sewn into the seams of my shirt and pants. I need them to complete my mission."

He stared at her for a moment, disbelief flooding him, and then stiffened when an unfinished matter occurred to him.

"Before we proceed one more step, I demand to know why you were wandering through an unsavory area in port when I specifically forbade you to leave the ship."

"What about my clothes?" Her face took on the stubborn look he had come to dread.

"You, my fine Miss Coulbourne, are in no position to bargain with me." He glared at her for a long moment before speaking again. "Would you agree to a compromise? We will retrieve your clothes, if they haven't disappeared yet. In return, you will tell me what you sought to accomplish when you sneaked into St. George."

"You have my word."

"Wait here." He put her down and turned to walk back into the drawing room. Roughly pulling the dazed Hollis to his feet, Jack demanded, "Where are her things?"

CHAPTER SEVENTEEN

Saturday, May 23, 1863
St. George Harbour, Bermuda
32°22'46"N, 64°40'40"W

"You wanted to interfere in my mission. I had to stop you," Lillie said, as if the explanation were simple.

Jack sat across from her in the surgery on board *The Kate* and watched the emotions flit across her face. They changed from angry to guarded to pleading. Her cheeks glowed like hot coals. She licked her lips angrily, and he could not trust himself to interrogate her alone. Thank God for Fergus.

"How did you presume to know my intentions?"

"I overhead you talking to Fitz."

"How the devil?"

"When you're confined to a small room for days on end, you learn all there is to know about such a tiny space." She jumped up and moved to the far side of the surgery. "You treat me as though I were nothing more than a witless child. How else should I react?"

"You leave me no choice," Jack said, and stood, clenching his fists. "Time is running out. If I were to allow you to remain on the island to catch the first mail ship back to England next week, you probably would not obey me. Secondly, I do not trust Hollis to leave you alone. The minute we haul anchor, he would have you back. And his plans do not include using you as a deckhand."

At that moment, Fergus abandoned the work on his medical inventory and gave Jack a warning look.

Jack glared back.

"So what's to be done about me?" Lillie asked with a dramatic little sigh.

"You will stay in your cabin in the evenings only. At all other times, you can help Fergus in the surgery," Jack said. Anger and frustration overwhelmed him, making him question his sanity. "Since he seems to be the only man on the ship I can trust to remain immune to your wiles, I leave it to him to keep you in check until we reach Charleston Harbor."

"And then what?"

"And then, my dear Miss Coulbourne, you are on your own," he said. He ignored her scathing looks by staring out one of the portholes.

He finally turned away without any farewell and climbed to the upper deck.

Sunday Night, May 24, 1863
On *The Kate*
Headed for Charleston Harbor

Lillie was amazed at the daily parade of crewmen who made their way to the surgery, claiming one ailment or another, ranging from toothaches to clap and various mysterious stomach complaints. For the latter, Fergus provided a universal cure. Glass bottles filled with a mysterious granular substance were given to each patient.

After so many dosings, she was curious.

"What exactly do you put in those little bottles?"

"It works." He made some more notes in his log and then turned to her with a boyish grin. "They either get better or don't come back again."

"I think my father employed similar cures." She picked up a tub of soiled bandages from the corner and headed up to the deck to pump some water for washing. This was the third batch she'd readied as dressings in case the ship came under attack again.

At least the grungy task provided a reprieve from staring at the four walls in her cabin. Her evenings were spent either practicing self-defense moves or repairing her meager wardrobe after the disaster at the hands of Armand Hollis and crew. Amazingly, though, her clothes had been returned with the gold coins and documents intact, as well as her weapons.

Although she tried to put Jack out of her mind, she glanced up each time footsteps sounded down the hallway toward the surgery. During her many hours alone, she had concluded her feelings for him were nothing more than hero worship. It would pass. She shrugged off the physical aspect of their relationship as an unfortunate aberration.

After an hour of scrubbing, she stood and stretched her back only to be dazzled by the spectacle of the sun slipping below the horizon. Bands of striated clouds glowed in hues of bright orange to blue, through a wide purplish layer high above. Stifling heat had forced her to abandon her hat. Her curls, which had repopulated her head at an alarming rate, sprang up all over. Snatching her hat with a sigh, she jammed it on her head and bent once more to carry the now clean load back down into the surgery for hanging on lines to dry.

When she straightened, hands came from behind and took the tub from her. The lingering light softened the stern lines on Jack's face when she spun around to see him haul the tub below.

They moved down the steps to the surgery in companionable silence and surprised Fergus.

Before either she or Fergus could say anything, Jack turned and clattered back up the companionway. After his departure, she moved to stand beneath a glass bevel streaming light from the deck above into a corner of the surgery. The last glow of day washed over her.

"If you stand there much longer, I'll be forced to do something I've vowed never to do."

"What?" She came out of her thoughts with a start.

"I'll have to give up the carefree life of a rootless swab and take you back to Scotland with me."

Turning to give him her full attention, she was surprised by the kindness in his soft brown eyes. His heavy, dark brows moved like exotic birds with the changes in expression on his face. She had never studied him in such detail and was struck by the handsome whole of his face. Lillie could not help but respond to his hearty laugh and constant sense of humor in the midst of ever-changing disasters. Incarceration as his assistant had been far from the unpleasant experience she'd expected.

The ease with which he moved in his surgery with the rolling of the ship, the elegant way he wrapped his long legs around the stool bolted to the floor at his desk, all had become part of their easy companionship. An odd thought struck her — maybe she could be happy as a surgeon's wife. Maybe.

"Never take a sailor from the sea," Lillie finally said, and broke the awkward silence. She moved reluctantly from the last light of day and walked toward him.

"What?"

"It's something my grandmother told me when I was a little girl."

"Why would she tell a child such a thing?"

"She was married to a man who left the sea to make her happy."

"I'm not a sailor, I'm a physician."

"Tell me you would not miss the danger and excitement, the faraway ports of call."

"I could live anywhere and be anything if you were with me." He stared back at her, uncertainty clouding his eyes, and then grasped her hand.

"I've never been a dutiful daughter, and I suspect I would make a miserable excuse for a wife," she said, and tugged her hand from Fergus's warm hold.

"You have to understand how important this mission is to me," Lillie said. "I could not live the rest of my life knowing I spent the whole of this war on the sidelines, like a pampered child."

"How old were you? Perhaps sixteen when this senseless war began?" He captured her hand again and drew her to him. "This is not your fight. War is about old men sending young ones off to defend their selfish causes." He stared intently into her eyes. "Helpless women and children are caught in the middle and left to suffer the consequences."

At that moment the entire ship shuddered and they were thrown to the floor. Although Lillie smacked her head on the side of the table on the way down, she sat up quickly in a fog. After slowly assessing the damages, she realized she didn't have any broken bones, and then staggered to her feet to search for Fergus. He'd been thrown to a far corner of the surgery where he sat dazed and fingering his shattered glasses.

"What can I do to help?" she asked, and kneeled beside him.

He stared at her for a moment as if she were a stranger and then shook his head. A steady stream of blood poured from a cut on his forehead.

"I'm fine. I always carry spare glasses for just such an emergency." He pointed to a box on a corner of his apothecary shelf. When he tried to lever himself up from the floor, she pushed him back down.

"You're not fine. Let me get you another pair while you sit here a moment and rest."

While retrieving his spectacles, she also grabbed several of the recently cleaned rags. Returning to his side, she knelt down again and folded one before pressing it to his forehead.

"Just stay where you are and keep this pressed to your head while I get the surgery ready."

"The surgery? What happened?"

"Fergus — do you remember where your home is?"

He stared at her for a few moments as if she were daft.

"Why, Glasgow — you know that, Lillie."

"You're going to be fine. Just rest, and everything will come back to you." She smiled and planted a soft kiss on his forehead.

When she rose to prepare for wounded sailors, she thudded into Jack's solid frame.

"What's wrong with Fergus?" he demanded, his face full of anger.

"He's had a nasty bump on the head, but I think he'll be fine in a few hours. He's just groggy and not thinking straight, doesn't remember the ship being hit."

"So not only have you turned into a physician, but now you are an expert on my ship's surgeon as well?" The stormy frown on his face unnerved her.

"Why, in the name of all that's holy, are you acting like a stubborn jackass at a time like this?" She bustled past him toward the cots lining the wall. "Help me get him into a bed, unless, perhaps, something might require your attention up on deck?"

He already had Fergus on his feet and was helping his friend limp toward the cot. He lowered him onto the sheet and then turned to her.

"Listen carefully, and don't interrupt. If you do not do exactly as I say, your life, and perhaps many others, will be in jeopardy." He spoke slowly and in soft, precise tones. "I need you to remain here and care for the wounded — Fitz will be sending down three more.

"We have a blockader to either side of us. Fortunately, they've stopped firing for fear of hitting each other. They're so excited at the prospect of a prize, they've crowded too close together. I'm going to surrender."

"But —."

"No interruptions." He spoke each word like a muffled shot. "No matter what you hear, or what you think, I must have absolute silence, from both you and your patients."

"Why —?"

He fixed her with such a glare she withered into silence.

"Just trust me," he said with a hiss, and spun away to race back up to the deck.

Jack took the helm while a small boat rowed across from one of the blockaders to tie up alongside *The Kate*. He had instructed his signalman to raise the flag of surrender, as well as the Union Jack, twenty minutes earlier. *The Kate's* engine was in neutral, but he had his engineer, Derby, give the order to build the fires of both boilers to full capacity.

"Those blasted devils," Derby said, eyeing the two ships lurking to either side of them.

"Come now. They're just a bunch of blokes like us. We shouldn't bear them any ill will."

"Beggin' your pardon, sir, — have you taken a blow to the head?"

"Absolutely not. In fact, on some distant day after this bloody war ends, I hope to raise a glass or two with the best of them. They serve under mind-numbing conditions for months on end with captures few and far between.

"It's embarrassing — the ease with which we evade some of them. And despite the aging naval fleet they have to work with, they're a game lot, keeping to their posts month after month, watching faster, steam-powered runners escape their net." He shook his head.

"Not to contradict you, sir, but I've seen an occasional steam prize out there they've taken into their fleet," Derby said.

"True. If this war drags on much longer, I've no doubt the odds will even out. They're all amazingly capable captains and officers."

As a British citizen and non-combatant, the worst he could suffer at the hands of the Yankees would be the confiscation of his charts and navigation tools. This time the stakes were much higher. He could not afford to lose. As an agent of the Confederacy, Lillie could be taken into custody and transferred to a Yankee prison. Women spies were rarely executed, but it could happen.

"We've never been caught, sir," his engineer said, interrupting his disturbing thoughts, "and we're not going to start tonight."

"Well, there was that time off Wilmington when we ran aground trying to get under the guns of the fort." Jack sighed involuntarily. "She was a brave little ship. Damned shame we had to torch her and escape to shore."

"She was a good old gel," Derby agreed, "but she earned the syndicate millions before she went down. Lucky for us they commissioned *The Kate* from the Laird yards in Birkenhead."

"Captain," Fitz said, suddenly appearing at Jack's side.

"Yes?"

"The boat and crew are right alongside now."

"So they are, so they are," Jack agreed, and gripped the wheel tightly. "Now, boys, now."

Derby signaled with his hand to a series of crewmen between the helm and the boilers and then raced back to his steaming hot post.

The ship shuddered beneath Jack's feet, the boilers whined to full pitch, and they flew ahead, cleanly slicing through the waves between the blockaders.

The Kate's abrupt departure took the other ships by surprise, allowing a wide margin of escape. Jack's crew steamed off at full speed before the boarding party could make it back to the mother ship. He saved the full force of her seventeen-knot speed for just such occasions, and she didn't disappoint him now.

"One of them's sent up a flare," Fitz said, and studied the night sky behind them.

When the signal's illumination ignited, Jack turned the wheel at a sharp, ninety-degree angle. At the same time, he shouted an order to his first mate.

Fitz waved to the waiting crewmen down the line, and a large cloud of smoke rose into the air from the boilers' pipes, instead of the usual underwater expulsion.

If his previous experiences with blockaders were any indication, a second line of the fleet would follow the billowing towers of smoke just released while they steamed off on another course.

Lillie grasped the shoulder of an injured crewman to keep from falling to her knees when *The Kate* turned sharply. Rows of medicine bottles bounced out of the restraining lips on the shelves and rolled across the floor.

Fergus seemed to be recovering gradually from his confusion, and the bleeding had stopped from the gash on his forehead.

"What happened?" Fergus asked. The sudden lurch of the ship caused him to rise up on an elbow and give her a questioning look.

"I have no idea, but I suspect Jack pulled a fast one on the Yankee squadron."

"You really are in love with him, aren't you?"

"Yes, blast it, but that doesn't change my resolve." Hands on hips, she faced him. "And you, my fine fellow, can just get up and work if you don't have anything better to do than devil your nurse."

He rewarded her with a slow smile and gingerly swung his legs over the side of the cot, testing his strength. He stood and braced against a cabinet.

"So, what have you done so far?" he asked.

"Stopped the bleeding, cleaned wounds, re‑set an arm, and gave your patients probably too much chloroform." She paused at his quizzical stare. "While your battered noggin was healing, 'His Highness,' Cap'n Jack, came down and threatened me if anyone so much as made a sound down here."

"Oh, yes — evasive maneuvers." Amused recognition danced in Fergus's eyes.

Much later that night, Lillie made her sleepy way back to her cabin. All she wanted was to wash the blood off her arms with nothing more than the water in the basin in the corner before she dropped off into oblivion in her bunk.

Odd how her priorities had changed in the few weeks she'd been at sea. She recalled Sarah's dire predictions that she would miss her old life, the parties, the fine clothes. She didn't miss any of those things. In fact, she couldn't recall the feel of clean, fresh frocks against her skin. As for parties, she never enjoyed them all that much. Unless she and Sarah were together to plot and make fun of all the silliness, most gatherings were boring.

She glanced down at the simple sailor's slops she wore day after day. They had become old friends, having seen her through an amazing number of misadventures, and she hadn't even yet embarked on her mission.

Since she hadn't bothered to bring a lantern with her, she nearly fell over a dozing form propped against her door. She lunged to a defensive stance before Jack reached up and pulled her down next to him.

"I need to talk to you before morning," he said, his voice slow and measured.

"What is it?" she asked, alarmed. "Are we in danger?"

"We are always in danger, little one."

She resisted the urge to touch his face, to feel the warmth of his smile.

"We've altered our course up the coast to evade the blockade fleet, which will put us a day off schedule."

"A day? That's not so bad."

"That's not all." He put a warning hand on her arm. "We took a hit near the waterline."

"Can it be fixed?" Her heart lurched. She had become fond of *The Kate* in the few weeks aboard her and couldn't imagine the beautiful ship lying at the bottom of the sea.

"Yes, but repairs will delay us another day."

"There's more, isn't there?" She chilled at his ominous tone.

"With delays, we'll have less time in the new moon to take on cotton and make the run back out."

"Which means I'll have fewer days to complete my mission and get back to the ship." She filled in the rest. Aching with anger at the delays, she needed to strike out at someone, but could not bring herself to blame him. "The run back out shouldn't be that difficult. Should it?"

"Lillie, the run back out is the whole reason I'm here. The syndicate hired me because they lose most ships on the return trip. I'm very good at that particular part of the game."

"So, how many days will I have to complete my mission?"

"Three, at the outside." He grasped her shoulders, pulling her close. "There can be no delay," Jack said. "We'll have to leave as soon as the cotton is loaded, whether you're back or not. This ship and her crew are my responsibility. They have to come first."

While she still reeled from his ultimatum, he stood and moved down the passageway.

CHAPTER EIGHTEEN

Monday Morning, May 25, 1863
On *The Kate* at Anchor
Off South Carolina,
Northeast of Charleston Harbor

Jack and Derby leaned over the starboard aft rail in the morning light and surveyed the damages to the hull.

"Looks like the hits were all above the waterline, but I'd sleep a lot easier if we could take her to Halifax and haul her out." Derby straightened to face him, pulling his jacket down over his considerable girth. "Could be a hairline crack down below seeping water deadly slow."

"There's no way we can take that much time now." Jack paused and stared out at the horizon to the south. "Our cargo has to make it into Charleston in the next day or two. Confederate troops are desperate for supplies."

"The rush to get there wouldn't have anything to do with that cabin boy of yours?"

Damn — was there no one on board the ship who didn't know the intimate details of his life?

"Derby, how long have you served with me?" Jack asked."Oh, near on to six years now." His engineer pulled off his hat and scratched his head trying to recall the passage of time.

"Have I ever deliberately caused the destruction of a ship?"

"Er, no."

"Have we ever been caught and forced to molder away in a Yankee prison?"

"No, sir."

"Well, then, you're just going to have to trust me, aren't you?"

"Yes, sir, Cap'n." His officer straightened and gave him a quick salute before moving toward the crew awaiting orders.

"Don't just stand there, lads. Haul that pulley platform out of storage so we can go over the side for a closer look at the damages," Derby said.

Jack let out the breath he'd been holding and then moved to supervise the crewmen heating rivets in a small portable forge for the temporary repair of the hull. He would have a long talk with Fitz later. It would never do for everyone to question his decisions.

Thursday Night, May 28, 1863
On *The Kate,* headed for Sullivan's Island
Charleston Harbor, South Carolina

Lillie knelt to repack her sea bag. This time she was much wiser than when she and Sarah first tried to figure out what she would need and how to stow it all. That day in the Williams townhouse seemed a lifetime ago.

She'd profited from her hard-earned lessons. Her pistol and dagger had to be on her person, with two backups easily accessible near the top of the bag. She had spent long evenings sewing the rest of the gold sovereigns into her clothes while awaiting *The Kate's* repairs. The dispatches were secure inside a long flap in one of her pant legs. God help her if she were to fall overboard. She would sink like a stone.

There was a light tap at her door, and when it swung open, Jack peered around the side.

"What are you hiding?" When she stared suspiciously at his left arm crooked behind his back, he produced a gleaming pair of scissors.

"I thought you might need some help refreshing your disguise." His slow smile seemed almost shy.

Just when she thought she would hate him forever, he had to do something like this.

He didn't force her to face him but instead pulled her across the room to settle on a stool. Kneeling behind her, he slowly pulled small sections of curls through his fingers and clipped an inch off each.

She gave in to the pleasure of his hands sifting through her hair and molding to her head.

"I'm curious, Jack. Why aren't you talking me out of my 'ill-advised' adventure?"

When she tried to turn to see his face, he pushed her back around while he continued to work his way through the unruly mass.

"No," he said, "I don't approve of this venture, but it's what you want. If I've discovered anything at all about the unpredictable Miss Coulbourne, it's that she'll do what she wants to do, the rest of the world be damned." He brushed a wayward slip of hair from her chin and then continued. "It remains to the rest of us to help her on her way if we can."

"You're not going to try to talk me out of my mission, or go behind my back to circumvent me, or lock me in my cabin till you return to Bermuda?"

"No," he answered, and knelt to scoop up the curls littering the cabin floor. She couldn't see the expression on his face.

She dropped to the floor beside him before he had a chance to stand again. Taking his face in her hands, she covered his mouth with her lips.

"Can't we live just one moment at a time? Let's not spend this last night pretending to be indifferent to one another," Lillie pleaded. When he opened his mouth as if to protest, she covered it again.

Friday Morning, May 29, 1863
On *The Kate* Near Sullivan's Island
Charleston Harbor, South Carolina
32°40'00"N, 79°57'00"W

Lillie rose with the dawn to the eerie silence of the ship lifting through the waves under sail power alone. The fires, of course, would remain banked, but the great engines and screws were silent. The approach to the mouth of Charleston Harbor must be near.

She threw on her clothes and moved across the cabin floor to test the door. It was open.

Bringing the pitcher of water and basin down to the floor with her, she splashed her face first, and then rinsed her feet.

All the while she secretly yearned to dive over the side of the ship and cut cleanly through the grey waters to cleanse all traces of Jack from her body so that she could start over. Loving him had cast some sort of spell over her. Even when they were apart, her body craved his company.

No matter. This interlude in her life was over. Within a few hours, they would cruise near Sullivan Island, and she would slip onto a waiting fishing boat. A light tap at her door destroyed all of the previous few minutes' rationalizations. Her fickle heart leapt and she jumped to open the door.

"Are you ready?" Abe swept past her with a grave look.

"Yes, I'm packed."

"I wasn't inquiring only as to whether you're packed."

"Yes, I've thought it through." She stared at him for a long moment.

"It's not too late to change your mind. No one would think less of you."

"You don't understand. I have to do my part. I have to stand up and be counted, as good as any man."

"Lillie, no one would blame you." He angrily pulled his cap from his head and slapped it back down over his hair. "Why don't you just go back to your mother and use your wealth to help the cause?" He leaned over and tipped her chin up to gaze into her eyes. "You don't have to sacrifice yourself. There's not much of a chance you'll get to your contact point and back before we make the run out again."

"Why do you care? If I were a man, would you urge me to abandon my mission?" She threw her arms wide when he turned away from her. "Of course not."

She pushed past him and out the door toward the surgery.

Fergus raised his head at the sound he looked forward to every morning. When Lillie slipped through the door, the lantern light cast a glow onto her dark curls. Someone had trimmed the riotous mass to a more manageable short, soft frizz. A stab of jealousy took him by surprise.

"I'll be gone soon, and I wanted to say goodbye before we meet the fishing boat." She moved toward him but kept her eyes downcast, as if suddenly shy.

"The offer still stands to come back with me to Glasgow."

"I know." She threw her arms around him and held him tight. "You are a prince among men, Fergus. You deserve much better." And then she was gone, running out of the surgery and up the companionway.

He listened while she raced to the upper deck and then sat down hard on his stool. Opening his log, he tried to begin an entry, but the words blurred on the page. He took off his glasses instead and faced the door, bracing his chin on his hand.

Weeks had passed since they left Portsmouth. He hoped to God dispatches and gold were the only things she carried with her on this dangerous journey.

Lillie sat on her bunk, thrumming in anticipation, once again going over the contents of her canvas bag. She stared at the stack of cloths she'd brought along for her monthly courses. A tear slid down her cheek, and she angrily wiped it away. Stashing the lot into her bag anyway, she settled in for the wait.

CHAPTER NINETEEN

Friday Afternoon, May 29, 1863
On *The Kate,* Dodging Blockaders
Charleston Harbor, South Carolina

Jack stood at the helm and frowned at the line of cruisers *The Kate* had dodged all afternoon. He cursed the time wasted in evasive maneuvers. They had to beat the moonrise at midnight.

Taking the glass from Fitz, he studied the enemy's movements. The third line of blockaders appeared to be about five miles away, at the wide mouth of the entrance to Charleston Harbor. One of them was a steamship the Yankees must have seized. His usual tricks might not work.

"What do you think, Fitz?"

"If the weather doesn't turn soon, sir, we'll have a devil of a time slipping in unnoticed tonight."

Jack studied the skies but couldn't find much there to cheer him. It had been a bright, cloudless day, and the night promised to be clear. When the moon rose, they would be sitting ducks.

"We could make a run for it to the north and then circle around toward Sullivan's Island at dusk," he said.

"Might work, might not," his first officer replied, and crossed his arms tightly across his chest.

"As usual, your faith in me is touching." Snapping the glass shut, Jack handed it back to his doubting mate. "Two points nor'east." He gave the helmsman directions and then moved on toward engineer Derby's boiler rooms.

Lillie sat on the floor of her cabin, meditating. She had abandoned her nervous pacing hours before but nearly lost her balance when the engines came back to life in full force. *The Kate* leapt ahead and once more cruised powerfully through the waves.

Enough was enough. She had to see what was happening. Jamming her cap low over her eyes, she left the cabin and raced to the upper deck, taking the steps two at a time. Jack would be occupied at the helm or the boilers. She could make herself useful if she stayed out of sight.

Abe was at the port rail, watching the shore with a glass. Striding to his side, she snatched it from him.

"What are you doing up here?" Abe asked. When he reached for his glass, she nimbly moved away.

"I'm tired of being closeted in that tiny cabin. Give me something to do. Let me help." She reluctantly handed back the spyglass. "Why are we heading north again?"

"We're bound for Sullivan's Island, but first we have to clear that line of blockaders. Cap'n's decided to make a run for it to the right."

Just then, a huge circle of air bubbles appeared on the surface behind the ship.

"What was that?" she asked, and stared at the rapidly dissipating ring. "Have we sprung a leak?"

"No," Abe said, "the boilers are working at full capacity, and they're releasing steam underwater."

He moved away from the rail and circled her slowly.

"Why are you staring at me that way?" Lillie asked.

"I was just admiring how you've refreshed your disguise. The black eye is a nice touch."

"Stop grinning at me like an ape at the zoo."

"Can't help it. Looks like someone helped you trim that wild hair back as well," he said, and ran his hands through his own windblown thatch. "Didn't know we had a barber aboard. Think he'd help me with mine?"

She punched her fist into his stomach and smiled when he doubled over in mock pain.

"All right — you've made your point." He turned to her, and the faint remains of a smile lingered on his lips. "You could check this end of the ship to make sure no lanterns are burning. When we make the final run at dusk, we have to be a ghost ship — no lights."

"And then what should I do?"

"Report to the aft pump and bucket crew, and then we wait."

Lillie leaned against the stern rail and jammed her cap down over her hair a couple of times to make sure all the strands were secure. Jack and his helmsman had played cat-and-mouse with the blockaders for hours, but each dodge brought them nearer their destination. She could now make out the far shore of Sullivan's Island without a glass.

She needn't have worried about inciting the captain's ire. He hadn't come near her all afternoon, and now even Abe had left her alone after delivering a litany of warnings.

"No sounds, no lights, not even a reflection from a glass — our lives depend on it."

Jack's crew was adept at creating the illusion of a ghost ship. Nothing had been left to chance. No food or garbage had been dumped overboard for days to avoid a telltale following troop of birds.

The setting sun hovered just above the island. The sky was so clear and the air so humid and still, even the swooping gulls quieted when the fiery orb dropped precipitously below the land horizon.

Lillie studied the shore, and visualized how *The Kate's* light gray hull would blend into the color of the low sand hills. Even her funnels and masts would fade into the scrubby pines covering the hillsides. At least that was her fervent hope.

After another half hour of slow progression toward shore, the engines came to life again. The powerful twin screws shook the deck beneath her feet, and the ship surged forward, forcing her to grab tightly to the rail. They shot past the far right cruiser in the line of blockaders and left the Union ship a mile or two to the south of them.

She sat down hard on the deck, dizzy with the forward propulsion, and peered through the thickening curtain of dusk. She prayed the evasion tactics had worked.

Friday at Dusk, May 29, 1863
On *The Kate* Near Sullivan's Island
Charleston Harbor, South Carolina
32°40'00"N, 79°57'00"W

Jack was at the helm, and none of his officers had spoken since they began the mad dash toward the island. He had used this maneuver so many times, he didn't even need a pilot.

The trick was to get as close to shore as possible and not run aground on a shifting sandbar. They would throw a lead line over once they were within a thousand feet and hope the currents had not shifted too much silt since the last time they'd anchored there.

He motioned to Derby to message down the line of crewman toward the boiler rooms — slow to one-quarter speed. One of the men levered a long line over the side with a heavy piece of lead on the end.

He relayed the depth of the water in fathoms by the number of fingers he held up. As they edged closer to the beach, he finally held up just five, and Jack gave the thumbs-down signal for two hundred fifty feet of chain to be released along with the anchor. Five crewmen on the bow of the ship wrestled the heavy iron anchor into the water by hand to minimize sound, and then let it run to the bottom while they hand-fed the long length of chain with it.

The Kate swung gently until her bow headed into the wind, and she steadied into the light offshore breeze.

Jack glanced up when a signalman strode toward him.

"Sir, there are light signals from shore — two men are on their way in a fishing boat."

It was time. He could no longer prolong the inevitable. Striding toward the stern of the ship, he looked for Lillie.

Lillie turned away from the rail where she'd been studying the shoreline. The grim set of Jack's face told her what she needed to know. She moved toward her bag and slung it over her shoulder before following him forward.

"Are you ready?" he asked. They were amidships where a rope ladder hung over the side rail.

Squinting several times, she could barely make out a single-sail boat slipping through the dusk. There was barely a breath of wind, so the two crewmen were rowing toward them, their oars muffled with large rags.

"How do we know this is the right fishing boat?" she asked and turned toward Jack.

"I've brought you this far, Lillie. The next step you have to take on your own." He moved close and placed his hands on her shoulders. "We've been receiving signals from shore for the last hour assuring us they were on the way."

"Who sends the signals?" she asked, and her teeth began to chatter in spite of the oppressive heat.

"Our friends from Fort Moultrie on the island. They always let us know when we're lined up to make our run between Moultrie and Sumner." His grip tightened on her shoulders. "You don't have to go through with this."

If only that were true.

"Three days, Lillie, and not a minute more," he warned. "You must meet me at the cotton wharf on the west side of Charleston."

She said nothing but slipped out of his grasp and clambered down the ladder. The men on the smaller boat tied off to one of the metal rings on *The Kate's* hull.

She hung from the ladder and noted two baskets attached to the wooden mast. Abe told her to look for them on the rendezvous boat. After a slight hesitation, she swung aboard and stowed her gear in the stern.

If she turned around, she'd lose her nerve. She didn't dare look into Jack's eyes again.

Her two companions were equally silent when she dropped onto the boat and they pushed away from *The Kate*. The only sound was the muffled slap of oars on water and the creak of stanchions when the wood strained against them. Picking up the rhythm, they turned toward the nearby shore, an open beach with little cover except for an occasional scrubby pine.

"Where are we going?" she asked.

The younger man said nothing but simply pointed toward the horizon around the next spit of land to the west.

She followed his hand and gasped. A Yankee gunboat headed their way.

When they lurched into sandy-bottomed shallows, she had to grip the gunnels to slow her forward motion. Jumping into the water, she helped drag the tiny craft up onto the beach.

By unspoken agreement, they split up to find driftwood and pine branches for cover. The younger fisherman returned first with an armload of brush and hastily dismantled the boom and mast, making their vessel blend into the contours of the beach.

After piling the bundle of scavenged driftwood in front of the boat, he pulled her to the sand behind the overturned craft. She had to stifle a laugh when she figured out a way to differentiate between them — Fish One, the elder, and Fish Two.

She lay there, barely daring to breathe, while a cruiser steamed round the point and headed east toward *The Kate's* anchorage. A blade of fear sliced through her stomach. She had to warn Jack. When she half rose to peer after the gunboat, Fish Two jerked her back down.

"Do you want to get us all killed?" he whispered into her ear. "Don't you worry about old Cap'n Jack. He's never been caught, and I don't think he's about to break his record tonight."

She nodded and tried to corral her jittery nerves. Fish Two was right. Jack would prevail. He always did.

Then she stared in horror when the gunboat slowed and dropped anchor down the beach from them. She and her two companions lay frozen behind their fishing boat, not daring to exchange even a whisper. Fish Two laid a gentle restraining hand on her back.

Jack draped his long frame across a bench in the wheelhouse and closed his eyes to catch a few hours of sleep.

A short time later the door cracked open. He could feel someone staring.

"It's all right, Fitz. What's wrong?" He squinted open one eye to address his first officer.

"There's a Yankee gunboat just steamed 'round the point and anchored up the beach from us."

Jack winced and tried not to contemplate the worst possible scenario.

"What are your orders, sir?"

"Spread the word to the crew to remain on full alert — and not a sound from anyone." He sat up, abandoning hope of a short nap.

"Do you think the gunboat crew suspects we're here?"

"No. They would have closed in for the kill by now." He ran his hand through his disheveled hair and rubbed his scalp hard to coax himself awake. "How close?"

"We can hear their conversations, sir."

"Damn."

"Anything else, sir?"

"Yes," Jack said, "let me know when enough time's passed for their boiler fires to have cooled. And, Fitz — "

"Sir?"

"Make sure Derby keeps ours banked to capacity."

When his first mate returned to the outside deck, Jack leaned back, determined to snatch a few moments of rest. However, the thought of what else the sudden appearance of the gunboat might mean kept niggling at the back of his mind.

He sighed when the truth hit him like a fist to his gut. He would not be able to rest easy until Lillie was back on *The Kate*, but he reckoned the likelihood of that happening was remote.

He must have dozed off, because some time later he came awake when Fitz shook his shoulder and motioned toward the deck. Jack followed him out the door and took the wheel.

It must have been after midnight, and a splendid three-quarter moon stared back at him from a star-filled sky. Although the dazzling light would work to their disadvantage, reflecting off *The Kate's* light gray hull, it was now or never.

Capture was not an option.

"Knock the pin out of the shackle on the anchor chain on the deck and ease the cable gently, <u>gently</u>," he stressed, "down into water." He whispered his instructions to Fitz. The lives of his men were worth more than one anchor.

"What shall I tell Derby?"

"Tell him to be ready to give us full steam power. I'm going to go ahead with one engine and astern with the other."

His mate passed the signal to the line of crew leading to the boiler rooms, and the entire ship pivoted violently, headed to seaward, thrashing the shallow water all around them. The engines shuddered with power and then all forward motion stopped.

"Damn." Jack pounded his hand against the wheel. They had run aground. After only a moment's hesitation, he pushed the throttle to full forward again.

Saturday Morning, May 30, 1863
On Sullivan's Island
Charleston Harbor, South Carolina

In spite of Lillie's vow to remain vigilant, she awoke with a start. She must have slept, but how long? A pink dawn painted the sky above the island's salt marshes. Gulls and terns made raucous rounds of feeding sites.

She rolled over in a panic only to confront the wide-open snoring mouth of Fish Two. Fish One was already awake, squatting and drinking from a stoneware jug of water. He handed it to her when she pulled herself up behind the boat and offered her a few chunks of hardtack.

"Is the gunboat crew still near the beach?" she asked, and tore off a bite of a tough biscuit while searching the horizon. She held a hand above her eyes to shade the early morning sun.

"They must have slipped away during the night, lad."

"Why would a patrol anchor for the night?"

"Why not?" Fish One reached for the jug and took another long drink. "They know as well as we do the tricks the runners use to get past them into the harbor."

"Do you think they caught *The Kate?*"

"Most likely not."

"How can you be sure?" Her voice quavered in spite of her resolve to be brave.

"You would have heard and seen a lot of firing from the gunboat, and Cap'n Jack and the crew would have torched *The Kate* before surrendering." Fish Two rose silently and reached for the water jug.

Lillie huffed out the breath she'd been holding and studied her companions. The family resemblance was clear. Both men were sandy-haired with light dustings of freckles across their faces. Fish One had warm brown eyes and a stocky build while the younger Fish Two had a taller, more slender frame and light green eyes.

"Do you live near here?" she asked, and shrugged off her damp woolen coat, spreading it over a nearby bush. Silence greeted her question. When she turned back to them, Fish One was readying the boat while Fish Two stood with his back to her, relieving himself in the high grass. Her cheeks burned, and she whirled around before forcing herself to turn back. She had to start acting like a man, or she'd be found out.

"The less we know about each other, the better. Don't you agree?" Fish Two turned to face her, and a slow smile quirked at the corners of his mouth. "That's my father Seamus, and I'm Ian. We do whatever we can to help the cause and drive the Yankees back."

"You can call me Rafe." She extended her hand and grasped his firmly.

Seamus finished with the boat and came over to kneel in the sand in front of them. He drew a series of lines with a stick and then looked up at her.

"Here's where you and Ian will head this morning."

"Aren't you coming with us?" She dropped down onto the sand beside him and leaned forward to study his crude map.

"I have to wait here for another runner."

"Which one?"

"Is there no end to your questions, laddie?" He pulled off the handkerchief tied around his neck and swiped at droplets of sweat running down his forehead. "Didn't your da ever tell you curiosity killed the cat?"

She slanted a sideways glance toward Ian, but the expression on the younger man's face gave nothing away.

"You two will hike back across the island," Seamus said, "about half a mile, to retrieve another sailboat hidden in the cove. From there, it's a three-mile sail to your meeting place on the other side of Mount Pleasant."

"That's all?" Somehow, she had assumed the journey would take much longer.

"Your contact is supposed to meet you there with a horse to get you to your final destination."

"You're not my final contacts?"

The two men stared at each other with odd expressions on their faces.

"Did no one fill you in on the details of your mission, lad?" Seamus stared at her, disbelief on his face.

"No," she admitted. "I've just been given rough bits and pieces along the way."

"This is your first time, isn't it?" Fish Two said.

"Yes, but I have learned much in the last month, the hard way." She stubbornly thrust her chin forward.

"Don't worry yourself. Ian will take care of you." Seamus stopped and fussed a moment with his pipe, minus the tobacco. "If there's a problem at that end, he'll contrive another plan."

Lillie straightened from the sand and pulled her jacket from the bush to stuff back into her bag before following Ian over the dunes.

Half an hour later, Lillie stared down into the inviting waters of the cove from behind a hillock of sand and sea grass. A stiff breeze tugged at her well-worn hat, and she clamped it tighter to her head.

A short trek angling back across the island took them through the lush, grassy interior of tidal backwaters and then onto the beach of the cove on the other side. For the hundredth time since leaving England, she swore she could not understand how men managed to survive in their heavy clothing in such climates. The humid heat had become oppressive when the sun burned higher in the cloudless sky.

Ian spoke little during the short hike, leaving her to wonder how much he really knew of her mission. Or perhaps he was just a man of few words, like her father. At the thought of her papa, she had to swipe at a tear sliding down her cheek.

Sullivan's Island was little more than a finger of land buffer between the mainland and the mighty Atlantic. Ian handed her a spyglass and pointed toward their destination — the hull of a boat overturned in the grasses several hundred yards down the beach.

She helped assemble the mast and boom before they shoved the boat toward the calm waters of the cove. A freshening breeze puffed, and she took a seat on the windward side to keep the boat flat.

Glorying in the temperature drop on the water, she adjusted the buttons on her shirt to cool her flushed skin, taking care not to expose the muslin binding her breasts.

"There's Moultrieville." Ian pointed to a cluster of houses along the point. "And Fort Moultrie is on across the island, facing the channel. Once the blockade runners get under their guns, they have a clear shot into the harbor."

She prayed Jack had made it in unscathed the night before with *The Kate*.

"Honestly," Ian added, as if sensing her fears, "We would have seen lots of fireworks if Cap'n Jack were captured last night." He leaned back and managed the tiller while angling out of the cove and into the rough waters of the open harbor.

When they approached the abandoned jetty just beyond Mount Pleasant, Lillie counted four men loitering along the rickety wooden structure.

"Something's wrong, Ian."

"How do you know?" His shoulders tensed and he strained forward, staring toward the group awaiting them.

"It doesn't feel right," she said. "Why would it take so many men to send me on to the next leg of my mission?"

"Down," he shouted, and pushed the tiller over all the way. The boom swung back with a vengeance, and they spun around away from the wind, rocking with the force of the sudden turn. He steadied the small craft and bore away from the headland.

When Lillie picked herself up from the bottom of the boat, pings hit the water five to ten feet behind them.

The grim expression on Ian's face confirmed her fears. Whoever those men were, they were shooting at them.

"Where are we going?" Lillie asked, leaning close to him to be heard over the wind.

"I'm taking you to a safe place, and someone with whom you have a great deal in common," Ian said, and turned to her with a smile. "You may be able to help each other."

Saturday Night, May 30, 1863
Northern Peninsula
On Charleston Harbor

The late afternoon sun was low on the horizon when Lillie and Ian finally rounded a small peninsula and pulled close to a dense stand of trees.

He turned the boat abruptly, grounding in shallows off the beach. He slid over the side and pulled them across the sandy, graveled bottom.

Ian retrieved a hidden pile of branches and arranged them around the sailboat and mast. Moving toward the center of the clearing, he began making soft birdcalls.

She was mystified but remained silent during the strange ritual. After a few minutes, a ragged young man materialized out of the woods. A battered hat and smudges of dirt on his face made it difficult to make out his features, but the creature seemed to be about her age and height.

Ian turned to her and made the formal introductions. "Rafe, this is Tom. Tom, this is someone with whom I think you will find much mutual interest."

For a few seconds, the two stared at each other and then Tom broke the silence.

"*Je ne parle pas l'Anglais.*"

"Oh, yes, you do speak English. Quit pretending," Ian said with a snort.

"It's all right," Lillie said. I can speak French if Tom would be more comfortable."

"Don't patronize me." Tom spat out, staring at her.

"Enough, ladies. Let's move to the heart of the matter." Ian spread his arms with the palms of his hands facing them.

"Jenna Dubois, this is —?" he asked while peering at Lillie.

"Lillie, Lillie Coulbourne," she replied defiantly.

They removed their hats and eyed each other, eyeing each other's disguises.

A sudden gust of wind off the harbor caused the canopy of tall pines above them to flail and moan. Lillie turned her head as she picked up a familiar sound above the keening of the wind — horses.

Soft whickers came from a source in the woods. Her annoyance at Ian for seeing through her disguise was replaced with hope. All was not lost. There was a chance she could still complete her mission.

"I'll purchase one of your horses," Lillie said, and turned to Jenna whose face filled with scorn.

"Who are you to tell me what I will do with my horses?" the other young woman demanded and moved threateningly toward her. "*Eh, petite poulet?*"

"*Vous êtes fou.*" Lillie replied with equal asperity.

Once again, Ian intervened. Lillie clenched and unclenched her fists as he held her back.

"Jenna, be still," he insisted. "Lillie has a legitimate need for one of the horses, and I believe she has contacts who could help you as well."

"How do you know who I am and what I can do?" Lillie asked belligerently.

"My father and I are harbor pilots for the runners. We don't take blind risks."

"I still don't see how this, this pampered chicken of a woman could help me," Jenna interrupted.

Lillie gazed at her adversary in wonder. The young woman was a beautiful mulatto with delicate, light mocha skin. Tight caramel-colored braids tumbled from beneath her tattered hat. They framed large, almond eyes staring back at Lillie in barely disguised disdain. Why on earth was she hiding horses on this remote spit of land?

"All right. I guess you two are at a standoff." Ian removed his hat and wiped the sweat from his brow. "It's up to me to explain your options.

"Jenna, you've been hiding way too long. Pretty soon your luck will run out and some bummers'll take both you and the horses." He turned back toward Lillie and added, "You are obviously in the middle of something gone horribly wrong. I have no idea what's going on, but those men at the jetty today did not have your best interests at heart."

He paused for a moment, but began again as neither of the two women seemed inclined to talk. "Why don't you join forces? You help Lillie get to her contact point, and she can help you get out of here until the war is over and your father is released from prison."

"What about you, Ian?" Lillie asked. "Can't you come with us?" She glanced at Jenna and caught a look of pure hatred.

"I have to stay close to Sullivan's Island to pilot with my da." He grasped both of their hands and forced them together. "You two are on your own. Come on. At least join hands and pledge to help each other."

They touched tentatively. Did the mulish expression on Jenna's face mirror her own?

"Good girls. Now, come help me shove off. Need to get back before dark." He turned suddenly while they were pulling the branches off the boat and moved toward Jenna. Taking her in his arms, he kissed her soundly before he pushed the boat into the water and hopped aboard and raised the sail.

They stared after him until he disappeared around a point before turning back toward each other.

"All right. Just where is it you have to go?" Jenna asked. "Although I can't imagine what a spoiled chicken like you could possibly do to help the cause."

Lillie sighed and bent to roll up one pant leg to retrieve a well-worn map from a hidden pocket.

Lillie cantered north off the spit of wooded land, close behind Jenna, her unlikely new partner in espionage. The whole episode might have been laughable if not for the fearful pounding of her heart. Who could have known about her intended mission? And which side were they on?

At least she would be able to face whatever lay ahead of her on a full stomach. They had managed a feast of grilled fish flavored with herbs from Jenna's cache before heading out.

The longer she was around her odd companion, the more a grudging admiration grew. The other young woman had deftly fielded her questions without giving much away. Lillie had discovered just a few things.

Jenna's father was a Confederate cavalry officer who had been captured and was now in a northern prison. She had received just one letter from him in the previous year encouraging her to go to her mother's family on their sugar cane plantation on Martinique.

Before the war, she'd served as a groom and occasional jockey for her father's racehorses. Now she was determined to save their two remaining horses until he returned.

Lillie shuddered at the thought of her own father languishing in similar straits.

They slowed the horses and pulled alongside each other on a narrow, firm path threading through the swamp·like salt marsh. She could tell Jenna had come this way many times before.

"Why are you still here instead of joining your family, as your father ordered?" Lillie asked, taking advantage of their slowed progress to probe for more information.

"Shush. Keep your voice down." Jenna leaned over and laid a hand on Lillie's arm for emphasis. "We may not be the only ones out here tonight.

"Would you run, little chicken, if your papa were in prison?" Jenna finally answered Lillie's earlier question with another.

"Of course not," Lillie said.

"Exactly. And, besides, how could I abandon Odysseus and Penelope?" Jenna bent forward and lovingly rubbed the former's neck.

"Why such odd names for horses?" Lillie asked.

"Then you've never read <u>The Odyssey</u>," Jenna said.

"Of course I have," Lillie said, raising her voice again.

"But you can't imagine a woman like me having read it?"

"That's not what I meant," Lillie said, embarrassed. "I'm sorry. Truce?"

"Truce," Jenna agreed.

They came to a raised grassy ditch and urged the horses out onto a road heading north, away from the coast.

"How far do we have to go?" Lillie asked.

"Oh, probably about fifteen to seventeen miles." Jenna patted the bedrolls attached to her saddle. "We'll hide in the woods once we get close and catch a few hours of sleep before daylight."

Lillie doubted she would get any sleep. Worries already swirled through her head — whether Jack made it through the blockade, whether she would get back to the ship in time.

And then there was the packet of unused cloths at the bottom of her sea bag.

CHAPTER TWENTY

Saturday Night, May 30, 1863
Northern Peninsula
Somewhere East of Charleston, South Carolina

"Here's as good a place as any to bed down for a few hours," Jenna said, and pointed toward a dense piney wood.

Pulling Penelope up short, Lillie gingerly dismounted. It had been too long since she'd spent so much time in the saddle. Her new friend was right. She really had turned into a "pampered chicken."

They led the tired horses through a thick stand of pines and tied them to two trees. Lillie gratefully accepted a threadbare blanket and scuffed pine needles aside in a clearing nearby before sinking to the ground.

"I'll take the first watch," Jenna said when she crouched to whisper in Lillie's ear.

Lillie barely mumbled her agreement before drifting off to sleep. Disjointed dreams plagued her and merged into a fearful awakening. Sounds of gasping and choking came from the direction of where Jenna stood guard. Ulysses and Penelope stamped and whinnied.

Shrugging out of the rough blanket, Lillie leapt to her feet and unsheathed one of her daggers from her ankle. Jenna struggled against a short, stocky man behind her. His hands closed around her neck and he was brutally choking her into silence.

Lillie didn't hesitate. She strode soft-footed through the trees at the edge of the clearing and circled around to his backside. Encircling the man's thick neck with her arms, she fisted the dagger tightly in her right hand and slashed across his jugular vein. With a shocked groan, he sagged to the ground, blood pouring down the front of his filthy shirt. Soft, gurgling sounds came from his mouth until he finally stilled.

Lillie staggered and tried to steady her breathing enough to think through their next moves.

"Deserters." Jenna mouthed the single word while pointing toward another man trying to steal the horses. Odysseus kicked and flailed at him while Penelope bared her teeth and strained at the rope. He'd not yet noticed the absence of the other thief and seemed oblivious to the two women.

Jenna tapped Lillie's shoulder and pointed to a large branch under a tree. Gesturing in a circle with her hands, she motioned for Lillie to distract the remaining horse thief.

"Please — don't take my horses," she pleaded, and ran toward him waving her arms. "They're all we have left."

He stopped and turned, scowling.

"Why ain't a man like you fighting with the army, instead of larking around the countryside?" he asked, and licked his lips while moving toward her.

Lillie's heart stuttered. Had he seen through her disguise?

In a move so silent and quick Lillie didn't have time to react, Jenna came from behind a stand of trees and rounded on the thief with the branch, landing it squarely at the base of his skull. He collapsed with an oath and a thud into unconsciousness.

"What should we do with him?" Jenna jerked her thumb toward the man lying motionless on the ground except for occasional snoring sounds.

Lillie knelt by his side, in dread of what they had to do. A rustling in the trees nearby brought her to her feet, but too late. Two more men walked into the clearing with guns leveled at them.

"Bet you thought you were pretty smart gettin' the drop on our boys," the newcomer said. A tall man with thinning hair, he made a sudden move toward Jenna and hit the side of her face with the butt of his gun. Lillie watched while her friend reeled from the blow, blood seeping from a diagonal gash on her cheek.

"We'll just see how far you get with us," he sneered. When she tried to stanch the flow of blood from Jenna's cheek, he pushed her away. "Never you mind about your friend. A little cut is nothing compared to what we'll do to you before the night's over."

Lillie kept her mind working while she resisted the nausea clawing at her stomach.

"You two — sit down in front of this tree." He motioned with his free hand for his slight, silent companion to tie them together and then turned away and spit to the side of his boot. "Damned if you're not a whole army on your own. Coulda' used you at Bull Run." He paused a moment to toe over the body of the man Lillie'd dispatched with her dagger.

"Christ, you got ol' Frank." He bent over his downed partner and felt for a pulse. The dead thief's head lolled over and blood flowed from his wound. "God-almighty — you kilt him."

Lillie considered her options. The rifles trained on them were much more powerful than her puny Derringers. With each breath she drew, she worked her wrists against Jenna's, gradually loosening the rope binding them together.

Jenna was the first to wrest herself loose and raced off into the woods.

When Lillie struggled to free herself from the remaining bindings, the tall thief thrust his rifle barrel into her Adam's apple. She leaned into the tree, gasped for air, and struggled to stay upright.

Willing herself not to give in to panic, she winced through a curtain of pain.

"That'll teach you to come here nosin' around where you don't belong," he said, and leaned so close, Lillie gagged at the smell of fetid breath.

The thief Jenna had bludgeoned began to moan and roll to his side. He was coming around. The odds against them were about to increase.

Out of nowhere, a high-pitched, blood-curdling scream split the silence. Three young women with dirt-streaked cheeks and unkempt hair rushed into the clearing brandishing farm implements.

Lillie's tormentor howled in agony and loosened his hold when a pitchfork pierced his leg. He collapsed forward into her lap. She ducked her head when a shovel came down solidly against his head and he rolled limply away.

The sun had just begun to filter through the pines from the east, and the bright backlighting revealed a chilling view of the woman towering above her with the deadly shovel. This must be what ancient Valkyries looked like in battle. The woman lowered her weapon once again, delivering a mighty crack to the back of the deserter's head. Lillie doubted he survived the first blow, let alone the second.

A younger woman appeared beside the Valkyrie and pulled her away from the bloodied man. An imp of a girl in well-worn muslin knelt next to Lillie and untied her wrists.

"Don't mind Mary Jane. She hasn't been right since the night it all happened. But she'll be fine now." The child continued to chatter away while helping Lillie stand on shaky legs next to the tree. "Sissy Nancy knows what to do."

Lillie swayed with a bit of dizziness on regaining her feet and had to rush to the side of a bush to be sick. When she turned to thank their rescuers, she caught a glimpse of one of the women helping Jenna drag two of the dead thieves deeper into the woods. Their rescuers looked so much alike, she assumed they were sisters.

"Do you love this child's father?" the tall, fierce farmwoman asked abruptly and moved to Lillie's side, searching her face.

"W-what?" Lillie stammered and turned away, avoiding eye contact.

"You know you're increasing, don't you?"

"No, of course not," she stammered in stubborn denial, and lowered her eyes.

"Don't worry. I won't say anything, but you should come back with us. Rest and have some food before you move on." The other woman shoved her hands into her blood-spattered apron pockets and added, "I know you don't want to admit you're in trouble, but I understand more than you think."

She looked at the other woman in surprise. Could she possibly suspect?

"I was married once myself," the Valkyrie said, a far-off look in her eyes.

"What happened to your husband?" Lillie asked.

"He's up north — fighting, I guess." After a slight hesitation, the woman darted toward her sisters and Jenna who were feverishly saddling the horses and gathering their belongings.

Lillie trailed behind the band of warrior women while they made their way down a remote dirt lane. She had hoisted the youngest sister onto Penelope's back with her. The talkative child had been the one to make formal introductions.

"I'm Annie Elizabeth," she said in pride. Sissie Mary Jane's oldest and Nancy's in the middle."

After Mary Jane insisted Lillie and Jenna return with them to recuperate at their farm, the eldest sister seemed to fall into a dark depression, refusing to converse, even with her siblings.

Jenna walked ahead of them, leading Odysseus with Nancy on board. Mary Jane walked alongside them and clung tightly to a rope with a grunting, squealing hog fighting her at the other end. The sisters had explained the band of deserters stole the animal from them.

After Annie drifted off to sleep, leaning back against Lillie, there was little talking among the women. She welcomed the solitude. Even after all her training with Weatherby, she was woefully unprepared for the aftermath of killing a man. Her heartbeat still hadn't returned to normal, occasionally racing erratically when she remembered the death grimace and open, staring eyes of the fallen thief.

Finally, a warm calm crept over her while Annie shifted against her chest and murmured in her sleep. Lillie gradually matched her breathing to the child's and adjusted her warm weight. What if Mary Jane was right? But her courses were late by only a few weeks. She pushed the unsettling thought out of her mind and adjusted the girl's drooping head to rest into the crook of her arm.

Her parents had battled throughout her life over her father's need to leave during his long and dangerous career as an army surgeon. Her mother spent six years at his side as his nurse before she had to stay behind with a baby.

Lillie couldn't bear to share so little of Jack's life. She knew him as well as her own heart. He would force her to live with her mother, or worse, stash her away at Clarendon. If it meant compromising her safety, or that of his child, he would not be budged.

When the small band of bedraggled women turned a corner in the road, they came upon a lane lined with a long canopy of oaks. At the end was a two-story plantation house with a pillared porch stretching across the front. Flowering magnolias clustered around the front steps, offering fragrant shade. The well-worn wood siding and shingles were in need of paint and repair, but the overall effect was of a cozy, welcoming home.

That night Lillie was so tired, her bones felt like lead, but she couldn't sleep. She lay next to Jenna in Annie's bed while the child doubled up across from them with her sister, Nancy.

She and Jenna had helped the women all day with farm chores before they all collapsed after an early supper.

Fidgeting, she tried to find a comfortable space and punched her pillow a few times. Finally giving up, she rolled onto her back and stared at the ceiling while listening to Jenna's soft breathing.

She must have drifted off for a time only to awaken to the sounds of Nancy moving around the room. She swung her feet onto the wood floor and bent down to pull on her heap of shabby men's clothing before following the other girl.

"Guess you couldn't sleep either?" With a broad smile, Nancy peered back at her from down the hallway. She glanced at Lillie's blood-splattered clothes. "Maybe there's something left in Pa's closet you could wear."

"Don't worry about me," Lillie said. "Is there something I can do for you?" She smoothed over the spots of blood dotting her ragged shirt and pants and added, "You saved our lives. The least I can do is help however I can."

"Those deserters have been hiding out in the woods and marshes hereabouts for months. They've threatened us and stolen nearly everything of worth."

Nancy hesitated. "I guess taking the hog was the last straw for Mary Jane. She just snapped — she hasn't been right since she lost the baby."

"What happened?"

When they reached the bottom landing of the staircase, Nancy held a finger to her lips and motioned for Lillie to follow outside. On the way through the kitchen, the other girl paused to punch down a pan of dough and knead it a few times before slipping out to the garden behind the house.

Turning back toward Lillie, she beckoned her on through the woods to a family cemetery in a secluded clearing.

"Are those your parents' graves?" Lillie asked, pointing to two fresh mounds of dirt at the outer edge.

"No." Nancy turned to her with a strange expression. "That one over there is Sam, Mary Jane's husband. The baby's buried with him."

"But I thought she said he was fighting somewhere up north."

"He was, but he came home unexpected-like one day."

A chill crept down Lillie's back in spite of the rising sun and balmy morning breeze.

"Mary Jane was pregnant. Only had about another month to go."

"Did he come home to help her with the baby?"

"No — he, he didn't know." Nancy hung her head for a moment and then stared back at her. Tears glistened on her cheeks.

"The baby belonged to a sailor who jumped ship from a Yankee blockader and ended up here. He threatened us all, and then Mary Jane made a deal with him." Nancy stopped and struggled to continue through hiccupping sobs. "She locked us in our room and made us promise not to make a sound or try to get out."

"What happened then?" Lillie didn't want to hear the ending, but sensed the girl needed to talk.

"We thought the deserter left the next day, but Mary Jane would never say what happened." Nancy sank to the ground and held her head in her hands. "The next time I came out here to put flowers on Mama's grave, there was a fresh hole covered with dirt."

"What did her husband do when he came home?" Lillie asked.

"He beat her, really bad." Nancy snuffled some more. "She lost the baby, and then he just wouldn't stop beating her the next day."

"What did you do?"

"I got him a bottle of Papa's liquor, and then we hid Mary Jane in the woods after he got to drinking."

"How did you get him to leave?"

"He never left," Nancy said, and another tear slid down her cheek. "We beat him to death with a shovel and hoe when he fell asleep."

"Then that's the other grave?"

"Yes, Miss, it is."

"Wait a minute," Lillie said. "You said 'we.' Who helped you kill him?"

"I know God will never forgive me — poor little Annie —"

Lillie folded the sobbing girl into her arms.

Early Sunday, May 31, 1863
Charleston, South Carolina
32°47'00"N, 79°56'00"

Jack shifted uncomfortably astride a hired horse at dawn in the cool shadows across the street from the Charleston Hotel.

It was only a matter of time before Wade would appear. He had a hunch the snake would slither out of his hole soon. An informant he'd paid to watch the bastard had come to the ship to tell him the agent had gone to a livery stable to arrange for a carriage for several days. He was supposed to pick up the conveyance that morning.

Edward was late. He and one of his crewmen were on their way to help, but if they didn't show soon, Jack would have to follow Wade on his own.

While Jack considered an alternative plan, his friend materialized out of the foggy dusk. The other man with him was compact and muscular, looking more like he belonged in the saddle than either Jack or Edward. He certainly didn't look like a sailor.

The man leaned forward before his boss had a chance to make introductions and extended his hand toward Jack.

"Name's James Weatherby. Pleasure to help you, sir. Known Miss Coulbourne's family for years. Fine people."

Edward's face registered shock while Jack struggled to absorb the latest development.

"And you just happened to be on Capt. Harken's ship?" Jack asked, disbelief in his voice.

"Yes."

Jack turned to Edward for confirmation only to see him shrug his shoulders. He made a split-second decision based on the capable look of the man and the fact they would need all the help they could get, regardless of the source.

"Right, then. Did he fill you in on our quarry?"

"Yes — double agent, money-hungry, absolutely no scruples. Did I miss anything?"

"You don't waste time or words, do you?" Jack said.

Wade chose that moment to burst through the hotel door and race across the street to the livery stable.

"And there the weasel is now," Jack said, adjusting his long legs in the stirrups and reining his horse back behind the stable.

"Where do you think he's headed?" Edward edged his mount close to Jack's and spoke in low tones.

"Can't be too far. Lillie's been gone less than three days." He absently swatted at a buzzing mosquito and squashed it below his ear. "Damn, these blood-thirsty devils won't leave me alone." He turned to his friend. "If you need to get back to your ship, go ahead. Weatherby and I can handle that spineless bastard."

"I don't know, Jack." Edward pulled at his collar and then unbuttoned a few buttons at the neck. "This whole affair makes me nervous. How can you be so sure he'll be there when she hands over whatever she's carrying for the Confederacy?"

"This entire situation has not made any sense from the beginning. Of all the seasoned agents in Europe, why would the French government choose a young, inexperienced woman to carry so much gold and God knows what else to the Confederacy?" Jack shook his head slowly. "I have to believe Wade engineered this ridiculous charade to compromise her in some way and get his grubby hands on her fortune."

"Wait a minute. Are you sure you're thinking straight?" Edward reached out and put a hand on his arm. "This could be a legitimate mission she's on. We could make a devil of a mess of things if we barge in unannounced and interfere with the exchange."

"I know this sounds like the maddest of plans," Jack said, "but I can feel it here." He punched his gut for emphasis. "Something is not right." He was grateful for the shadows, since he had to clench his fists at his sides to resist the urge to use physical violence to silence Edward's doubts.

Weatherby interrupted diplomatically. "Captain — he's right — sending a nineteen-year-old on a mission of this importance is at the very least questionable."

"Jack, you must have good reason to feel so strongly," Edward said. Then he added cautiously, "You have to admit you're not acting like yourself. I can't ever remember a time you left a ship under your command except for reconnaissance under wartime conditions."

"Right." Jack released his breath and ignored his friend's concerns. "As soon as Wade ventures forth, we'll give him a twenty-minute start and then follow." He moved to steady the skittish mare they'd procured the night before at the livery. "Good God, man — could they have given me a more unsuitable mount?"

"There's a war going on, you wooden-head." Edward smiled and moved closer, extending his hand. "You were lucky to get that nag. Ours cost a bloody fortune."

Weatherby moved his mount smoothly behind them. "I'm thinking the two of you are probably evenly matched with those two plodders." He softened his words with a wink and a smile.

Edward whistled low and threw Jack a wry glance when they circled to a side street to await their quarry.

Sunday Morning, May 31, 1863
Northern Peninsula
Somewhere East of Charleston

Lillie was surprised when she tucked into the modest breakfast their benefactors managed. Although she'd been ready to upchuck her innards earlier in the cemetery, now, only an hour later, she was ravenous.

"Could I please have another one of those wonderful biscuits, Nancy?" A hot blush crept onto her cheeks at the odd looks of her companions around the table.

"Of course. I'm glad you like them so much." Nancy picked up the basket and passed it to her. "I'm sorry there's no butter, but there's plenty of Mary Jane's blackberry jam."

"Those bad men took our milk cow early this spring, but we still trade for a little milk from our neighbors," Annie said, with a guilty glance at her older sisters. "Sissy always makes me drink the milk, so there's never enough left for butter."

"We managed to get the blackberries last fall," Mary Jane said, breaking her long silence. "We picked them as soon as they ripened, to cheat the birds and the thieves. I keep some jars hidden in a basket on a loop of rope down in the well."

Lillie had helped gather eggs from the few cantankerous hens left on the farm. Their fierce, warlike tendencies must have saved them from the same fate as the milk cow. A couple of potatoes retrieved from a cave behind the summer kitchen rounded out the simple fare.

"What is the strange flavor I taste in the coffee?" Jenna asked, and took a long sip. "It's different, but good," she hastened to add.

Nancy and Annie exchanged glances and then broke into a fit of giggles.

"We mix browned okra seed with dried, ground sweet potatoes," the younger sister volunteered while she sent mischievous looks at her siblings.

"Miss Annie, our guests probably would rather not know what deprivations they are sharing with us." Mary Jane leaned sharply across the table while chastising her sister.

"You get used to living off the land, you can eat pretty well," Jenna contributed. "Once you get past the fat, groundhogs can be pretty tasty." She glanced around the table. "And Ian brings me lots of fish." Her cheeks pinked, and she cast her eyes down at the mention of the young man who had brought them together.

Annie adored Jenna and followed her everywhere. She leaned against her shoulder, like a kitten basking in the morning sun.

"Jenna, you have such beautiful skin. I wish mine were more like yours." Annie reached up and stroked her hero's cheek with feather soft movements.

"Which plantation are you from?" Nancy shyly asked.

"Papa and I have lived at Rosehill all my life." Jenna stuck out her chin and stared a challenge at the other two sisters. "We raise and train racehorses. Mama came from his plantation on Martinique to be the housekeeper at Rosehill." She faltered then and stared down at the table. "I'm his only child."

"Her father is a cavalry officer, in a Yankee prison." Lillie rushed to fill the awkward silence.

The girl circled her arms around Jenna's neck and hugged her tightly.

"When Pa died, we had seven slaves, but they all left earlier this year after they heard about the emancipation," Mary Jane said.

"Didn't you try to stop them?" Lillie bit her tongue and sneaked a look at Jenna as soon as the words left her mouth.

"Why? We can barely feed ourselves. Workin' five-hundred acres is beyond us," Mary Jane said, and spread her arms to encompass her two sisters. "I didn't have the heart to try to make them stay." After pausing for a moment, the Valkyrie added, "I hope they found a way to keep body and soul together. I sent half of the potatoes and a chicken with them." She leaned forward and rested her chin in her hands. "I don't know. I hope they were lucky and found their way up north."

"When Pa was alive, he never taught us anything about growing rice," Nancy said. "Of course, we all grew up helping with the livestock, thank the heavens."

"Do you have a pair of scissors I could borrow for a moment?" Lillie asked in a fit of inspiration.

The rest of the group around the table stared at her, curiosity on their faces.

"I just want to repair a hole in my pants before we go back on the road." Excusing herself from the group of women at the sunny breakfast table, she hurried up to the bedroom and stripped off her well-worn clothes. She knew what she had to do.

CHAPTER TWENTY-ONE

Sunday Afternoon, May 31, 1863
Northern Peninsula
Somewhere East of Charleston

After Jenna turned in Odysseus's saddle and motioned for her to stop, Lillie slid to the ground and bent from the waist to massage her aching thighs and calves. Jenna disappeared into the bushes, returning a few moments later to drop at her feet with a sigh.

"What were you really doing this morning, Little Chicken, when you went upstairs?" The young mulatto woman leaned back onto the cool grass and placed her hands behind her head. She lifted her face to the sun and looked sideways at Lillie. "You have no idea how to mend a pair of pants."

"Of course, I do —," Lillie said.

"Come on — you can tell me."

"Oh, all right. If you must know," she said, "I left them part of the gold I was carrying."

"What brought on such a fit of generosity?" Jenna sat upright, pulling her knees under her chin and hugging her legs to her body. "What happened to the old blood-and-guts woman who was ready to do or die for Dixie?"

"I'm beginning to think the best thing I can do for the cause is to help just one family," Lillie said. She wrung sweat from her handkerchief and swiped at renegade droplets sliding down her nose. "They came to our aid like avenging angels. The gold will help them start over after the war.

"I've also decided I'm going to buy your passage on the first ship south to the islands. You should stay with your mother's family on Martinique until the war's over and your father's released from prison."

"How enlightened of you," Jenna said, and turned, spitting on the side of the road. "Did you come here just to throw money around to satisfy your guilty conscience?" She pushed her chin out and moved her face closer to Lillie's while she rubbed furiously at tears sliding down her cheeks.

"What do you mean?" Lillie snapped back.

"Why do you think you know what's best for everyone else? What makes you think I want to leave? This is my home," Jenna said. "What if I want to be here when Papa returns, not hundreds of miles away?"

"Believe me, Jenna, it's for the best — I've thought this through."

"You don't know nearly as much as you think you do," Jenna said, and poked a finger at her. "You should put yourself inside another person's skin for a change."

Lillie said nothing, but moved toward Penelope's broad back and fetched a jug of water tied to the saddle. After taking a healthy draught, she passed it to her friend. The pungent smell of the ocean and the intervening salt marshes wafted across the morning breezes and calmed her anger. On an impulse, she encircled Jenna in her arms and squeezed.

When Lillie began to mount her horse again, Jenna pulled her back.

"What is with you and all the throwing up and dizziness?" she asked. "Are you all right?"

"Why do you ask?" Lillie kept her expression and voice tone wary.

"Mary Jane took me aside and said she thought you were pregnant, asked me to look out for you."

"Honestly." Lillie stamped her foot and tried to move away, but Jenna held tight.

"I care about what happens to you." Jenna's face reflected genuine concern.

"The truth is, I have no idea. My courses are only a few weeks late. I don't think so, but—." Lillie paused and for the first time considered the possibility.

"Who is the father, and why did he let you come on this dangerous mission?"

"He doesn't know, and the truth is, he didn't want me to do this. He thinks I'm risking my life needlessly."

"Then why isn't he here?" Jenna raised her voice and squeezed Lillie's arm more tightly.

"He couldn't leave his ship." Lillie's voice caught in her throat in spite of her determination to be strong.

"Couldn't he speak to his captain, explain your problem?" Jenna asked.

"Jack is the captain, and he doesn't know there's a problem," Lillie admitted, resignation in her voice. "If I'm not back in three days, he'll have to leave without me," she said miserably.

"So what is this baby's daddy like?" Jenna asked.

"Very tall, very British, very angry," Lillie said.

Jenna shook her head and helped Lillie back onto Penelope's back.

Sunday Afternoon, May 31, 1863
Annadale Plantation
East of Charleston

After an hour of steady progress north on the wide dirt road, Lillie had nearly abandoned hope of finding the turn-off for the final meeting place.

"Do you even know where you're going?" Jenna asked with a whine, when an ornate wooden sign suddenly loomed ahead of them. Ornate lettering revealed — "Annadale."

"This is it," Lillie said. "This is the place the solicitor described as the last stop on the map before I turn over the gold and documents."

She and Jenna paused at the gate to the winding entrance and stared for a few moments. This was not at all what she'd expected. Her destination was an elegant plantation, and here she stood in tattered pants and shirt, like a filthy tramp. The instructions after this point were unsettlingly vague. Spiders of fear crawled up her spine when she recalled the initial rendezvous point where the mysterious thugs had tried to shoot her.

"What now?" Jenna asked as she turned, surveying the surrounding area.

"We should dismount and lead the horses through the woods. We don't want to give advance notice of our arrival," Lillie said.

"I have a better idea," Jenna said, and slid down from Odysseus, pulling the reins over his head. "Let's tie them in that meadow back there."

Rubbing Penelope gently while Jenna tied her to a tree, Lillie smiled at her initial feelings of inadequacy at the sight of the grand entrance to the plantation. War changed everything. She doubted they would encounter any finely dressed belles tripping across manicured lawns.

She looked around, assessing the woods at the edge of the tall grasses. There was something she had to do before walking into this unknown situation. Like any good poker player, she would hedge her bets.

Wade sat and stewed in the shade of the wide pillared porch, smoking a cigar and drinking glass after glass of lemonade. One foot bounced a nervous tattoo. He'd delayed his usual addition of alcohol in anticipation of a confrontation with Lillie. One of the deserters he'd sent to harass her had reported she'd probably show up early that day.

He considered her determination with grudging admiration. She'd evaded every roadblock he'd thrown in her way. He could have ended her "mission" early if she'd only followed directions and gone in at the first jetty. He'd disciplined the trigger-happy agents who started their barrage early in spite of his instructions.

The details surrounding her death behind Confederate lines would be murky, and no one would question his possession of the title to her property after the war. He toyed with the idea of explaining her actions as a "donation" to the cause.

Success was within his grasp, so he didn't dare leave anything to chance. He would take charge of the situation and silence her for good. She'd never again humiliate him.

The front door opened then slammed shut as three other men joined him. The elevated site of the mansion atop a knoll would give them the advantage when she approached.

"Is everything in place?" he asked.

"Of course." The leader frowned at him and selected a cigar from the humidor on a wicker table next to Wade's chair. "Why don't you calm down? I don't know why you're so worried. She's just an ignorant, young, albeit rich woman."

"Roy — you wouldn't be so confident if you knew her the way I do."

"I can't imagine why you've gone to all this trouble just to take one troublesome woman in hand." The other man raised his hand and rubbed the stubble on his cheek, revealing a gun strapped in place under his jacket.

Wade didn't answer, but simply glared at his companion.

"Ah, I see — it's personal," the man said. "You do realize there's only one reason we're here. No one wants to see France support the Confederacy at this stage of the game."

Lillie's mouth was so dry, she doubted she could breathe, let alone speak, if her life depended on it. After crawling through underbrush up the backside of the bluff, they were crouched at the side of the house. Bits of the cold-blooded conversation on the porch drifted down to them.

Her companion tapped her shoulder and made signs of leaving to check on the horses.

She let out the breath she'd been holding when Jenna retreated out of harm's way. Her friend had no more than disappeared into the woods than cold metal jabbed hard into the back of Lillie's neck.

She tried to duck and sprint out of her assailant's grasp, but he snatched her by the back of her shirt and slammed her into the side of the house. Fear silenced her when he took handcuffs from his pocket and secured her wrists behind her back.

"That's it — that's my girl. We don't want to mess up your pretty little head." He grunted while she struggled to kick and out-maneuver him. "Someone did a good job of training you to fight — too bad I'm better." He jerked her up painfully and prodded her with his gun pressed lower into her back. "Walk to the front of the house, please," he ordered.

When they rounded the corner, Wade's smirking face came into view. The other men on the porch hastened down to the lawn and restrained her while their leader pulled a document from a pocket inside his jacket.

"Miss Lillie Coulbourne, I'm Special Agent Roy Vickers, and you are under arrest for acts of treason against the United States of America." He waited expectantly. "Do you have anything to say for yourself before we take you into custody?"

She remained silent and hoped Jenna would have the good sense to stay away.

"All right, then," the man said. "Let's take her to the root cellar out behind the summer kitchen. There's a strong padlock on the door." He wheeled without another word and led the way. The other two men grasped her feet and arms, lifting her between them.

After his companions dumped her inside, the lead agent helped her to a seat on a cot. "Mrs. Moran will join you in a few minutes to take charge of whatever it is you're concealing."

"You could make it easy on yourself and confess," he offered. In the face of her silence, he added, "a Union judge might be more inclined to leniency if we had a signed confession from you."

"It really doesn't matter, does it?" She glared at him, disgusted. "Wade wants to destroy me. That's why I'm here, isn't it?" Sweat poured down the inside of her heavy shirt. Rivulets of moisture trickled onto her forehead from her short mop of hair.

"No, Miss Coulbourne. It's about the incriminating papers you're carrying from the French government. How could you be so gullible?" He stared at her, disdain on his face, and then hauled her up and handcuffed her to a support beam in the cellar.

She quelled the urge to shout denials at him and curved her lips into a belligerent smile. He was goading her for information. In spite of her rising temper, she would not give him the satisfaction of losing control.

After waiting a few moments, he added a final warning over his shoulder. "We both know this will not bode well for Dr. Coulbourne. No one will believe this was your idea alone. At the very least, he'll be court-martialed."

He shut the door, plunging her into darkness. At the sound of the key click in the padlock, despair threatened to swallow her.

"Stop." Jack shoved his elbow back against Edward, nearly knocking over his friend in their headlong race through the woods. Weatherby brought up the rear.

"Do you hear something?" Jack raised his hand for silence.

"What?"

"That." Jack pointed toward the thick underbrush ahead of them where something was causing the branches to sway violently.

The thrashing increased in volume as a young woman broke through the brush with two magnificent horses.

"Who the devil are you?" Jack demanded.

She slid down from the back of the huge animal and stared at him.

"You're the captain, aren't you?"

"How did you know?" Jack bit back the impatient words forming on his lips.

"Never mind. Come with me." She tied the two horses to nearby trees and motioned for the men to follow her. "You'll have to be as quiet as possible," she cautioned. "That monster has a small army with him."

"Good," Weatherby said, and abruptly pushed his way ahead, taking the lead toward the mansion.

Sunday Night, May 31, 1863
Annadale Plantation
East of Charleston

Lillie struggled to keep a smile off her face. The thorough Mrs. Moran was sending ugly glances her way after a search of her clothing yielded nothing more than a couple of seams full of gold coins.

"It's useless to try to hide the truth from us. The documents you carried have to be somewhere nearby. We'll find them, Miss, and then you'll pay. You're nothing more than a dirty little Confederate pawn."

They'd never find the hollow tree where she dropped the documents while Jenna was busy tethering the horses. The possibility of the papers being worthless had occurred to her. She had not actually seen them, since the packet was closed with the seal of France. However, Wade would have to produce something official in a Yankee courtroom to have her sent to prison. Without the documents, he had nothing.

As soon as the officious woman closed the cellar door, Lillie picked up a stick from the corner and moved to the doorframe. She hadn't been handcuffed again to the support beam. Someone else must be coming to question her. Falling to her knees, she felt her way around the opening and probed for a weak area between the earthen wall and wood frame. At the sound of a key turning in the padlock, she scrabbled back crablike. Wade burst through the doorway.

"I was expecting you," Lillie said, and squinted in the glare of the lantern Wade held above his head. "I suppose you've come to gloat?"

"No, I've come to offer you a deal."

"A deal with you — a liar and a cheat? Never."

"Never is a long time," he said, and produced a sheaf of papers from inside his shirt. "This is a deed transfer for your Sea Island property adjoining our land. All I need is your signature."

"My signature?" she said with a sputter. "You expect me to sign over my grandparents' home just like that, because you say so? You can torture me, but I won't.

You have nothing on me without the French documents, and you'll never find them."

"I don't need them," Wade replied. "I could re-create the documents, but that's really not necessary. You've already been caught in an obvious plot to provide aid to the Confederacy." He pulled a painted miniature of a tiny dark-haired girl from his coat pocket and placed it in her hand.

"Where did you get this?" she asked, stunned.

"From your father. He put up quite a fight, didn't want to let it go," he said. "He's in our custody now. You could both hang unless you sign the property over to me."

"Where is my father?" She reached out and grasped his shirt, pulling him close. "You have to tell me."

When Wade pulled away from her and attached the lantern to a hook on the wall, she threw all of her weight on the back of his legs, forcing him to his knees. The lantern fell to the floor, fizzled out and rolled away, leaving them in darkness.

She scuttled to a far corner and waited.

"Come on, Lillie. You can't escape, and even if you do, there's nowhere to go," Wade said, his voice cajoling. The sound of his breath coming in jerky gulps betrayed his reasoning tone. "If I don't come out soon, they'll send someone to check on us."

He lied. More likely his fellow thugs assumed he would take his time to humiliate her.

"Yankee and British agents are all around us. They believe you've hidden incriminating French documents. They mean to stop Bonaparte's plotting and interference for good with proof of espionage," Wade said.

With great stealth, she inched her way around the tight prison toward the opening, certain he hadn't barred the door from the inside in his haste to gloat.

"Please, Lillie," he begged. "Why can't you cooperate so I don't have to hurt you? If you weren't so stubborn, we could share everything. You could learn to love me. For God's sakes, just talk to me." After a few seconds of silence, he added, "If you cooperate, we might be able to work something out so your father doesn't hang."

She strained to pick up any sounds of movement, but he stayed quietly in one place. Feeling her way by touch, her fingers finally encountered the sturdy wood frame surrounding the door. She had one chance, and she took it, dashing out the door as soon as she felt the inside latch hanging loose.

Her heart stuttered when she was jerked from her feet and dragged to the side of the cellar entrance. She tried to turn her head and identify her attacker, but he had his hand clamped so tightly over her mouth, she couldn't move.

Lillie smacked her head back against her assailant and then dropped and rolled to the ground out of his grasp. She scooped up a handful of dirt. When he stooped to grasp her arms again, she threw the grit into his eyes and jumped to her feet. She'd gone only a few steps when a hard object connected with the back of her head and she dropped like a stone.

Lillie awoke slowly, her vision blurred. Unfortunately, her condition didn't keep her from seeing the acid green floral wallpaper lining the walls. Someone had laid her on a settee and covered her with a blanket.

This time her hands were bound tightly with rope. She searched carefully for a nearby weapon she could use and smiled at her jailers' thoughtfulness. A candle burned cheerfully on a nearby table.

She scooted to the edge of the couch and tried to ease off. Instead, she rolled onto the floor with a thump and waited in fear for a few minutes, praying no one had heard her. She folded her knees into her chest before moving onto them and raising herself onto her feet.

After a few tries, she grasped the candleholder behind her back with her hands still bound together. Once she set the curtains on fire, it was easy to extend her hands into the flames with short, quick bursts until the rope gave way. She winced at her singed fingertips and flattened against the wall closest to the hinged edge of the door. At that moment, the smoke must have reached the agents down the hallway. The sound of men running thundered toward her.

Jack and Edward circled the mansion and followed Weatherby while he methodically took out three agents.

Jack stood awestruck as Weatherby crept up behind each guard before covering their mouths with a rag soaked in some cloying, sweet-smelling substance. When the men passed out, Jack and Edward dragged them away and tied them to a sturdy oak tree.

Weatherby stood by one of the windows and counted the remaining agents inside, using sign language to communicate – another three in addition to Wade. Jack moved closer to the open window and identified at least two of the men as British by their voices.

"What are you thinking?" Edward asked Weatherby.

"If we walk into the house, we lose the element of surprise," he said, "but if we start shooting, they may hurt Lillie. The problem is," Weatherby said, "we don't know where they're holding her."

"What can they do to us?" Edward asked in a reasoning voice. "After all, Jack and I are British citizens, and as for you, well—."

The sudden clarity of what he had to do struck Jack like a cannonball to the deck.

He took the front porch steps two at a time before pushing through the door and bursting into the midst of the remaining agents.

They sat crowded onto an overstuffed couch while Wade slumped on a wing chair.

"Who's in charge here?" Jack demanded, swinging his gaze around the room.

Wade stared at him, his mouth open. "What are you doing here? Why'd you leave your ship?"

"Never mind," Jack snarled. "Where is my wife?"

"Your wife?" Wade repeated numbly.

"Yes — Lillie and I were married in Charleston before she embarked on this misbegotten 'mission' of yours." Jack closed the distance between them and leaned in to menace Wade more. "If you've done anything to harm her... As my wife, she's a British citizen and entitled to the full protection of the law. And of course, there's the earl, my brother. I doubt he would approve of his sister-in-law being incarcerated in an American jail."

At that, Jack swung around and glared at the British agents. "I say, aren't you fellows a long way from Whitehall?"

"And you are?" one of the men finally managed to ask.

"Charles Augustus Finch-Barton."

The remaining British agents rose and walked out of the house with the Union men following close behind.

After they were alone, Wade began to clap slowly. "Bravo, old man. Not that I believe for one moment you would sully your aristocratic family name by making that little strumpet an honest woman."

In just two steps, Jack crossed the room to where Wade sat and confronted him. "Get out of that chair, you miserable little bastard."

"Why? What have I done?"

Jack lifted Wade by the front of his shirt and braced him on his feet before smashing his fist into his face. "Now, unless you want to end up in the graveyard, I'm giving you one last chance to tell me what you've done with my wife."

Blood streamed out of Wade's nose, and he flailed his arms in hopeless defense against Jack's ire.

"I wish I knew where she went. We've scoured the woods. I hope you have more luck hanging on to her."

Jack's rage overwhelmed his good sense. His fist connected one last time with Wade's head, and the double agent flopped back onto the chair, unconscious.

When Jack walked out on the porch, one of the British agents held out his hand in a gesture of peace. "I'm sorry we were mistaken in the lady's identity, but she's gone."

"Where?" Jack demanded.

"After she escaped from the root cellar, we locked her inside one of the back parlors. She hadn't been in there more than an hour when smoke began to roll out under the door."

"What happened? Is she hurt?" Jack's hand curled into a fist again, and he leaned toward the man.

"When we rushed in, the curtains were engulfed in flames. By the time we put out the fire, she was gone."

"How could you lose her?" Jack's gut clenched, anger spiraling.

"We don't know," the agent replied. "We tracked her into the woods, but then lost the trail."

Jack shoved him aside and raced down the steps. He shouted Lillie's name over and over but after a few moments, he stopped, did a slow turn, and strode toward the root cellar.

When he jerked open the door, a small figure hurtled into his arms. Soot marks covered Lillie's face. Short dark curls frizzed out all over her head, and tiny burn marks sprinkled across the back of her shirt.

"Jack — you came." She hiccupped and sobbed into his jacket. "Why did you come? You shouldn't be here. You belong on *The Kate*. You should..."

His heart didn't really stop, but it stuttered for a moment. He gripped her arms tightly and growled softly into the top of her smoky curls. "Don't ever do anything this foolish again."

His anger flared and then floated away like morning fog burned off by the sun. When she tipped her tear-stained face up to him, he silenced her nervous chatter with a kiss.

When he finally drew away, she asked, "How did you know where to find me?"

"Your friend led us to the house and then, God help me, I'm beginning to think like you. I realized you'd hide in the last place they'd look."

"So Jenna got away?" she asked.

"She's fine," he replied impatiently.

Still gripping her arms, he shook her. "There's no time to waste — we have to find a church before we return to Charleston."

"A church?" Lillie eyed him suspiciously, hands on hips.

"Yes. Your continued safety in this Godforsaken country depends on you being a British citizen. I told them we were married, but it needs to be official."

"And you did this without asking me first?" Lillie's voice took on a belligerent tone. "How —?"

Weatherby joined them, cutting short her complaints.

"How did you get here?" she asked, her eyes wide.

"I'm afraid I've been posing as one of the worst crew poor Edward ever had," he said with a chuckle. "But there can't be any more debate. I must leave now, and you, for once, must listen — to Jack, but most of all, to your heart."

"Where is my father?" she asked, fear creeping into her voice.

"Where he belongs. In a battlefield surgery saving men's lives."

"But they had the miniature of me he carries all the time."

"You mean this?" Weatherby produced a cloth-wrapped packet from inside his vest. "He keeps this in his breast coat pocket, next to his heart." Then he gave her a slow wink. "But no surgeon operates wearing his jacket." He carefully placed it back in its hiding place. "One of those weasels up in the house stole it. Wade's been planning this for a long time."

"How did you know?" Lillie asked.

"The miniature was taken months ago, causing your father to suspect you might be in trouble since he also received a letter from your mother bragging about your work with the Confederate spy organization. That's when he contacted me."

CHAPTER TWENTY-TWO

Wednesday, June 3, 1863
Charleston Harbor Cotton Wharf
32°47′00″N 79°56′00″W

The moment of truth Lillie dreaded had arrived.
Should she tell Jack about the child? Hell, who knew if
there really was a child? For all she knew, the delay in
her courses could be attributed to the worst case of
nerves in her entire life.

Jenna, however, was convinced. She nagged her
daily to confess as she held Lillie's head while she
heaved up her breakfast into a bucket. Her friend had
decided to leave the ship soon, before the phase of the
moon changed. As captain of the ship, Jack would
officiate at her marriage to Ian, the young harbor pilot
who had led Lillie to her.

Lillie promised her she would write to her father to
see if he could discover where Jenna's father was being
held and try to negotiate his release.

Ever since she'd returned to the ship, Jack's mood
had gone from hurt to angry over her escape from
Wade's clutches. How was she supposed to know Jack
was coming for her? Especially after he'd repeatedly
warned her she was on her own. And then there was
her rejection of his marriage ultimatum.

In spite of his unreasonable moods and his stubborn
insistence they marry as soon as possible, she still
wanted a life with Jack. She wanted his child as well

but was afraid she couldn't have both. If she stayed with Jack, his life at sea would separate them.

Propped up in her small bunk, she ran her hands through her tangled hair in anguish. Would she ever be able to close her eyes in sleep again? Throwing on her ragged pants and a clean shirt one of the crew had given her, she headed up to the deck to watch the stars and think.

Jack trod so many laps on the deck in front of the wheelhouse that Derby came out of the boiler room and shook his head. "Will ye stop yer pacin' and tell me what's wrong?"

"I have to get that woman off my ship before she destroys my sanity."

"And why would you be wantin' to do that?"

Jack stared dumbly at his engineer.

"Marry her and then listen to her complain about your bein' gone all the time," Derby said with a grin. "The homecomings are always sweet, though."

Lillie drew her knees up under her chin and rocked back to get a better view of Venus – first star of the evening – her favorite.

"A penny for your thoughts," Edward whispered, causing her to spin around.

"What are you doing here?' she asked. "I thought you were back on your ship."

"We're all waiting for the dark of the moon for the run back out," he said with a sigh and sat down cross-legged across from her. "I came over to give you something." He pulled a much-folded letter from one of his pockets and handed it to her.

"Where did this come from?" she asked suspiciously.

"Weatherby," Edward replied. "I should have told you sooner, but I forgot in all the excitement when we tore back to Charleston."

Lillie rolled her eyes at him, even though the gesture was probably lost on him in the dark. She ripped open the letter and immediately scanned for the signature – "James Weatherby."

Edward touched her arm and said, "I'll leave you to it."

"But how?" Lillie muttered.

"He gave me the letter just before he left, made me promise this would be for your eyes only." With that, he stood and moved toward the stern of the ship.

She unfolded the missive and began to read:

"My dearest Lillie,

By the time you read this, I'll be on my way to join your father in Vicksburg with Grant. I owe Dr. Coulbourne my life, and much more than I can ever repay.

Your parents asked me to watch over you, but I knew you could take care of yourself with some help from Edward and Jack. Please apologize to both of them for the delay. I'm afraid that was my doing.

But know this — I'm proud of you for standing up for your beliefs.

Your father wanted to be here but couldn't leave his post. However, he wanted you to understand that his absences during your childhood were not because he chose duty above his love for you. The differences between your mother and him were more to blame, I'm afraid.

I came in his place with, I hope, the same devotion any father would muster.

Martha believes Captain Jack is a good man. Both she and your father love you and want you to follow your heart without worry about the past.

The rest, my girl, is up to you.

Your loyal friend,

James Weatherby"

When Lillie refolded the letter and stashed it inside her shirt, a single tear slid down her cheek. She realized there was a secret, tangled reality among her parents and their old friend that she didn't want to examine too closely.

She turned to locate Venus again and found a large shadow blocking the view.

"Jack —," she said with a start. "I thought you were resting before the next watch."

"Couldn't sleep."

"Why not?"

"Can't stop thinking."

"About what?"

"You."

"Me?" she asked, her eyes wide as he stepped closer, making it hard for her to breathe.

"Yes, you — I worry about what scrape or escapade you're going to get yourself into next, but most of all, I'm afraid."

"Afraid of what?" she asked, and tried to stifle a smile.

"Afraid you'll leave this ship, and I'll never see you again — afraid you'll spend the rest of your life in the arms of another man."

"Jack, I've never seen you afraid of anything."

"Well, you see me terrified before you now," he assured her and pulled her up off the deck to gather her in his arms. "Right now, I'm afraid I'll ask you to marry me again and you'll say 'no,'" he murmured onto the top of her head.

After a lengthy silence, she faced him squarely. "I will marry you on one condition."

"Which is?" he prompted.

"I will always be your navigator."

He narrowed his eyes at her, but finally agreed. "You have my word," he said solemnly.

"The word of an Englishman?" she said with a snort.

He smothered any further impertinence by scooping her up and heading back to his cabin.

EPILOGUE

1867 — Portsmouth, England

Lillie bounded off the settee at the sound of horses in the drive and raced to the door to peer out the cottage's high windows.

Outside, Jack jumped from the carriage and turned to help a gentleman climb down. The stranger was wrapped in a heavy woolen coat, layers of scarves, and wearing a turban. More importantly, snugged beneath one of her husband's arms was a long, narrow box tied with a red ribbon.

Just then a commotion swirled around her skirts, and she bent to gather Charley into her arms, along with his newest "patient" from the litter of kittens in the stable.

When she hoisted the small boy to the level of the windows, his eyes grew big.

"Papa's home," he chattered excitedly. "Present..."

"Yes," she said "but we have to be on our best behavior. Papa has a guest with him. Let's go back and wait."

He pouted but returned to the sitting room, quietly fidgeting until Jack burst into the room and swung him up over his head.

After setting the child back down, he rescued the mewling kitten from his clutch and inquired, "Which creature are we healing today, Dr. Charley?"

"Eddy," his son replied and then climbed onto his mother's lap to take charge of the mysterious box balanced there. He made short work of the ribbon followed by the lid, which he tossed onto the floor.

Lillie made faces at Jack over the top of the boy's head while he ripped mounds of tissue out of the box and threw them to the floor also. She saved a rich silk robe in shades of lavender and sky blue that Charley lobbed aside in his dive to the bottom where he retrieved a hidden toy soldier.

After the child's nurse gathered him for bed, Jack put his hand over Lillie's and pulled her to her feet toward the mysterious stranger who had settled into the chair closest to the crackling fire.

"I want you to meet my friend, Kaimakam Yilmaz."

"Madame, the pleasure is all mine," the man said as he rose and bowed slightly.

"Yilmaz came to London to ask me to work with the Turkish Navy," Jack said.

"So that explains the extravagant gift," Lillie said, her face flushing hot. She slammed the gift box onto the floor and spilled glowing silk onto the dark carpet. "It's meant as a bribe for me to stay at home like a good wife while you go back to sea, isn't it?"

"No," Jack answered patiently as he knelt and retrieved the robe. "It's a bribe for you and Charley to come along. They've asked me to design port blockades, so I'm going to need a navigator."

Lillie smiled at the anxious look on her husband's face while he awaited her answer. She made him wait.

THE END

AFTERWORD

The adventures of my heroine, Lillie Coulbourne, are based on some of the exploits of Lillie Hitchcock Coit, beloved San Francisco icon who lived from 1843 to 1929. She spent time in Paris during the American Civil War and also ran the blockade back into the South at some point with her mother, Martha.

Charles Augustus Hobart-Hampden was the British Navy post captain and aristocrat behind the Civil War blockade runner who went by the name of Captain Jack Roberts. He was never caught and went on to become an admiral in the Turkish Navy. He spent his later years penning memoirs of his seagoing adventures with the help of his younger, second wife. He was born in 1822, the third son of the 6th Earl of Buckinghamshire, and died in 1886. He is buried in Istanbul.

His memoirs, *Never Caught*, and *Sketches of My Life*, are available for download from Google Books.

Most of my research into setting and details I owe to the kindness of the librarians at the Mills College Library in Oakland, CA, where Lillie's personal correspondence, photos, and memorabilia reside. My good friend and co-worker, British delivery Captain Tony Plummer, obtained additional information from the Admiralty on Captain Roberts's actual name and naval background.

AUTHOR BIO

Andrea K. Stein lives and writes at 9,800 feet in the Rocky Mountains, just fifteen minutes from the Continental Divide. A retired newspaper editor, she is a USCG certified sea captain who spent a number of years delivering yachts out of Charleston Harbor to destinations up and down the Caribbean. Many nights her ships were moored near the site where blockade runners took on loads of cotton for the run back out through the Union blockade during the Civil War.

www.ingramcontent.com/pod-product-compliance
Lightning Source LLC
Chambersburg PA
CBHW022140170626
46807CB00005B/2012

Although Lillie and Jack were fascinating characters, the events in this book have absolutely no connection to their actual lives.

FINAL NOTE

Thank you so much for taking the time to read *Fortune's Horizon*. Hopefully, you enjoyed the journey. If you did, I would love for you to leave a review at the retailer where you purchased the novel.

And please stop by my website, **http://www.andreakstein.com** for information on additional titles coming out over the next few months. While you're there, sign up for my newsletter for occasional updates, links to bonus materials, and peeks at what's coming next.

There's nothing I enjoy more than connecting with readers, so feel free to drop me a line at **andrea@andreakstein.com** with any comments or suggestions.

Twitter
@andreakstein

Facebook
Author Andrea K. Stein